THE AVERAGE HUMAN

A NOVEL BY ELLEN TOBY-POTTER

MacAdam/Cage Publishing
155 Sansome Street, Suite 550
San Francisco, CA 94104
www.macadamcage.com
Copyright © 2003 by Ellen Potter
ALL RIGHTS RESERVED

Library of Congress Cataloging-in-Publication Data

Toby-Potter, Ellen, 1963—.
The average human / by Ellen Toby-Potter.
p. cm.
ISBN 1-931561-33-8 (Hardcover : alk. paper)
1. City and town life—Fiction. 2. Incest—Fiction. I. Title.
PS3616.O85 A97 2003
813'.6—dc21

2002153551

Manufactured in the United States of America
10 9 8 7 6 5 4 3 2 1

Book design by Dorothy Carico Smith.

THE AVERAGE HUMAN

A NOVEL BY ELLEN TOBY-POTTER

MacAdam/Cage

FOR MY PARENTS

WHO KNEW HOW LONG the pond had been there? An ancient glacial pothole, perhaps, jettisoned by the northward-retreating ice. Through cold, quiet centuries, the pond waited with the patience of a natural epicenter, appearing placid, yet all the while churned, like a witch's cauldron, by a wealth of perch and largemouth bass and black water snakes that cleaved its dark surface. For some time, a band of Cayugas stopped regularly to bring their sick to bathe in its depths. Then silence again, until the land around the pond became Land Grant Lot No. 77 and No. 78.

It was then that two great farming families—the Libargers and the Mayborns—decided to settle on either side of its banks. They were great in the sense of the large number of dairy cows that they owned and in their mutual progressive decrepitude, truly blue-blooded in nature, if not in fact. Powerful, with thick Viking foreheads, and slow-moving as their herds, the two families were probably of similar stock. Year after year they alternately feuded and mated until, by degrees, the Libarger family was absorbed by the hungry, pink-faced Mayborns, who suddenly had a glut of boy children at the same time that the Libarger property was overrun by white-haired little girls, pulsating through the farm like a muscular constellation.

The inevitable marriages left only one Libarger, the aging, widowed father, Jake's Jake Libarger, to run the farm on his own. At the age of sixty-two, he was a sinewy, robust man, dressed always in knitted suspenders and a high-crowned John Bull hat, a careful dandy even shin-deep in cow manure. Less a farmer than a master breeder, having meticulously tracked his livestock's lineage for twenty-seven years, he had a fine herd to show for his trouble—sleek, docile creatures with milk that flowed easily from their teats, even during lean seasons. On the other side of the pond, the Mayborn herd was a hardscrabble collection of beasts that were forever succumbing to milk fever. Jake's Jake was loath to have their mouths touch the same pond water as his own exceptional herd, and whenever their bull broke loose he kept his rifle aimed until a Mayborn came running and recaptured the animal.

In the summer of 1875, during a dry spell that turned the fields into crackling brown steppes, Jake's Jake's house went up in flames. He escaped by crawling out a window, shattering his hip and right leg when he hit the ground. Miraculously, the barn and the cows went unscathed ("The good Lord takes and gives like a strumpet, praise God," said Garvey Mayborn. "Who are we to question Him?").

In the end, Jake's Jake's right leg was amputated at the thigh. This, along with his broken hip and chronic dizziness from taking in too much smoke, left him an elegant cripple. There was nothing to be done but for Jake's Jake also to be absorbed by the Mayborns—along with his cows and barn and most of his land, for which the Mayborns paid a niggling amount. A Mayborn carved him a crude peg leg and one of his daughters smeared mutton tallow on his burns. All in all, they treated him as tenderly as a captive.

With innocent, irreproachable maliciousness, so typical of the Mayborns, they placed Jake's Jake in the best room, the one with the French doors that opened out onto a small verandah, braced by a wrought iron railing. From the verandah he could see the pond and the cow pastures, so that on any given day Jake's Jake could witness his life's work being undone as the lumpen Mayborn bulls mounted his fine cows. He could watch the Mayborns brutally switch at the flank of his best heifer, her udders tight and full with evening milk, primed by sweet July grass, ready to flood the Mayborn buckets, to spill herself at the tug of their thick fingers. Painful—yet the view compelled him to watch, day after day. He sat out there on the walnut rocker that his sons-in-law had provided, his peg leg pistoning up and down in his boot as he rocked, his John Bull hat sitting on his lap. Strapped to the hat by a cream-colored silk band was a sheaf of papers, neatly rolled up and tied with a ribbon.

"Must be his Last Willin' Testerment," the Mayborn husbands speculated. That made their pale lips go damp. Often, they found him penning in his papers fitfully, but when they came near he'd quickly roll the papers up again.

His life lost its precision. Without his ritual tasks, the days bled one into the other. Seasons occurred in no particular order, laborious floorshows: one day the sky was shot through with snow and the next day pinpoint beads of heated rain steamed against the basking roof. Never a drinking man, Jake's Jake now made a friend of whiskey. The Mayborn boys were delighted by their father-in-law's new interest, and took pains to keep him well supplied. They sent the children up with a fresh flask of whiskey each morning. In the afternoon, the children again came up with more and occasionally tried to peek at Jake's Jake's secret papers. They clambered on top of him in his rocker and clawed at his hat. He swatted them off.

"I swear, I have grown sincerely fond of the old man." This was said at the dinner table, between mouthfuls of boiled potatoes, by Thomas Mayborn, chewing so vigorously that he appeared to be able to dislocate his jaw at will. "Too bad the change come about now, after he's a cripple and no good to no one nor hisself. If he hadn't been such an uppity proud bastard all his life, he might have been safe under our roof, here, when his house took a-fire."

"Maybe," one of the wives said, "his house wouldn't a took—"

"It would have took a-fire, because it *done* took a-fire. That's what you call happenstance. You can't go tracking down happenstance like a hound. If a person was to go tracking down happenstance, he'd find hisself at God's doorstep. Knock, knock, God." The children at the table snickered. There were plenty of them now. Every few months there would be a terrific squalling in the house, and a new one was born (Jake's Jake never heard any womanly screams—his daughters gave birth as surreptitiously as cats). The baby girls were all born with tiny black fingernails. Rotten and truffled, the fingernails rose up off the skin in the center, like small black flies struggling to escape. Jake's Jake pitied the children. As a breeder, he knew that when a line kept producing an abnormality, the offspring would be deeply unsalvageable. As they bred, the problems would worsen, working from the outside in. At first it might be skin rashes, then later bone abnormalities, then finally the organs would be affected: heart defects, convulsions. He sincerely hoped his granddaughters were infertile.

"Knock, knock there, God," Thomas Mayborn continued, rapping hard on the table. "Sorry to disturb you in your nightie-gown and slippers, but I come about Daddy Libarger's house. It is my opinion that it is all your fault. Now, listen, here's my logic. If you had not gone and made this world and then stuck people in it, if you hadn't gone and made fire and wood to catch fire, and if you hadn't made Daddy Libarger such a rare cranky bastard with a herd that's got teats so stingy a man gets cramps in his hand just to squeeze out a few drops…" Thomas spread his hands out, wide. "Happenstance. You enjoying those potatoes, Daddy Libarger?"

Jake's Jake nodded without looking up from his plate. His hat with the rolled-up papers was on his lap and his face was newly soft, relieved of its former rancor. He was, however, still as dignified as before; more so, even, because having lost everything he felt himself to be as weightless and influential as an element, like fire or wind.

The end of the Libargers came one day in early May, just as the bullfrogs were beginning to clamor in the pond, a rapture of mating and belching on top of water lilies, which bobbed under their lust. Their noise kept Jake's Jake up all night, but he made good use of his time. He lit a lamp, took the roll of papers from his hat, and made a few amendments on the pages. After the children had brought him up his morning whiskey, he dressed and made his way to town.

During the past ten years, the town of Loomis had grown with the sort of breathless mass energy that produces lynchings and bad storms. The population swelled with an onslaught of Finns, ferreting out cheap land. Honest and plain, they would have made fine husbands for his daughters. But never mind—they had arrived too late. He passed their farms, stuck here and there, the crops already vaulting out of the ground. The clapboards on their houses were so new that they were still white.

He followed the footpath that ran along the bottom of Mercy Hill, the stretch of woods that rose up high and thick along the backbone of the town. It wasn't long before he began to hear the section gang. They spoke in urgent, thrusting Italian, punctuated by the cracks of their shovels into gravel. Jake's Jake found his usual smooth maple stump and sat down. Below, a few feet down the embankment, the section gang was hard at work. Their dark, damp heads were bent, and their bodies lifted and dropped with the movement of their shovels. They jabbered carelessly to each other, like people who were accustomed to sleeping in the same room. Jake's Jake sighed. He took his hat off his head and put it on his knee.

Searching the gang, he found the young Italian who, in turn, looked up at him and nodded, recognizing Jake's Jake as the man who had been coming to sit and watch them each day for the past week. The young man wore a pair of striped coveralls, shredded at the bottom from the gravel, and cheap thin boots. The foreman, who was also Italian, yelled something at the young man, who fell back to work placidly. A rush of tenderness for the boy brought boozy tears to Jake's Jake's eyes. He thought of his poor, mistreated herd. The young Italian's hair was dark and slick as a wet hide, and his eyes were eager with expectation of cravings fulfilled: shade and cigarettes, girls with strong, white teeth. Enlisted in—some would say sold to—the section gang by an older brother, the young Italian was now tethered beneath the open sun by the brute, living rhythm of production. Monastic in demand, production burned off the bloom of his meat and bread, consumed his vigor, each morsel of motion given up for a thing far greater than himself, and a paltry wage. Tomorrow the section gang would be gone, their work completed. Before long, the great trains would roar through town. The dairy farmers would have to hustle their morning milk to the station. They would have to hunker down to progress. Everything in its turn.

The foreman shouted and clapped his hands, and the gang dropped their shovels where they stood. They dispersed into shade to smoke and take a drink of water from a tin that was passed from man to man.

Jake's Jake stood then and hobbled unsteadily down the embankment, keeping his hat off out of respect to the bareheaded young man. Removing his flask of whiskey from inside his boot, Jake's Jake offered it to the boy, who pressed a cigarette to his lips before he reached for the flask and took a swallow. The whole time he kept his eyes on Jake's Jake with dumb, contemplative suspicion. When he handed the flask back, Jake's Jake closed it and replaced it carefully in his boot.

He took the papers from his hat, unrolled them, pulled out a single page, and pushed it toward the boy. "This is for you," Jake's Jake said.

"Che cosa è questo?" the boy asked, nodding toward the paper without touching it. He had been initiated into the section gang through the exchange of just such kind of papers. Jake's Jake smiled encouragingly and jiggled the page toward the boy. The young man shook his head and repeated his question more forcefully. He would not be sold again; he had learned his lesson the first time.

Crouching beneath a tree, the foreman had been watching them. Now he stomped out his cigarette and strode over. Without a word he snatched all the papers out of Jake's Jake's hand—the one he was trying to give to the boy as well as the rest— and stared hard at them as his lips moved over the incomprehensible English. Then, with an exclamation of disgust, he crumpled the papers in his fist. Jake's Jake cried out and the young worker grabbed the papers away, convinced now that they must benefit him— perhaps more money, perhaps even a lot of money. The young Italian had a cousin who had settled in Loomis a few years before. He would take the papers straight to his cousin's house and ask him what they meant.

Clasping the papers against his chest, the boy turned and ran, following the tracks that they had laid. But the foreman was quicker and caught him, grabbed him by the back of his shirt. The rest happened very swiftly: a knife appeared in the young man's hand as if manifested from the hot wind and gravel dust. Blood splattered in all directions. The foreman weaved and cooed, then dropped, the knife plunged deep in his neck. The young man did not look surprised. He stood over the dying foreman, nodding approvingly, like a father whose child had finally learned his lesson the hard way. Then he turned and fled, still clutching the roll of papers, now stained with blood. No one went to catch him, and though Jake's Jake stumbled after him for a few steps, pleading loudly for the boy to keep the paper that was meant for him but to return the others, the boy would not come back.

Jake's Jake started for home after dark, well soused, having been bought many rounds of drinks by the men at the inn, who wanted to hear the story of the murder. He drank until he was light and sweet as a toddler, and in this mood he walked back home, across the black pasture, and sat by the pond, swaddled in the rushes. The bullfrogs were all around him, singing loudly, mating, even as the rain fell. Jake's Jake didn't mind the rain at all. It was a fresh, early spring rain, and he curled up in his cradle of cattails and rushes at the water's threshold, like a wizened Moses, and listened to the cows lowing in the barn, until he lost consciousness. Gently, gently, the pond rose up, just enough to cover Jake's Jake nose and mouth, which was tipped so near to its edge, and smothered the life out of him. That was how the end of the Libargers went.

By morning, the young Italian murderer was discovered in his cousin's icehouse. He was delivered at riflepoint to the sheriff and it was there, in the sheriff's office, that Jake's Jake Libarger's papers were first examined.

Records of the murder, Loomis's first, can still be found today in thin local-history chapbooks, tucked away in the dim recesses of the Loomis Town Library. A lithograph hangs in the police station, depicting the execution of the Italian murderer, his face a mass of cross-hatchings to indicate the darkness of his skin contrasted with the ghastly whiteness of the noose and the man's upturned eyes. But Jake's Jake's papers vanished shortly after their discovery; destroyed, most likely, because of their profane implications.

According to those who'd seen them, penned across the first page in large, careful letters was the heading A RECIPE FOR SHIT SOUP. Beneath that, and on the succeeding pages, was a comprehensive genealogy of the Mayborn family, starting with Bartlett Mayborn, who was an old man when Jake's Jake was a small boy, all the way down to Lila Mayborn, who had been born that past April. It took a second glance, however, to notice some curious lines which doubled back on themselves and shot off in odd directions. It appeared that some very strange and unnatural couplings had occurred in the Mayborn household. The offspring of these unions often had the same date marking their birth and their death, provoking some monstrous conjectures of infanticide. Within an hour of their discovery, news of the papers had traveled to the dry goods store, the inn, and the creamery. By dinnertime every home in Loomis had heard of the papers.

Some said that there were legal papers mixed in with the Mayborn genealogy, and others claimed that the murderer's cousin had hidden some of the more valuable documents; he was an Italian, after all, and shifty by nature.

Although the Mayborns continued to prosper, their wealth hitting its peak in the 1920s, then plummeting after World War II, the scandal of those papers survived hard in the minds of their neighbors. Tales of Mayborn monstrosities lingered through the generations, gaining strength and veracity, in part through sheer endurance. More than a century later, when Loomis Pond mysteriously began to dry up, children (and others besides) searched the mucky pond bed for the legendary bones of the misbegotten Mayborn babies, who had reputedly been pitched into the pond and drowned at birth. People searched under the very shadow of the Mayborn house, still standing on its knoll above the pond. Its filthy white paint was curled back and clinging tenaciously to the rotten clapboards. Long ago, the cow barn had collapsed in on itself after a hard snow, the herd having been auctioned off a decade before that. The vast Mayborn acreage had been sold off in plots, leaving just enough land for a forlorn front lawn and, in the back, a dog run and a burn barrel.

CHAPTER ONE

JUNE MAYBORN LAY FACEDOWN on the bed, arms at her side like a soldier. Harnessing her wide, freckled back was a yellowed bra. Ed had never tried to remove it, gleaning, perhaps, that she wore it like a wristwatch, and that its absence would demand some creative recompense on his part. Now he was jamming his legs into his pants while she lay there, her head twisted to one side, watching him. The bell hanging on the candy store door downstairs tinkled for a second time.

"What the hell already?" Ed said, shoveling his shirt into his pants.

"It's Teachers Conference Day today," June said. "We always get out at one o'clock on Teachers Conference Day." Ed looked at her.

"Why the hell didn't you tell me that before?"

"What's the hurry, Ed?" June stretched out her legs, pushing at the footboard until it began to crackle.

"What's the hurry, Ed?" he mimicked her. "Slow down, Ed. So all my little friends can stuff the whole store down their pants, Ed." He ran out of the room with the backs of his shoes curled up against his heels. June was flattered that he thought she had so many friends.

She passed her nose across the pillow as if she were reading exquisitely small print. She could smell the oily heat where her temple had pressed against the fabric. She could smell the bloom of her own saliva. She could detect where the corner of the pillow had, at some point, slid down her neck and wedged itself into her clavicle—here, the odor was succulent with exhaustion. Crawling backwards, she inhaled; the sheets were saturated with the wooly, suspicious bilge water of Ed's efforts, an odor that seasoned the air.

For the past week, June existed in a state of gorgeousness. Time was unbundled. She shut her eyes to blink and the blink lasted for the entire day. Her body dissolved into the bed; there was nothing left of her but mattress and nerve endings. When she left to go home, she was reduced to a bat-squeak drifting across the dried pond bed.

June listened to the sugar riot downstairs. It made her smile to think that she could stamp her feet on the floor, and some of her own classmates might look up at the ceiling. Just weeks ago she had hardly noticed Ed Cipriano, except to mark when his back was turned. Which was mostly never. Once, he had been an athlete of the slight and unassuming variety, and his body still retained its instinct to perform for a win. As the children crowded into his store, he moved up and down behind the counter, taking in cash, slapping down change, grabbing for ice pops. And all the while he patrolled his premises with dark eyes that had only four or five eyelashes to a lid, sticking straight out like visors.

How things started between them seemed simple enough; he noticed her and, having been noticed, she lingered.

Rolling onto her back, she gazed around the room. On the night table was a scrap of Ed's wife's embroidery cloth, stretched and trapped in a wooden hoop. A needle with purple thread, the juicy purple of a cluster of grapes, was stuck lightly in the cloth in a dreamy, extramarital punctuation.

There were other things marking Mrs. Cipriano's abrupt departure. Her closet door was left open, and at its base lay hangers that had dropped to the floor as she'd hastily pulled her clothes from them. A nervously plundered jewelry box sat upon the vanity, spilling out a jumble of glass-bead necklaces, one of which, in trying to untangle, she had broken. The little beads had rolled across the floor and under the bed. One wound up, inexplicably, in June's sneaker, and she kept it as a memento. She liked to feel Mrs. Cipriano's presence in the room; not the bleached, vague Mrs. Cipriano who speared bags of chips on the store's wire spinner. No, *her* Mrs. Cipriano felt like a runaway older sister—having fled three weeks before with a furnace repairman—whose bedroom, with its concentrated vapor of brand-new lust and its wealth of experience, June had inherited.

But there was something about the needle in the cloth.

June had, along with the rest of her family, a rudimentary moral conscience. It was not corrupt, exactly. It had simply been left behind in the wake of evolution, blithely treading in its primordial state. Still, every so often a seemingly innocuous object would pinch at something inside of her. Lately it had been the upright needle in the cloth on the night table, poised like a moment about to be resumed. It tweaked her at odd times because, when the night table was jostled during lovemaking, the needle would twitch like a Geiger gauge, and she could not take her eyes off it. She might have moved the table over a little so that it did not touch the bed, but the twitching needle had become part of the whole experience, and she was afraid to force it to be still.

It was twitching now. The old man next door, the boarder, was knocking on the wall behind the headboard for his meal. June had never seen him—he was sickly and kept to his bed—but his demands had interrupted her and Ed often enough. He banged again and the needle shuddered.

June slipped out of bed and put on her white peasant blouse, its elastic hem ending just below her last rib, and a denim miniskirt with frogs embroidered on each of the back pockets. On the vanity was an opened box of the packaged crackers that Ed gave to the old man as a snack. June grabbed one of the packages and walked quietly down the hallway to the old man's room.

He was sitting up in his bed, very small, with his hands folded on top of his blanket. His hair was perfectly white with dry ringlets on the ends. He looked alarmed to see that it was she and not Ed who had come to feed him. But then, when his expression did not change, June realized that it was fixed on his face. He was very ill. June could smell it.

"Quit banging," June said.

"Where's Cipriano?" the old man asked. Although his eyes had the glassy crust of illness, they were sharp beneath, like dimes on the bottom of a dirty pool.

He scrutinized June with some interest, and since people generally took little notice of her, she was happy to let him stare. She walked into the room, clasping the crackers behind her back with both hands, and looked around. The room must have belonged to a child, but a long time ago, so that the child might now be older than the man in bed, or dead perhaps. A wallpaper printed with trains that were puffing out faded, particolored steam was split and rotten at every seam. The plaster ceiling was covered with hairline cracks. The only ornamentation was one of Mrs. Cipriano's framed cross-stitch pictures of a large hand gripping, almost strangling, a bouquet of flowers on the wall opposite the bed. Beneath that was a low, scuffed dresser and, nearby, an ancient black stove.

"What have you two done with Mrs. Cipriano?" the old man asked.

"Killed her and stuffed her in the freezer like a Popsicle?" He took pleasure in this notion. His eyes shut for a minute and his mouth stretched into something like a smile. His tongue protruded slightly. His teeth were very small.

"I didn't do nothing to Mrs. Cipriano," June said.

"Well said! Tell me, Sister. Are you ignorance bliss or a cunning little blister? Perhaps Mrs. Cipriano can answer that for us on her return. I must say, you wouldn't have been my choice. One would feel the need to bathe you first. Oh, I would have passed on you, Sister, with those hard, beady eyes. And it wasn't so long ago when I had my pick of many a young lady such as yourself. There was Julie. And Kitty, ah, Kitty. Poor, sweet Kitty. She was such a tender little shoot. She loved me so."

"You're dreaming," June said.

"I had a young bride, too," the old man continued. "Her name was Iris. Lovely Iris. *Ravishing* Iris. She's mine still, you know, if she's not dead. She ran off with some dude. He was a fledgling—what?—filmmaker, plumber, I can't remember now. She had shitty taste in men. Most beautiful women do. A holy man can catch a girl, but only a son of a bitch can keep her—" The old man had a coughing fit, giving his body a fascinating vitality. When he was done he seemed spent and soft.

"What's the matter with you?" she asked.

"Why? Can you fix it?"

"Here." June handed the package of crackers to him, but he fumbled so much with the cellophane that she took it back, tore it open with her teeth, and spilled the crackers out onto his blanket. While he ate, he held the crackers with two hands, like a squirrel, and gazed ruefully out the window.

"Have you noticed the clouds?" he asked. The window looked out past the Pick-A-Part junkyard onto the woody rise of Mercy Hill. The trees only recently began to fill out with new leaves, closing ranks with the staid pillars of firs. The low clouds shadowed the uppermost part of the hills to a singed green.

"Black, thick clouds since the day of my arrival. They hang over the hills all day long. 'A frown upon the atmosphere, that hath no business to appear.' All my life things have conspired against me. Tell me, Sister. How many are there left?"

"Left where?"

"Mercy Hill," he snapped impatiently. "Who lives up there now?"

June thought for a minute.

"Hunters go up in the woods and fall asleep in the trees. I don't know. Oh, and Leon. He still lives up at the old commune. He's black. He doesn't wash."

"Leon! *My* Leon?" He looked out the window, as though he might be able to see Leon up in the hills, and smiled. "He's a strange boy with strange appetites. I wouldn't turn my back to him, Sister."

He turned to June suddenly and examined her with great interest.

"You strike me as a very lonely young woman, Sister. Few friends? You make people uncomfortable, my dear. But that's not your fault. That's your gift. I saw that the moment you entered my room. The world will always shun you. Never mind. You'll visit me as much as you like."

"I can come again tomorrow," she said. She felt slightly intoxicated by the attention.

"Then come again tomorrow. And bring poor Leon with you."

"You can see him for yourself tonight. He goes to the Casablanca Bar on Tuesdays. He watches the fights. But he doesn't talk too much."

"Casablanca Bar." He was again overcome with a coughing fit.

She sat down beside him and watched his little body convulse. The odor of his sickness was sharp in her nose, but she rarely took offense at smells. In her pocket was a book of matches. When an odor became too distracting, she would strike the match and blow it out. The warm rush of sulfur helped to numb her sense of smell and take the edge off the odor, even if it was only for a minute or two, so that she could clear her head. She often struck matches in Loomis Park, where the exposed pond bottom emitted such a cacophony of ancient fumes that it made her eyes water and her head ache. But the old man's smell was simple rot. She adjusted the elastic hem on her blouse so that her belly button was showing.

"I am in the family way, Sister," the old man said quietly to her. "Fifty-eight years old, and in the family way." He placed his hand on his stomach. "He's a big bastard. They've tried to poison him, to starve him. They have shot their ray guns at him. But he's a fat, vengeful pig of a boy. I'll kill him, anyway. We'll put an end to this trouble. Kaw…" He winced and took June's hand and placed it on his belly. "There. Can you feel him kick?" His stomach was rubbery and hot to the touch.

"Your fingers—" he said. He was staring down at her hand. All June's fingernails were black and grotesquely shriveled. She looked at them, splaying her fingers out in front of her as though she were assessing a manicure.

"It's not dirt," she said. "I was born that way." The old man leaned close to June's face, his eyes passing across her features with alarm.

"Lee?" he whispered. His breath smelled like the inside of a laundromat dryer. "Lee Utter?" His membranous gaze made him appear to be staring blindly into pitch darkness. June met his eyes, fascinated with the way her own face curved across his damp pupils.

"Are you here to plague me about your brother?" He still whispered to her, and his breath fizzed and broke against her skin. "I did nothing to that baby. My hands are clean in that matter. Ask Leon. He knows everything. Ask him." June could hear Ed's clumping footsteps on the stairs, and she rose and adjusted her skirt so that the frogs were in the right place.

The old man looked up at her, his lips a grimace. He licked them and they changed to a smile. He pulled the blankets back over his lap and clasped his hands.

"Well," June said. "I'm off."

"Like a prom dress," the old man said as she walked out and shut the door, and she heard his laughter for five minutes after, through the walls.

Chapter Two

June returned home that afternoon to find her father's white van, mud-splattered and rust-eaten and resembling a decomposing whale, parked on the front lawn. He had come back. No one had expected him. June ran inside through the kitchen door, where her mother was mixing raw chopped meat with her hands. A large pot of boiling water steamed up the windows.

"Where is he?" June asked. Ruby nodded toward the living room.

"Hey," Ruby said.

"What?"

"School called. They said you haven't been for a while."

"Nope."

"What have you been doing, June bug? Come over here." Ruby lifted her hands out of the meat, fingers spread and greasy. She had a long, sallow, acne-scarred face and thick black hair that reached her lowest vertebra. She looked like a pirate's wife.

"You been smoking in the woods?" Ruby asked.

"No," June said.

"Mmmm, June bug," Ruby growled. "Let me smell your breath." June blew into her mother's face. Ruby wrinkled her nose.

"Smells like fruit candy," Ruby said. "Hey, what all does that bottle say, Junie?" She nodded toward a squat white jar with a black lid that stood on the kitchen counter. June picked it up and read the label.

"A divinely rich lotion that will pamper the most sensitive skin."

"What's the flavor?" Ruby asked. "Your daddy brought it for me."

"It doesn't say."

"Are you sure?"

"It doesn't say," June showed the label to her mother. Ruby waved it away—she had never learned to read properly.

"What did they call it again...divinely rich? Divinely rich." Ruby snorted.

Jack Mayborn was stretched across the couch, his denim jacket still on. He'd put on a little weight since June last saw him. His pale hair was tied back in a ponytail, and his face was a sunburnt moon. His eyes were shut. June put her hand on her father's belly and pressed down. He expelled a rush of fermented air. His eyes opened—they were the same milky blue as his daughter's—and he smiled up at her.

"I didn't know you were coming," June said.

"Neither did I but here I am anyway. Lucky you all. Want to see what I picked up along the way?" He pulled up his shirt. Across the side of his blond belly was a fresh, pink scar. June bent down and sniffed at it.

"You like that?" he asked. June nodded.

"I got my appendix taken out of me. You believe that?"

"Sure."

"Sure you do. Do you feel sorry for your poor old dad? Yeah, you got a heart, June. Where's your goddamn brother? Probably saw my van and hightailed it in the other direction."

"Nah. He's working."

"Is he? Making money? Yeah? That's good. Is he treating you and your mother good?"

"Nah."

Dinner was half gone when Frank walked through the kitchen door, followed closely by his bullmastiff, Keeper. Frank must have known his father was home—he couldn't have missed the van in the driveway—but he showed no sign of it. He removed his muddy boots and placed them on a square of worn doormat. He washed his hands in the kitchen sink and wetted down his face. Frank was a large man, like his father. But whereas Jack was beefy, Frank's body had a supple, quick-primed quality. His face, however, favored Ruby's: the long, narrow Slavic eyes with faint crescents beneath them; features that had the look of rough usage, as if the bones in their faces had been shattered and reset one too many times, and yet Frank managed to come up handsome on third or fourth inspection.

Frank sat down at the table, his mouth set inscrutably. Without a word to his father he began to serve himself spaghetti out of the green plastic bowl, while Keeper slunk beneath the table and whined.

"Good to see you too, son!" Jack's voice betrayed no offense whatsoever. On the contrary, he seemed more cheerful in the face of his son's rebuff.

"Gee, I do miss you all while I'm away," Jack continued. He squeezed Ruby's arm from across the table and she winked at him. "But it does seem to be Frank's name that comes up most often. Why, just a few weeks ago, you were the center of a very interesting conversation, Frank." Frank kept his eyes on his plate while he ate, as though deaf to his father's conversation.

"It so happened," Jack continued, "that I picked up a hitchhiker from just outside of Boston. He was a kid, eighteen or so, just a few years younger than yourself, Frank. But, you know, completely different—smart as a whip. A college boy. In fact, he was on his way home for summer vacation when I picked him up. He tells me he studies biology.

"'Biology,' I say. 'Now that interests me. It's a subject I happen to think a lot about. Here's a question for you,' I say. 'It's something that's troubled me for a long time. You got this fellow Darwin who says that things keep getting better all the time. Says the world is oiled to improve. So,' I ask the kid, 'how come my son is stupider than I am? How come every goddamn Mayborn that comes into this world is just a little bit lousier than the goddamn Mayborn before him?'" Jack leaned across the table toward Frank, his face pink with pleasure. Frank looked up for the first time.

"So," Jack continued, "the kid says to me, 'Sir, it's got to do with adapting. Maybe, once, your people were king of the hill. You look like you are a lot stronger than my father, for instance. Thousands of years ago, you would have crushed someone like my father. But now, he can crush you. He is very well adapted. Which means he knows all the right people and has the money to pay them. That's putting it in the simplest terms, of course, but a species has to adapt to its environment if it's going to improve.' He was a very bright boy. He kept me in good conversation for the next forty miles, and I commented several times that his father must be very proud, indeed. 'Well,' I said to the boy when I stopped to let him out, 'you have been very informative, and I thank you. That will be twenty-five dollars for the ride.' He looks at me. Wah? Huh? He doesn't have the money, you understand.

"'It's not very smart of you,' I said, 'as a member of the human species in these modern times, not to carry any money on you, son.' I took the heel of my shoe and I stuck it into his ribs and launched him right out of my van onto the side of the highway. You'd never seen a more surprised face. I held onto his bags for fare." Jack smiled at his family. "Who's king of the fucking hill now?" He laughed out loud, and from beneath the table Keeper whined louder in order to be heard.

"Frank got himself a contract from the town, Jack," Ruby said. "They hired him to renovate Loomis Pond. He's draining it and laying down the grass, turning it into a regular park. Him and his friend Boulevard. Now isn't that something? A hundred years from now, me and you will be dead, Jack, and we'll be lucky if anyone even thinks to piss on our graves. But people will still be sitting in *Frank's* park. That's something for us Mayborns. All right, just get your hot breath off of my legs." Ruby rose, taking her plate with her. Keeper followed her out to the mudroom, where he knew she'd feed him his food and hers, too.

June stretched her legs across her mother's empty chair and lay down in her own chair, her head hanging off the edge.

"Look how long my hair is getting," she said. She amused herself by tilting her head back so that her straight, yellow hair hit the floor and buckled out.

"Well, it's plain that you're not too happy to see me home, son," Jack said. "I understand your point of view. I'm not unreasonable. You've grown accustomed to life without the sight of me. That's all right. The bad news is I'm stuck at home for awhile. I've had some shit luck on this last trip. Got in a little bit of a fix at a racetrack down on Long Island and, I'll be direct with you, I haven't a dime left. That means I can't buy any knives from the company. And they won't sell me any on credit anymore neither. So here I am. Home again. Until I can find my way toward some capital."

"Enjoy your stay," Frank said.

"Maybe I'm not saying this simply enough for you to understand,"

Jack's voice lost its self-derision, and a pink energy welled up in him. "This afternoon, I stopped by my piece of land over by the bridge. Noticed that the stumps had been cleared. And there were two new window panes on the house."

"I've done a little work on it," Frank said.

"That's mighty big of you. Considering that the land isn't even yours."

"Not yet."

"Pretty confident, are you?"

"I figured you'd need the cash sooner or later."

"And you have the cash, son?" Jack made his face look stern but there was sharp curiosity in it. "How is that possible, may I ask?"

"I've been saving."

"How are you going to save that much money on your Mickey Mouse wages?"

"I've been saving for seven years," Frank replied. Jack was silent for a moment.

"You've been saving for my land since you was sixteen?"

"That's right," Frank said.

"Well," Jack said, tilting his head contemplatively, "I have to be honest. When you first told me you wanted to buy my land, I didn't like the thought of parting with it. It's a beautiful parcel, everyone knows it. But now I'm coming round to the idea. How much did I ask for it...forty-five thou?"

"Thirty-five." Frank watched his father carefully. June swung up to a seated position.

"Blood rush." She pressed her hand to her forehead.

"Thirty-five!" Jack said. "Well, that's robbery but all right, thirty-five if you say so. Cash in hand, not that I don't trust you. It's a shameful bargain, but I make it with your mother in mind—she hates us fighting, I know it. It tears her apart. What do you say, Frank?"

"I can give you twenty thousand now. The rest when I finish Loomis Park."

"No, no, no. I need it in full. I have some debts that are pressing. If you can't pay it, I'll find myself another buyer. I'll lease it out to a farmer."

"We'll be finished by August, September latest."

"Goddamn, can't you do nothing straight? Have them pay you up front."

"No one's going to pay a Mayborn up front," Frank said. "You'll just have to go without your whoring and gambling for a few months."

"Ingrate!" Jack cried just as Ruby came back into the room, her plate glistening with Keeper's spit. Ruby looked hard at the two of them until both of them looked away, and she sat back down.

After dinner, Jack went out to the van and returned with the college boy's duffel bag. He told June she could pick out whatever she liked. She chose three T-shirts and a poster of a young woman emerging from a swimming pool. The girl was pulling herself up on the edge of the pool, the water breaking around her hips, skimming off the back of her shoulders. The pool was minty blue. Her legs, still submerged, were distorted by the water and looked toadlike, amphibian. June taped the poster up on her wall and sat on her bed staring at it. She examined the girl piece by piece: the brazen throat, the eyes blue as the water and brilliant with some private ecstasy. Her golden shoulder blades buckled with the effort of her ascent.

CHAPTER THREE

STILTED ON A HIGH-RISE of bluestone foundation, the Casablanca Bar was a white stucco cube, with a front door shaped like a child's drawing of a cave entrance. This, coupled with the fact that there was no sign on the building, made it seem as if a homesick Tunisian had set up camp on Loomis' Front Street and was, even at that moment, reclining in a nest of carpets and sipping sweet Turkish coffee. In actuality, the bar's interior was perfectly plain. It was owned by Edie Pelto, a local woman in her late forties, of Finnish extraction. She kept it clean and dour, which spoke as much of her own heritage as the Tunisian's carpets and beaten silver.

On Tuesday night everyone else in the Casablanca Bar could go to the devil, as far as Edie Pelto was concerned. She made their roast beef platters and asked after their gout and their wives, but all the while her eyes were fixed on the door as she smoked fitfully. She knew he would show up, but until she saw him, she could not relax.

It was crowded Tuesdays, on account of the fights on the big-screen television, which she had purchased with him in mind; and because of the roast beef sandwiches, which she made with him in mind. The irony being that she spent the night perspiring over the grill while half of Loomis obscured him from her view. Somehow, it was always like this for them.

Finally he arrived. The front door opened and there he was in a pair of powder blue corduroy pants and a blue and white Dolphins T-shirt. He was the only exotic concession to the facade's exotic promise. Neither black nor white, he expressed the combination with limpid, deep-set eyes and the brown, scrolled lips of an Arab. His head drooped slightly, giving the impression he was slow.

Edie put her cigarette out in a little saucer of butts by the vodka bottles and examined him. He needed shoes. His sneakers were ripped open along the seams, and one of them had no laces. He needed a hundred things. His pant cuffs looked raggedy. She made a note of this in her head.

Edie was a woman of limited needs. Even her physical form had been rationed to lean specs: the slight, serviceable body, the snub nose, blunt as a .38, and precise lips with nicotine-stained teeth tucked well out of sight. She had no husband and no children. But her life was full of things needing tending—dogs and Java Rice finches and three garden plots. It was enough. She hadn't really wanted to have children. But she *had* wanted one child in particular, someone else's child.

The first time she spotted Leon, he was a little sway-backed boy emerging from a swim in Loomis Pond. He collapsed in the sun beside his mother, a fine-featured black woman. One of his sharp little knees was raised. His eyes shut against the sun but snapped opened like a young terrier's at any small noise.

Edie was sitting near them, under the shade of a willow, book in hand. She caught the boy's eye and he stared back at her. At that age, he had frank and clever eyes.

"Did the fish bite your toes?" Edie asked him. The boy's mother opened her eyes, alert like her son, but hostile, too. When Leon didn't answer, his mother said sternly, "Have the fish bitten your toes, Leon?"

"No."

"No, what?" his mother prompted. Edie wished that she had never spoken.

"No, ma'am," he said. His voice was smooth. Tropical. Slippery as a peeled mango. He stood up to avoid any more civilities and began to sink stones into the pond.

With her gauzy, soiled headdress that she did not remove, the boy's mother was certainly from the Mercy Hill commune. The commune members often came to swim at the pond or shop at the grocery. They were a strange, unsettling sight in the beginning—outsiders, hippies from downstate. No one wanted them in Loomis. But they kept to themselves, mostly, bound together by a guru called Joseph. Edie had always imagined gurus to be fat and from India. But this man was from New Jersey or Long Island—something like that. He was short and slight, slim as a cowboy. He looked like nothing special. She once saw him eating a Snickers bar in the laundromat.

Leon's mother did not have the same loose, easy way as the other commune members. She was harsh and she wanted to be left alone. She had removed her worn boots, but kept them tucked protectively between her bare, dusky feet, as if she were bunking in a den of thieves. And in a way she was right. From the moment Edie saw the woman's son, she coveted him. It was absurd, irrational. She imagined taking the boy home with her. Feeding him, spoiling him. Washing his grimy hands in the sink, between her own hands, and guarding his sleeping face as it passed through a subset of dreams.

Edie was not a person to seek out human challenges but that day she put down her book and began to fight her way into the lives of both the mother and the son.

No sooner had Leon sat down at the bar than Phil Mason stalked over, sliding his clenched, squat body onto a stool next to Leon. Leon flinched, as if the man intended to assault him, pushing off the edge of the bar with his fingertips like a swimmer.

"What do you think of this?" Phil said, ignoring Leon's reaction. He put a large paper bag on the bar counter and pulled out a sizable rainbow trout.

"Jeez, Phil! I knew I smelled a stink," Edie said.

"How can it stink when it was fresh caught this afternoon?" Phil replied. "What do you think of him?" Leon took the fish and held it out in the palms of his hands.

"Loomis Pond used to be crammed with trout twice that size," said Shane Eskeli. He was a big redheaded man. Some years back, he had inexplicably moved to New York City. He returned a year later, but his little adventure had forever branded him an oddball—a reputation he privately relished, being an essentially dull man. "I remember when you could practically dip your hands in the pond and pull them out."

"I never saw you pulling out a trout the size of my boy here!" Phil said. "He's pure gorgeous, ain't he, Edie?"

"Goddamn Town Council," Shane Eskeli continued. "None of them know a damn about ponds."

"Yeah, you're the expert, Shane," Phil snorted. His nose had been broken three times and his nostrils were uneven.

"Just a plugged spring. Nothing fancy. They can stick in all the trees they want, but in the end the water will come back and they'll be dragging the bottom for park benches. I'll lay a hundred dollars cash on that wager,

I'll tell you what."

"Why'd they have to go and hire a goddamn Mayborn for the job, that's what I want to know?" This shot back from one of the corner tables.

"Who else is going to work like a dog on the cheap?"

"Frank probably wants to turn up the rest of his ancestors' bones. Do you know the Denney boy found a tiny little leg bone in March. Yea big."

"I'll tell you what," said Phil. "Last spring, that Frank Mayborn come around to my sister's house to take care of her lawn. Him and that retarded fellow, Boulevard. Well, at some point they knock on her door and Frank asks her if Boulevard can use her toilet. You know Becky. She's got no discretion. She'd ask the devil in for a glass of lemonade. Well, Boulevard goes to the toilet, and she's left in her living room with Frank, who says nothing at all, and his eyes are wandering around her house while she's getting the pricklies on the back of her neck, thinking that the kids are going to be home any minute and wondering how fast she can make it up to her linen closet where her husband keeps the revolver."

"So what happened?"

"Nothing *happened*. But Becky swore she'd never felt so close to physical violation in all her life."

"Now, now. The Mayborns only violate their own kind."

"I always say someone ought to call Social Services on behalf of that Mayborn girl, June. Who knows what all goes on in that house. What with her brother."

"Oh, for pity's sake, Phil," Edie said. "I can't stand that kind of gossip!"

"Now I'm not blaming them! A Mayborn girl is like catnip to her relatives; they can't help themselves and that's the unvarnished truth."

"A hundred dollars," Shane Eskeli pointed his finger up in the air. "I'll wager a hundred that the water comes back."

"I'll take that bet just to shut you up, Shane!" Phil said. "Now what do you think there, Leon? Can you do something with him? You know I'll pay you fair." Leon didn't answer for so long that Phil glanced uncomfortably at Edie for a translation.

"The head will have to come off," Leon said finally.

"What's wrong with his head? It's a beautiful head!"

"Rainbow trout's got too much fat in the head. Even if I treat it, the maggots will get to it sooner or later."

"What good's a mount with a headless fish?"

"I can get you a plastic head to fit on it," Leon said. Phil squinted at him suspiciously.

"I ain't never heard of that. You want the fish head for yourself, is that it?"

"What the hell does he want your fish head for?" Edie said. "What's he going to do with a fish head?"

"I don't make judgments on a man's lifestyle," Phil said, holding up one thick palm toward Edie. "What he does up in that cabby-shack in the woods is *his* business."

"Give him his goddamn fish back, Leon," said Edie. Leon handed the fish back but was no longer paying attention to either of them. Up on the big-screen TV, the first fight had begun. Two rangy black fighters were dancing around each other, looking nervous and put upon.

A new rush of customers arrived before the main event started, along with a flurry of dinner orders. Edie retreated back to the kitchen, taking Phil's fish with her and stuffing it in the icebox so it didn't smell up the bar. She snuffed her cigarette out on the floor and overturned a bowl of diced potatoes onto the grill where they sizzled loudly.

She wondered, as she often did, if Leon was happy. "As much as any of us, I guess," she told herself promptly. It must be lovely now up in the woods with all the wild flowers blooming and the cool, shifting ceiling of leaves and light. She believed she could live like that quite happily. But somehow Leon's reclusiveness seemed like a vigil, self-imposed and joyless.

The front door opened, and through the kitchen window Edie could see a small, elderly man with pure white hair limp into the bar. He paused at the piano and leaned against it for a moment to catch his breath. In fact, he looked like he might topple over, and Edie glanced at her customers to see if any of them would get up and help him to a seat. Most everyone was staring at the television, and the ones who weren't only stared at the newcomer and showed no sign of moving to help him.

"Savages," she said. She wiped her hands on her apron and pushed open the kitchen door, ready to offer him her arm. But when he turned her way, she realized that the man was not old at all—fifty, fifty-five perhaps, though his hair was absolutely white with tiny curls on the ends. He was clearly ill but he was not elderly, and Edie feared she would embarrass him by offering her arm. Instead, she went to the bar and told Phil to get up.

"There's a man there who could use a seat." She nodded toward the door.

"Where's his sickle?" Phil grumbled before getting up. Well, she admitted, it was true: the man looked like the angel of death come for someone. Weak as he was, though, he seemed to have a purpose in mind. His eyes swept the room as he advanced toward the bar. Some others noticed him, but turned back to the television, because the fight was now in full fury, the television commentators shouting above the crowd.

Edie watched as he slowly, and with apparent pain, maneuvered onto the empty seat beside Leon. Right then she realized who the man was. Sickness had changed him greatly. The yellowed skin, with its odd, plastic sheen, adhered loosely to the bones of his face. His eyes were wide, glassy, almost unblinking. But beneath the illness, Edie recognized the man. Joseph. The Mercy Hill guru. Her heart sank. She wanted to grab him and drag him outside before Leon noticed, but it was too late.

"Hi, Leon," Joseph said to the young man's back. Leon's head, which had been raised toward the television, now drooped again, but he did not turn around.

"Aren't you going to look at me, Leon?"

"I know who you are."

"Our troubles have made us strangers," Joseph said very softly. "You're angry with me still. I deserve it. We did some bad things, the two of us. But you were a boy and you can't take all the blame for your actions. I'll take the lion's share. Turn around and look at me, Leon." Leon turned to cast a wary glance at Joseph. Shocked by the state of the man, it was a few seconds before Leon spoke.

"What are you doing here?"

"Looking for peace of mind. Looking for forgiveness."

"I forgive you," Leon said and turned back to the television.

"That's kind. But who will forgive *you*, Brother?" Joseph began to cough violently. His shoulders curled in and his head bobbled on his neck.

From behind the bar, Edie watched, smoking. She thought about giving Joseph a glass of water, but didn't. After a few moments, the cough subsided. Joseph took in a dry, wheezing breath and wiped his mouth with a handkerchief from his pocket.

"So," he said huskily, "have you heard from Iris Utter?"

Leon shook his head.

"Mmm. Perhaps she's dead," Joseph mused. "No, no, she's not the type. I'm sure she's lost her looks by now. Women like that tend to. It's the fast living. It wreaks havoc on the soul and the soul punishes the body. She made a most unnatural mother, as you and I both witnessed, most pathetically. Monstrous—to abandon your own son. He was my son, too—"

One of the boxers was knocked down, and the crowd in the bar roared and thumped their fists on the bar counter. The noise smothered Joseph's words, so he stopped speaking for a moment and sat up straighter on his stool. When the boxer struggled back to his feet, the crowd settled.

"Might I have a ginger ale?" Joseph said to Edie. Reluctantly, she threw some cubes of ice in a beer glass, sprayed ginger ale into it, and set it in front of him. He sipped at it with his dry, colorless lips, then pushed it away.

"I've made my share of poor choices, Leon," Joseph said. "Iris Utter was one of them. The worst one, yes. She ruined me. And she didn't even have the decency to do it for spite. She was simply brainless. That's what pains me the most. Imagine if I had chosen Kitty instead…sweet Kitty, who would have never left me. Mercy Hill might still be thriving. I would not be alone now, wasting away without anyone to notice or mind. Terrible to be alone. Well, you know all about it, Leon. You have made your own share of poor choices, haven't you, my lamb?"

At this, Leon slid off his barstool and, without a word, walked to the door.

"What?" Joseph called after him, his bony hand curling back against his chest. "What have I said?" When Leon didn't respond, Joseph turned back around, saw Edie staring at him through a shroud of her own cigarette smoke.

"I don't know what I said to offend the young man," he said to Edie.

"What do you want from him?" she asked Joseph. He looked at her for a minute, then seemed to recognize her. He smiled. Long, curved indentations formed along his cheeks.

"A small thing, Sister."

"I'm not your sister," Edie said.

"But we both love Leon, don't we? We have that in common at least."

"I didn't show him love with the back of my hand," Edie replied.

"A boy must have two parents. A mother of rectitude and a father of retribution. Light and dark. Vishnu and Shiva."

"Oh God, what crap," Edie said. Joseph nodded and smiled, or grimaced—she couldn't tell which—and dropped his eyes. The skin on his eyelids was puckered like the skin on raw chicken. His hair was so fine and white. It looked to Edie like the hair of a child, and she was conscious of a desire to touch it.

"Tut, I've gone and scared him off," Joseph said. "He's such a sensitive boy, always was. Now he'll scurry back up to Mercy Hill and we won't see hide nor hair of him for weeks."

He's right, she thought. Leon will just hole up in his little cabin, afraid of coming back to town and running into Joseph. It struck a chord of fear in her and she stubbed out her cigarette, came out from behind the bar, and rushed out the door. She saw Leon in the distance, walking in the direction of Mercy Hill. Even from far away, she admired the way he moved, swift and smooth, like a cat. She called to him, but he would not stop or even turn around. So Edie began to run. She felt the roughness in her lungs, reminding her of her longstanding plan to stop smoking. Her heels clicked clumsily against the pavement, and the sound seemed too loud and too urgent. Leon stopped. Maybe he felt sorry for her. She didn't know what he thought, or felt, about her.

"Just let him talk," she said when she caught up with him. "Give him five minutes, that's all. Just let him talk, say no to whatever he wants from you, and that will be the end of it."

Leon didn't answer her for a long time. He blinked off into the darkness, his eyes drifting across the rows of houses. Here and there, lit windows offered patchy, intimate glimpses.

"After that," Edie said, "you'll be rid of him."

Leon nodded slowly, without conviction, as if he were humoring a farfetched belief as a courtesy to the believer. Together they walked back to the bar, and Leon took a seat at a table nearest to the door.

"Thank you, Sister," Joseph said as he hobbled past Edie and sat down across from Leon. He coughed hard and wiped his mouth with the handkerchief.

"I'll be direct," Joseph said. "I've got the cancer, same as your mother. I've been to nineteen doctors and three surgeons. I've been cut open and poked at and they've done everything short of bleeding me with leeches. Nothing's worked. So I've come back for the water."

"What water?" Leon asked.

"A simple man is the Lord's most precious child, Leon. But a simpleton is despised by all. The water, the *water!* The water from the spring."

"There is no spring," Leon shook his head. "There never was a spring."

"It's there, Leon. We weren't digging in the right places."

"We dug for it everywhere. It doesn't exist."

"Are you denying me this?" Joseph's eyes, dark and marginal, had been staring out of his skull like a suffering immigrant. But now all their latent authority rushed in, as blood rushes to a wound. Leon's head dipped so low that from behind he appeared headless.

"Your mother was a righteous woman," Joseph said. "I never said a word against her. When she died, you became a son to me, since my real son was taken. Do you understand what I mean? Is there a shovel on the grounds?"

"Yes."

"Yes. You'll start digging tomorrow." He stood and took a deep breath, his ribs expanding like a greyhound's beneath his shirt. "When two people know as much about each other as we do," Joseph added, "it's not prudent to refuse such a small favor."

CHAPTER FOUR

THAT FOLLOWING DAY, WHEN June walked into the store, Ed eyeballed her as she hung back in the corner, spinning the rack of comics, making it squeal irritatingly. She was waiting out the other kids. She didn't even look his way, not like a normal girl who would have given the whole mess up with sloppy, teenage mooning.

Ed had been grateful for her secretiveness at first. He was no creep. She was fourteen. Yeah, he knew it. But he was no child molester. He'd had kids bouncing round him for over twelve years, and never once did he have a sexual thought about any of them. He wasn't that way. After all, he'd seen June hundreds of times, never thought of her in any way except as a Mayborn and a little thief.

It wasn't until his wife left him that he actually noticed June. Noticed that her neck was hard and white and how, now that the weather had turned warm, she wore blouses that exposed her long, smooth belly with its slight meatiness pinched in by her jeans; noticed how all the other kids ignored her, not deliberately but as a matter of course. And when they did talk to her, it was as if they were muttering some small reminder to themselves. It had touched him, the way she accepted her lot in a silent, bovine way. He began to reconsider the Mayborns. He wondered if they'd been dealt an unfair hand by the whole town.

Today, as he watched her spinning the comic book rack, he thought about her future. Likely, ten years down the line, she'd be stretched thin with a litter of squalling kids, maybe some of them with blackened fingernails—that weird Mayborn trait—and each from a different father. It depressed him, sure, but there was nothing he could do about it.

The moment the last child had left the store, Ed, without coming out from behind the counter, said, "Go on, June. Go on to school."

She pulled a comic from the rack and came over to him.

"L'il Lu is so cheesy." She tucked the comic into her knapsack. It irked him that she didn't pay for it, but he let that go. Coming around to meet him behind the counter, June pushed her bangs up off her forehead. "Feel my head."

"I can't tell that kind of thing."

"Just—if it feels hot. Just put your hand." She took his hand and placed it on her forehead. It felt sticky and he pulled his hand away.

"Yeah, I guess you feel warm. Listen, June, get going. You can't miss school again."

"It doesn't matter. Today's the last day of school. They don't care if you go on the last day of school." She sighed and let her body swoon against his, her arms slung around his collar. "I just feel like lying around all day today. Like a big, fat slob."

She was tall, nearly as tall as Ed. Her upper lip was lifting a little against his cheek, and he thought she would kiss him—a thing she had never done since their affair had begun. It was an omission that had bothered him. Once, he had tried to kiss her tenderly on the lips and, after a bewildered pause, she suckled his tongue as though she were sampling cheese. Now he kept perfectly still, feeling her cool teeth against his skin and then hearing the *hinnnn* of air being reeled in. She was smelling him. He pushed her away roughly.

"Go on, girl. Go to school." She looked at him ruefully, without appearing the least bit offended, and sailed out through the tinkling front door just as the two Hannula boys came in. They were quick, crafty boys. He'd never caught them at anything, but he knew they were up to something all the same. Worked like a team, the way they spread out across the store. He stood up on his little stool behind the counter to get a better view.

June walked around the back of the store, reentering through the service door, which Ed kept unlocked on Wednesday mornings for deliveries. She edged past the fresh, sealed boxes but stopped to grab a handful of Three Musketeers out of an open carton and slip them into her knapsack; then a can of pop and three bags of Sugar Babies.

Sidling behind Ed without being noticed, she walked quietly up the steps, toward the bedroom. Halfway up, she began to detect a strong odor. Stopping, she pressed her tongue against the roof of her mouth and pulled the air deep into her nostrils. She frowned. The odor was thoroughly familiar, but it was mixed with some other thing too, casting a fatty, dark-yellow smell. She continued up the stairs cautiously, her sneakers padding lightly on the wood. Just as she reached the landing, she caught a quick glimpse of the back of a woman dressed in a nightgown. The woman's hair formed a woozy, careening aureole as she walked down the hall and disappeared into the bathroom. Mrs. Cipriano was back.

A small whimper came from June's throat. She inhaled the vaporous trail left in Mrs. Cipriano's wake. It was fading but the strident pulse of its origin signaled to June from the bedroom.

Her head felt hot. Her breath came fast and quick as she opened the bedroom door, then approached the bed itself, the full weight of the odor bearing down upon her. It was a stink; her stink and *their* stink and something more; the bed was drenched in a precise chemistry of all three of them and had formed a fourth organism: violent, exotic, repellent even to June. She remembered her matches and dug into her pocket to retrieve them. The first one she struck so frantically that it ripped before it lit. The second match lit and she held it beneath her nose, breathing in the soothing sulfur, feeling it short-circuit her sense of smell. Down the hall, she heard the shower turn on. Her head felt a little clearer now. She looked around the room. The closet door had been shut. The jewelry box, too, had been closed and the spill of beads had vanished. Beside the bed, the embroidery hoop remained as it was, the needle still masted up through the grapes. June sat down on the bed, unzipped her knapsack, then carefully placed the embroidery hoop inside.

The effects of the sulfur didn't last long, and the stink began to assault her afresh—a corruption of her own happiness, the theft of her triumph, for which she did not blame Mrs. Cipriano at all. Not at all. She *cherished* Mrs. Cipriano like a sister.

June struck another match. Slowly, experimentally, she touched the flame to the edge of the quilt and was a little surprised when it caught. A demure flame. She sucked in the lovely fumes, held them in her nose as long as she could until the fire sputtered out. She struck another match and brought it to the quilt again. The flame slipped easily beneath the top layer of cloth and crept toward the center. The stink cowered back wonderfully, and June stayed on the bed, breathing in the purity of the flames until they forced her to stand. She stood there until the heat and smoke drove her back, out the door, which she shut solicitously, like the bedroom door of a sleeping infant.

Chapter Five

June slept late into that beautiful, beautiful day. She might have slept on, nestled in the light that poured through the French doors of her bedroom, but the elastic on the sleeves of her nightgown was bothering her. She pushed the sleeves up and down her arms, but could not escape the sensation of rough cuffs. She had to take the nightgown off, and by then her sleep was completely broken.

She got up and rummaged through her dresser until she found a pair of shorts and a sun-colored halter top. She tied the straps around her neck, but her fingers felt dismantled.

Opening the French doors, she stepped out onto the little verandah attached to her bedroom. Loomis Park spread out before her, a few hundred yards off. She lowered her head, suddenly reminded of yesterday's painful odors, and cautiously took in a small noseful of air. It was okay. She could smell the park, but no more or less than usual. To her sharp nose, the earth was still swollen with the carrion dust of trout and bluegills and bowfin. The savage smell of new grass stung her nasal cavities. In the park below, her brother, Frank, and his friend, Boulevard, hammered rebar into a retaining wall of stacked railroad ties. Boulevard gripped the rebar with both hands. His head jerked back a little each time Frank struck the rebar with the sledgehammer, but his gangling arms kept a fixed triangle in front of his body.

There was not another soul in the park. Even though it had been years since there was water in the basin, people still superstitiously skirted along the old banks. At night, the window-light from the houses above skimmed across the top of the park without dipping into the empty crater, as if refusing to acknowledge that there was no water surface to deflect its touch.

The branches of an old pear tree poked through the verandah's railing. Here and there, tight-fisted young pears hung from their stems, giving off a green odor. June leaned over the railing. She could hear the voices of the girls sitting on the park's mounded bank, nearest her house. The girls, who were all in June's class at school, were huddling and flexing and minutely active while doing nothing at all. June could hear their chatter, cloyingly punctuated with the *hsssst* sound that confident young girls make, but their words were indecipherable.

The girls themselves were prohibited to June; June's ancestors, by simply living their lives, had secured these girls against her. If someone had bothered to tally up all the Mayborn crimes, all their misfortunes, and accidents, the sum would likely be no greater for them than for any other family. But their mythology had forged a substratum that gave the town its form and contour, as much as its rolling hills and rock-laced fields.

Reaching over the balcony, June plucked one of the little pears, releasing its fledgling aroma. She hurled the pear at the girls amiably. It missed them by yards and they never even noticed it. But still, the girls all rose together at that instant, instinctively cued by a collective knack for self-preservation, since, of all Loomis's citizens, it was the young girls who were most at risk of being absorbed into the Mayborns by a trick of Eros, like their bygone Libarger sisters.

June went back in, put her sandals on. Her eyes drifted over to Mrs. Cipriano's embroidery hoop. It hung on the wall beside the poster of the girl emerging from the pool. The threaded needle still pierced the cloth and the purple embroidery floss dangled in a loop. The hoop had relaxed its grip and the square of cloth wilted in the middle, the needle threatening to topple. June pulled the cloth taut again and turned the hoop's butterfly clasp a fraction of an inch. The needle snapped upright, sending a pang through June's body. It was not unpleasant, like the nudge of ovulation; a whisper from the human coven that kept up a secret, mass communication of morals and standards—a communication constantly eluding June. She was left to navigate by impulse and scent, following a vague trail. Yet she longed to be pinioned to society's strictures, and had she been privy to them, she would have made an admirable puritan. But each rule that she grasped and acted upon revealed yet another that she had unknowingly violated.

June headed out to Cipriano's, cutting through Loomis Park. The sun burned hard against the recently tilled topsoil; June could smell the fevered coma beneath it, and the longing of the pond bed—dry, unsatiated, furious.

As she approached her brother, he stopped working and looked at her.

"Tie your straps tighter," he muttered. She had forgotten that her top was still tied carelessly and was dipping low in the front.

"Hey, June," Boulevard said. "Hey, where you going, June? To see your sweetie pie? Do she have a sweetie pie, Fank?"

"I'm going to Cipriano's," June said.

"She going to *Cipriano's*, Fank. Oh, jeez." Boulevard rubbed his hands against his sides and laughed. His protruding eyes, behind their thick glasses, never left Frank's face.

"Cipriano's burnt down yesterday," Frank said. He reached out suddenly and grabbed the straps at the back of her neck. The bow was tied so loosely it came undone instantly and he pulled her backward, as though he were yanking on the reins of a horse. "You want the whole town to see your tits?" he said, then retied the straps roughly in a tight knot.

"Stay away from Cipriano's," he said. "There's burnt shit still falling off the building."

"I want to see what it smells like now."

"Leave the smelling to the dogs," Frank said. She continued on, ignoring the hoarse laughter of Boulevard.

The plastic letters of the CIPRIANO'S CANDY sign were now yellow drippings fused to the black, blistered siding. The store was brittle bones. June looked at it for some time, pulling the biting, black air into her nose.

A movement in one of the second-story windows caught her eye and she saw the passing figure of a woman. Mrs. Cipriano? Ducking under the yellow tape strapped across the doorway, June opened the front door. The bell tinkled in a faint, mangled trill. Inside, the floor was littered with seared flakes. Fire had conquered every odor, burned off the scent of a hundred chocolate bars. It struck June then that when she would finally leave Loomis—and she knew one day she would—she would like to go out burning. She wanted every place she'd ever been to smell only of June Mayborn for months afterward.

She climbed the stairs quietly. If it was Mrs. Cipriano, she didn't want to alarm her. She only wanted to talk to her, to explain about the fire.

The bedroom door was wide open, but there was no one inside. She walked in and stood in front of the bed. It was the blackest thing she had ever seen. She ran her hand over it. The burnt cloth lifted and curled around her fingers. Carefully, she laid herself down upon it and closed her eyes. It felt as though she was stretched across a blade-thin layer of ice, already crackling under her weight but holding—miraculously holding. She tried to conjure up the sense of well-being she had experienced in the bed, but without the old smells she felt lost.

A slight twist of her spine and the mattress shattered beneath her. She dropped into its charred depths, the tremendous sponge that had soaked up Ed's semen and all the odors of June's body and those of his wife. Fire had conquered all these things, too.

From the other side of the wall, the wall that the old man had used to knock on for his food, June heard a voice, soft and faint. Not Mrs. Cipriano. She thought of the young girls the old man had told her about, the girls he could have had. Iris and Kitty. Did they come back, those girls, to see him?

She got up and brushed herself off, then walked down the hall and into the old man's room. The woman inside stood in the center of the room gazing about, a cardboard box cradled in her arms.

"Where's the old man?" June asked. Linnet Denney shrieked and turned. She blinked at June, her little mouth curled in the shape of an egg.

"He's dead." She uttered the words with unseemly fascination. She was a private groupie of the dead and usually took pains to hide the fact. But, seeing that the girl was a Mayborn, and therefore pagan, Linnet took less care.

She was a thickly built woman, with massive cheekbones and knotted jowls giving her face the hourglass silhouette of a 1930s movie starlet's body. Her shoulders were masculine and rounded, as if she had been harnessed to a plow her whole life. This aspect often made people forget

Linnet's position as the minister's wife. Conversation regularly turned rough in her presence, full of scandal and cussing, until someone noticed that Linnet's pink, child's lips were smiling imploringly at the offender, as if to say, "The last thing I want to do is spoil your fun, but for heaven's sake..."

"I smelled death on him the other day," June confided.

Linnet's eyebrows lifted. She wanted to put her head close to the girl and whisper, "Tell me more ..." but she caught herself in time and nimbly secured the appropriate expression: "May the good Lord have mercy."

"Amen," June said. It was a response that she had heard somewhere, television maybe, and it seemed right. The two began to feel more comfortable with each other. Linnet put down her carton and sighed over the poor Ciprianos, who were left without home or livelihood and whose few salvageable possessions she was now collecting for them.

June's resemblance to her father was not lost on Linnet. June had the same attractive cragginess, the small, lewd mouth and square face, the flaxen hair. Linnet reddened slightly as she noted this, and the cilia on her jowl rose.

Linnet knew the church had done sorry little in the case of the Mayborns. If the truth be told, they had abandoned the family altogether as hopeless. And who among the members would have wanted the Mayborns in their church, in any case? This struck Linnet as terribly wrong now. A lapse in Christian charity.

She looked at the girl and wondered...What if Linnet herself made the first move, and tried to bring the Mayborns into the church. Starting with their daughter. It would be difficult, maybe impossible. It would make people angry. But Linnet was a bold, hearty country girl and the notion appealed to her magnificent constitution.

"Tell me, June. Do you like to bake?"

"I don't know." She drew in Linnet's odor. It was damp and briny beneath a dry dusting of powder.

"I'm sure your mother must bake. Occasionally."

"Our oven broke. We use the stove top."

"Ovens can be fixed," Linnet said strictly. A case against Ruby was already beginning to harden in her mind. "The church's Ladies League will be holding a benefit bazaar to help the Ciprianos through their hard time. Would you like to help, June?" Linnet asked as formally as a swearing-in.

"Yes," June said eagerly.

"We'll need volunteers for the baking—" Linnet began, and June's hand shot up in the air and stayed there, her fevered blue eyes boring into Linnet's dampening blue eyes.

"Well." Linnet looked away to hide her pleasure, her eyes drifting across the walls and settling on the view out of the window that the firemen had shattered. "I wonder if we've been entertaining an angel unawares." June gazed into the air around her as well.

"It's possible," June said to be polite. But she imagined that if the old man's spirit *was* in the room, they had said nothing that would have entertained him, he had seemed to have such a weird sense of humor.

CHAPTER SIX

Ruby was kneeling in the mudroom, her head pressed against the waist of a tremendous Saint Bernard. Holding his hind paw backwards, she snapped at each of his thick, black nails with a guillotine nail clipper. The dog jerked forward at each snap, wrestling his head around to see what was happening; but his owner, Edie Pelto, kept him steady by wrapping her arms around his brisket, her right wrist flexed severely to hold a cigarette away from his fur.

"June had a seizure last night," Ruby said.

"I thought she was through with that," Edie said.

"So did I. She hadn't had one in two years. But she came home with a fever yesterday, and in the middle of the night I heard her thrashing around in her room."

"What does the doctor say?"

"Never been," Ruby said. "They bug me." This was slightly ironic considering that Ruby was dressed in head-to-toe doctor's scrubs, her grooming uniform that she'd picked up at a yard sale. "How's *your* boy?"

"Taking it bad," Edie said, appreciating the fact that Ruby always referred to Leon as if he were her son. She had always liked Ruby, whom she had known since they were girls. Ruby was hard and self-contained, a loner who only seemed inclined toward Mayborns. But Edie had never detected a single drop of malice in her, never heard her say a bad word about anyone, though Lord knew people always had plenty to say about Ruby.

"Pass me a little puff, will you?" Ruby said. Edie extended her cigarette over the dog's back and Ruby took a drag from it. "Why did that Joseph fellow come back to Loomis anyway?" Ruby took up the dog's other hind paw and resumed clipping.

"According to Leon," Edie said, "he came back for the water."

"*Our* water?" Ruby shuttered her dark brows skeptically. "Our water tastes like bung."

"Not the town water. There's supposed to be a mineral spring up on Mercy Hill. An underground spring. Before Leon's mother passed away, she gave me an earful about the commune. A lot of it was against the place, but other things...now I'm telling you, that woman had some healthy common sense, but she was convinced that the commune was built on a sacred site. She said at night she felt the strength of the place swirling under the ground.

"Joseph had an idea that there was an underground spring and they brought up all kinds of dowsers and witch doctors and what-all to try and locate it. I guess they never found it. But here's the strange thing. When I was a little girl, my grandfather used to tell me about a place up in Mercy Hill that the Indians believed was the spot where people were first created. An Indian Garden of Eden, he called it, and he also told me about a spring that ran under the earth that could heal sick people. He took me up to the site once. It was completely cleared, even though there hadn't been anyone living up there. My grandfather said that no trees ever grew in that spot. I found some buttons made of deer antlers that were polished and burnt black on one side. And there was a stone piling too, made by the Indians, my grandfather said. Big around as a truck tire and higher than my head. It gave me the heebie-jeebies, and I wouldn't go near it."

The dog screamed and yanked its paw away from Ruby. One of its nails was tipped with blood.

"Oops, hit the quick. Well, go on you old bastard," Ruby said, smacking the dog on his rump. "Go off in the corner and sulk, I'm done with you anyways." She stood up and the dog slipped out of Edie's arms and chuffed off to lick its nail in the corner.

Against one wall was a massive bookcase that held no books but displayed a complicated jumble of items, neatly arranged in a Pig Latin logic that only Ruby understood: a length of rusted chain, coiled and speared with a Coca-Cola pencil; a magnifying glass; an industrial-size jar of peanut butter; three tiny bottles of cologne; a puckered gourd in a bird's nest; five boxes of disposable douches for taking out the smell of skunk from a dog; a small fossilized stone; the red L-shaped flag from a mailbox; and, among many other items, a stack of ribbons, from which Ruby now chose a navy blue.

"Leon came to my house this morning," Edie said carefully. "He asked if he could stay with me for a while."

"No kidding?" Ruby rolled out a length of ribbon, snipped it, and with her quick fingers worked up a large bow. "I thought that boy would never come out of the woods."

"Neither did I. Something spooked him up there last night. He said he heard crying, like a baby crying. It was so clear that he got out of bed and walked around outside, to see where it was coming from."

"A coyote maybe?" Ruby stuck her forefingers in through the ribbon loops and spread them.

"That's what I thought. But he said coyotes don't sound like that."

"Well, are you going to take him in? Puff."

"Hell, yeah." Edie put the cigarette to Ruby's lips, then stubbed it out in the sink. "He lived with me before, you know. When he was fifteen, after his mother passed away. It was what she wanted, and Lord knows it was what I wanted. But it wasn't what Leon wanted. He kept running away, back up to Mercy Hill. And there I'd go, chasing after him into the woods and hauling him back out of the commune. I guess he hated me then. But, for Pete's sake, they lived like animals in those tarpaper cabins, scrounging food, living under the thumb of that madman. I don't mean to speak evil of the dead, but jeez, things had deteriorated so bad up there. That's why Leon's mother asked me to keep him in the first place. I just couldn't figure out the appeal."

"Jack used to prowl around up there, too," Ruby said. Her bow was finished but she was fidgeting with the loops, poking her finger through each and stretching it tight. "The appeal being all them young girls."

"Mmmm, Ruby."

"I wonder how he'll take the news."

"How I'll take what?" Jack asked. He was leaning against the doorframe, holding a can of beer. He wore a blue Hawaiian shirt splashed with pineapples, unbuttoned to his stomach.

"Goddamn, Jack, I hate it when you sneak around," Ruby said.

"What news am I supposed to take?" Jack asked. Ruby grabbed a handful of the St. Bernard's fur, right behind his ear, and tied the bow to it.

"Cipriano's burned down the other day," Ruby said.

"With Cipriano in it, I hope," Jack said. He winked at Edie and rolled his can of beer across his chest.

"No. The Ciprianos are fine. But they were keeping a boarder. That Joseph fellow from the commune. He'd come back to Loomis a few weeks ago," Ruby said. "He died in the fire."

"Joseph? He died? Well, goddamn." Jack shook his head, blinking into his beer can. After a minute he looked up. "What about a funeral?"

"There's nothing to bury, I guess," Ruby said.

"I heard they're going to spread his ashes," Edie said.

"So," Jack ventured carefully, "I suppose all them Mercy Hill people will come back to Loomis for that."

"All?" Ruby rolled her eyes. "Some. Maybe. If he's lucky."

Jack tipped his head back against the wall and looked up at the ceiling to avoid his wife's eyes. He knew that she knew what he was thinking: she knew he was wondering if Iris Utter would come back to Loomis to spread the ashes.

Jack turned away, went outside. The sky was a thick gray, threatening rain. He walked around out back, stirring Keeper, who was stretched out across the driveway. The dog lifted his head and followed Jack with his slothful, judicious eyes. Sighing, the dog rolled his body upright and trailed Jack to the back of the house.

A few yards from the house was a low projection of stacked stones— the only remains of the ancient Mayborn barn. It was obscured by tall clumps of phlox, rangy weeds, and, here and there, some daylilies, their freckled orange petals flexing backward. Jack sat down on the stones, scraping at the lichen with the bottom of his beer can. Keeper sat close but at a distance, where he would not be suddenly kicked.

Iris Utter had been Jack's golden moment. His prize. She had appeared one night at Mercy Hill, manifested out of the damp evening air. Sixteen or seventeen years old and hauling a greasy backpack, wearing layer upon layer of clothing, her hair matted. She was a runaway, but she was also not anything so decided as that—a filthy Venus, a visitation. He wouldn't have dared to approach her. But she chose him, *she* chose *Jack Mayborn*. And in response, he was like a monster released from a spell; his vision cleared and he saw his life for what it was: the blistered ceilings, the illiterate wife, the half-wit son who had grown inside the illiterate wife.

Between Iris Utter's legs he battered down his life, crushed it against her cervix. He was not what he was. He was lifted up, resuscitated. And then suddenly, without explanation, she was finished with him. He never asked her why. He knew instinctively that Iris Utter would always be exempt from blame. He just retreated back down the rugged trail through the woods, back to the slumping house on the top of the hill, and he never saw her again.

CHAPTER SEVEN

T HE SIGN IN FRONT of the Fellowship Church was changed the first
Wednesday of every month. Linnet chose the slogans herself,
plucking them from the *Christian Life Journal*. In general, the "words of
wisdom" reflected Linnet's large, impertinent, almost manly sense of
humor, such as "Forbidden fruits create a lot of jams." Today, before
entering the church, June stopped to read the sign, whose message was
more succinct than usual. "Eternity…smoking or nonsmoking?" Beneath
that, squeezed in with black plastic letters, was a notice for the Fire Relief
Bazaar to benefit the Ciprianos.

June walked inside, passing through the double set of wooden doors
into the chapel. It was the first time she had ever been inside a church. It
was empty, silent, dark. The odor of bananas drifted above the vacant
pews and circled the pulpit, an odor so thick she might have been standing
in a hot, tropical grove.

"How delightful!" Linnet came up behind her, dressed in a very short, adolescent summer dress, tied at the back. Beneath that she wore a pair of denim pants with a floral cuff. There was a white, powdery dusting on the sloping shelf of her breasts. She smiled at June, flushed with the hubris of success and the thrill of imminent opposition to her success.

"Is Mrs. Cipriano here?" June asked.

"No, no. Just the Ladies League." She drew her arm beneath June's. "Come inside. We're finished with the breads and we're onto pfeffernüsse."

Together they went up the aisle, June escorted like a bride by Linnet, and through a door hidden behind a wall of mossy draperies. As they walked down a short hallway with a pale green cinderblock wall, the smell of bananas grew stronger.

They stopped in front of a metal door, the sort that might have been marked for high voltage. Linnet shoved hard on the bar handle and ushered June inside the church rec room. It was a large room with an orange and yellow shag carpet and three sets of couches and chairs, arranged in each corner, like a living room showroom in a secondhand store. At the far end, five ladies toiled away in a kitchen. They looked over when the door opened—five earnest, pleasant faces.

"Mrs. Trott, do we have an extra apron for June?" Linnet said. By degrees, the ladies' expressions turned from confusion to distress.

"Well, I'm not sure as we do," said Mrs. Trott, a thin older woman with close-cropped white hair.

"Then she can take mine," Linnet pulled off her dress, alarmingly, until she revealed a blouse underneath it. She cupped her fingers around the dress's neck hole and placed it over June's head.

The kitchen was very small but the ladies managed to give June a wide berth as Linnet taught her how to cream the butter and sugar. The ladies resumed their work in stony silence, but Linnet was undaunted. She reasoned that the idea of the Mayborns must be brought back into the church in the most natural way possible. Slowly, but with great intent. The other church members would certainly resist. But the thought of their resistance only bolstered Linnet's determination. She *would* bring a Mayborn back into the arms of Christ. Perseverance was the ticket. And perhaps, if she saved the one, she might go so far as to save them all.

The butter was hard and June struggled awkwardly with the wooden spoon. Her arm ached a little but she remembered that the ache was for Mrs. Cipriano. She imagined the new clothes that Mrs. Cipriano might purchase with the bazaar money; imagined that she would go with her to help pick them out, trying things on together, laughing. Maybe Mrs. Cipriano would buy something for June, a little trinket. She listened to the metallic scrape of the sifter, smelled its chafing heat. That was how Ed's mouth had tasted—tinny. Like canned meat.

"Do you know where Christ is, June?" Linnet asked suddenly.

"Right now?" June asked.

"Now. All the time." The ladies did not raise their eyes from their work but they were listening hard. June shook her head.

"He is standing at your door, June. He's knocking to come in. Will you let Him in?" June hesitated, looked around at the ladies. They kept their heads bowed. They all seemed to know the same secret and they weren't telling. Their silence hinted at the same puzzling message as the twitching embroidery needle.

"Would *you?*" June asked.

"I have," Linnet answered, her voluptuous face radiant with pleasure at June's question and at her own reply. "I have and so have all of us here." For the first time, the other members of the Ladies League lifted their eyes to meet June's.

The bazaar was a success. The baked goods had raised $321; they had collected two cartons full of clothes, old pots and pans, and chipped china. The loot was piled into Linnet's Ford Festiva, and she and June drove to the mobile-home park where Ed and Mrs. Cipriano were living with Ed's mother.

On the way Linnet warned, "Remember not to sound your trumpet, June. Good deeds should be done very, very quietly."

June nodded but wasn't really listening. All her thoughts coiled around Mrs. Cipriano. She pictured Mrs. Cipriano's face when she saw all the gifts. She imagined catching Mrs. Cipriano's odor, an odor she had never really smelled, except when it was already spoiled by the bed. And after they gave her all her gifts—the shiny cookware, the ceramic trivet with a mother duck and her ducklings, the summer quilt with squares of cornucopias—June wanted to explain to Mrs. Cipriano about the fire.

It was a tidy mobile-home park, the trailers set up one behind the other in tight military formation. Each home had a precise, clipped rectangle of lawn that was mowed every other week by the management. Ed Cipriano's mother lived in the back of the park, where a heavy bulwark of hanging begonias lined the trailer awning.

Linnet and June walked up to the door, each holding a big carton stuffed with donations. Linnet put her carton down and pushed the buzzer. A few seconds later June knocked loudly.

"Patience," Linnet said. The door was opened by a heavyset elderly woman. She had a lame leg and rocked backward and forward on the good one.

"Yes?" she said and stared at both women, up and down.

"We're from the Fellowship Church," Linnet said.

"I don't keep money in the house," the old lady said.

"No, no, we've brought things for *you*," Linnet said. She opened up her shoulder bag, pulled out an envelope, and handed it to the old lady.

"Three hundred and twenty-one dollars. To help your son and his wife get back on their feet."

Ed came up behind his mother. At the sight of him, June felt a vestigial twitch between her legs. She clutched the carton tighter against her body. He looked from June to Linnet, then back to June again. His face was unfriendly. He slipped his hands in his pockets, where they played nervously with some coins, while the old woman limped off, back into the depths of the trailer.

"And these are the rest of the donations," Linnet explained, picking up her carton and depositing it just over the door's threshold without walking in herself. "June...now give him yours."

"Where's Mrs. Cipriano?" June asked without giving up her carton.

"Why? What do you want with her?" he asked, his voice full of suspicion, his eyes boring angrily into June's face. "She's out." His eyes dropped to June's legs, which were bared in a pair of shorts. She didn't shave and her legs were covered with fine, golden hair. Linnet noted Ed's gaze, admonished him mentally.

"Then I'll wait for her to come back, Ed." June shifted the carton in her arms and moved toward the door, but Ed blocked her way.

"What's the idea bringing her here?" Ed said to Linnet. "I don't want her here."

"Why not?" Linnet asked. "What in heaven's name has she done to you?" Ed did not reply, but the coins jingled faster in his pockets.

"Well, if *you* don't know, Ed," Linnet said curtly, "I'm sure June doesn't either. This child is a member of our community. This child is not an animal to be kicked at and scorned, regardless of who her family is." Linnet took the carton out of June's hand, wrested it out, really, and set it down on top of the other one. She hooked her arm in June's and pulled her away from the house, both of them ducking beneath the hanging begonias.

"She's a menace!" Ed called after them. "She shouldn't be allowed loose on the streets, mark my words, she's done bad and she'll do worse!" June looked back at him. She felt a downward tug on the muscles around her lips and her throat seemed to swell within her neck. She thought she might cry and then suddenly she was crying, very quietly. The lining of her nose throbbed, then swelled and clogged.

They drove off in the little Festiva, Linnet silently consumed with her own outrage. June watched the wooden cross hanging from the rearview mirror as it swung back and forth with the curves. A two-tone dark brown and tan Buick approached and passed them by, and June thought she saw Mrs. Cipriano in the driver's seat. June craned her neck to look back but the car turned and disappeared.

"It's not your fault, June," Linnet said finally.

"I just wanted to talk to her," June said.

"I know. It's not fair. But you carry the burden of your family on your back. Listen, June dear. There is a certain type of sin…" Linnet persued this line carefully. It required tact. It was the issue that had been foremost on her mind ever since June had set foot inside the church. "There is a sin within families. *Some* families. I believe it is a sin in your family, June. And it has to stop. It's the wedge that is driven between you and the rest of the community. It sets you apart from everyone else. From the other girls, from your neighbors. From people like the Ciprianos."

"What is it?" June asked. Linnet was hoping that the girl would simply understand, so that she wouldn't have to go into details. But never mind, she would speak frankly. And besides, Linnet was a big old country girl at heart. She knew that life was often crude; the body was an organ of sensation, of overeager nerve endings and rushing blood, curiously made so as to be perpetually at its own mercy, defying its own salvation. Linnet adjusted her rearview mirror, adjusted her seat belt, and bravely plunged into the subject of incest.

CHAPTER EIGHT

THEY WERE CLOSE TO Loomis now, driving through a tangle of back roads. Lee Utter wore a perfectly plain, black dress, while Lee's mother, Iris, was dressed in a haze of lilac. On Lee's lap was a physics textbook opened to a section on electrodynamics, the page held down by a spiral notebook covered with a frustration of figures and pink specks of eraser dust. Lee gripped a mechanical pencil in her right fist, its tip poised against the paper, but her eyes were following the landscape, scrolling out beneath a bruised late-afternoon sky.

Along the side of the highway the houses they passed were lonely encampments of peeling paint and leaning barns affixed to stretches of healthy cornfields. The smell of cow dung, like salt water gone rank, peaked and flagged but was always present.

"If I don't stop and eat something I am going to pass out," Iris exclaimed. "I swear I am going to pass out right at the wheel and kill us both." She was a beautiful woman. Yet on close examination, her features—

the length of her nose, the set of her eyes, the cut of her chin—were just a hair's breadth away from being unbeautiful; they pushed the limits yet hit the mark, making her beauty seem all the more exquisite and rare.

"We're almost there," Lee said. "Let's just get this thing over with. You can eat after."

"I'm dying for pancakes. You can't get good pancakes in the city. Why is that? You're going to give people nightmares with that dress, you know."

"It's appropriate for a memorial service," Lee replied.

"It's ghoulish."

They passed a tractor hauling a spreader, creeping along the edge of the road. The farmer held up his hand in greeting without looking at them.

"He waved at us. Did you see that? How hysterical!" Iris was stretching up in her seat to get a better look in the rearview mirror. Her spirits were high, Lee noted with some apprehension.

They passed a hitchhiker on the opposite side of the road, standing in front of a motel. She was a young blonde girl dressed in a shirt with a tuft of green feathers around the collar, her thumb extended. She looked to be around Lee's age, maybe even younger.

Lee shook her head.

"What?" Iris said.

"Nothing. There was a girl back there, hitchhiking," Lee said. Iris looked in the side-view mirror.

"Maybe she's a hooker," Iris said offhandedly. The comment annoyed Lee at first; but then she recalled that the girl had been standing in front of a motel. It was possible, Lee supposed. The girl suddenly seemed less defenseless, and she drifted easily out of Lee's thoughts.

About a mile outside of Loomis, a diner's gleaming chrome signaled, and Iris turned the wheel sharply and pulled into the parking lot.

"This will make us late," Lee complained as they got out of the car.

All eyes turned to them as they entered the diner, then lingered on Iris. They took a table near the counter where two overturned coffee cups in saucers anticipated them on paper placemats advertising the powers of raw bee pollen. A chunky, chapped-lipped girl in a blue jumper handed them menus, their laminated pages rubbed raw. Before she left them, the waitress blinked suspiciously at Iris's beauty, as if it were a trick.

"Well, I know what *I'm* having," Iris said, slapping down her menu after a minute. Her eyes passed over her daughter quickly.

"I hate your haircut," Iris said.

"It's the same one I get every time."

"It makes you look like a nun. I don't see why you won't let me cut it for you."

Occasionally, people said that Lee resembled her mother—but that was generous. In fact, she only resembled Iris in the same irritating way that a poor reproduction mimics the original: the similar features were coarsely rendered, the forehead a little too high, the lips too thin. At sixteen years old, Lee was dark, lank, ordinary, except for a certain stiffness that was uncharacteristic of someone so young. She wore no makeup. Her dark hair was cut precisely. Although Iris worked in a hair salon, Lee never allowed her mother cut her hair, but instead went to an elderly Austrian barber, who cut it neat and straight and exactly the same way every time.

The waitress reappeared, cocked one thick hip, and held her pen above her dupe book. Lee ordered a coffee only—she was too nervous to eat—and Iris asked for pancakes.

"It's after five o'clock," the waitress said. "We only serve breakfast until eleven-thirty. It says it on the menu." And she reached past Lee to pick up the menu, flipped it open to the first page, and pointed to the small print below the word "Breakfast."

"I have had pancakes on the brain since I woke up this morning," Iris confided to the waitress without looking at the proffered menu. "Pancakes stacked this high, soaked with syrup. Do you ever get that way—what did you say your name was?" Iris asked, even though the waitress had not told them her name before.

"Carolyn."

"Carolyn!" Iris repeated brightly, as if it was the most unusual and delightful name she had ever heard. "Do you ever just have a *craving*, Carolyn?" Iris was flirting gently. It was how she fought the tiny battles in her life, a tactic that confused her boyfriends and made them wonder, after the relationship was finished, what exactly had ended it.

"I guess that's obvious," the waitress said without humor, as though she suspected Iris was making fun of her.

"Those are curves," Iris assured her. "I'd give anything for curves like yours." The waitress rolled her eyes and smiled a little for the first time; she wished her mother was there to witness such a sleek and ornamental person paying her a compliment about her figure.

"Well, I can ask the cook about the pancakes anyways," the waitress said. "The worst he can say is no."

"We have nothing to lose by asking," Iris agreed.

Almost all the other customers in the diner were men. There were loud men and silent men and nothing in between. Sometimes the loud men stopped talking. Their bodies curled over their stained mugs of coffee and they became the silent men.

Iris leaned her head back against the plastic orange booth partition, blinked her green, sloe eyes around at the other diners.

"I don't know what it is about country people," Iris said. "All the men look like rapists."

"Shhh," Lee said. She opened up her physics book and tried to focus. She loved the beautiful correctness of physics; the way it parceled things out, forcing the mute, evasive world to explain itself. And it carried the heft of a promise.

She had been accepted for early admission into Cornell University and was slated to start in the fall. She'd given her mother the financial aid forms to fill out, but Iris had put them between the leaves of a *Glamour* magazine and promptly forgot about them. The deadline for the forms passed. With no aid, Lee could not attend. She'd have to wait until next year. But her guidance counselor had told her about an exam in September for a competitive scholarship; if she won it, she could start college in January.

"I hope they don't think that I'm going to touch his ashes," Iris said suddenly. Beneath the table her leg was jiggling so hard that it shook the booth partition. "I'll help scatter them if they're in a cup, but I won't use my hand."

"That will make a good impression," Lee said.

"I don't care what they think of me. I have nothing to prove to them," Iris said, her voice rising.

"Shhhh," Lee said.

"I know they hate me. I know they thought I was the one who made Joseph go crazy. But the man wasn't well from the beginning, with his underground springs, his vows of silence, his vows of celibacy. Was it my fault that he fell in love with me?" She frowned and stared out the window at the highway, her jaw working and forming divots along her jaw line.

Lee watched her mother's face carefully, waiting to see which direction Iris's temper would turn. In truth, she hoped that Iris would give way to her fury and decide to turn around and head back to New York. That would be best. It hadn't been a good idea to come in the first place. Iris was too unpredictable in difficult situations. She was a creature made for pleasure in the present moment. The past was a nag, a bullying totem of angry or hurt faces—discarded boyfriends, infuriated employers.

"I hope that Joseph didn't die in pain," Iris said now, turning back to Lee. "I keep thinking about that. I hope he slept through the fire." Her concern seemed genuine, and for the first time since they had learned of Joseph's death, Lee too felt a pang of sorrow for the man. She had once loved him like a father, when she was little, before she grew to hate him.

"He used to sleep very soundly, I remember," Iris continued. "Noah could cry all night long and Joseph wouldn't wake up."

The mention of Noah shattered Lee's composure with one brute blow. Her lower lip drooped and the blood rushed into her stomach. She clamped down on herself, clenching her toes hard within her shoes. For so long, she had put all thoughts of her younger half-brother out of her mind. It was useless to dwell on him; it only upset her. He was gone, and that was the end of it. And since neither she nor Iris ever spoke of him, it was as if he'd never actually existed. Now, at the sound of his name, her nerves bristled.

The waitress approached, an oblong plate stacked with pancakes in her hand.

"The cook said no at first, but I sort of sweet-talked him," the waitress said as she placed the plate in front of Iris, smiling at her.

Iris looked down at the plate, then lifted one of the packets of syrup by its edge and flapped it toward the waitress.

"Do you have any real syrup?" Iris asked. The waitress's smile collapsed.

"That's syrup."

"No, it's sugar water," Iris replied.

"It says syrup right on the label," the waitress countered. She looked confused, off-balance. It was a look that Lee recognized; she'd seen it before on the lovers who were summarily told by Iris that she could no longer see them; that it was beyond anything she could explain.

"It says 'maple-*flavored*' syrup."

"Well, that's all we have," the girl snapped back.

"Then why even serve pancakes if you don't have syrup?" Iris's voice was pitched, her face pinched with agitation as she appealed to Lee. "I mean, what's the point?"

"Fine, then. I'll take them back," the waitress said and she reached over and picked up the plate, but Lee grabbed it back.

"We'll keep them," Lee said. The waitress hesitated, then her gaze dropped to Lee's hand. Each one of Lee's fingernails was black and shriveled, as if they had each been torched individually. The waitress dropped her grip on the plate, perhaps to avoid making contact with Lee's nails. Lee's face burned red, and she quickly placed the pancakes back in front of Iris, then curled her fingers in and tucked them into her fists.

"You should have thanked her," Lee said after the waitress had left.

"I did."

"No. You didn't. Are you eating them or not?"

"I've lost my appetite," Iris said. She pulled out some singles and slapped them down on the table, then shimmied her body out of the booth. Lee followed, squeezing past tables of men who hummed in Iris's wake, and avoiding the glare of the waitress who was angrily conferring with the other waitresses, all of them like the polar coordinates of Kepler's laws, the motion around a central point, like planets around the sun. They existed in reference to the center, were defined against it, expressed by its parameters. Iris held that monopoly. She consumed all that was connected to her, and she did so as if she had a right to it, to everything that caught her eye. You could not fight her. You could only step aside and hope for the best.

CHAPTER NINE

JUNE WAITED AT THE edge of the highway, in front of a vast cornfield. She wore a red and white striped tank top with a plume of pale green faux-ostrich feathers around the neckline, and white pedal pushers. One foot had slipped out of its sandal. Her bare toes pinched up bits of gravel and deposited them on the rigid body of a hummingbird. Behind her, goldfinches darted through the field, flying low. The heat poured out of the filmy sky and burned at the top of June's scalp. She stuck out her thumb. The car passed without slowing.

"Later for you," she said. She grabbed more gravel up in her toes and dumped it on the bird's head. She wondered if she should hold a sign that said what her destination was, but she had no particular destination in mind; these were day trips, and she always came back to Loomis before dark.

The first time she had stood by the side of the highway, just a few days before, it was in the hopes of seeing Mrs. Cipriano in her two-tone Buick. She had an idea of flagging her down, so that the two of them could talk, finally. She could explain about the fire; they could go for a ride and June would explain the whole thing. But the Buick had not passed by. Instead, other cars stopped for June. Strangers. People who had no idea that June was a Mayborn. And since they opened their car doors for her, she naturally stepped inside.

The last ride she had taken, the boy hadn't asked where she was going. He was nineteen or so with a pale orange goatee. He shed a nervous internal odor that astounded June. He was timid with her; he wanted to please her. He had no idea who she was. Somewhere outside of Millboro he pulled off onto a narrow gravel road. They spent half an hour at the base of an oak tree. Afterward, she left him with a tract from the Fellowship Church. It had a smiley face on the front of it and beneath it asked "Do you ever feel like nobody really cares?" She had stolen a bundle of them out of the minister's desk, with its drawer handles carved like acorns, and carried them with her all the time. At the end of each ride, she opened her pocketbook and chose the tract that she thought would best suit the driver.

Not all of them were men. Once she rode along with a family that bought her a hamburger at McDonald's. Once she rode with an elderly pair of French ladies in an RV, who fed her lunch and gave her a box cutter for self-defense. But there was also the man in a poncho. He wore a fishing hat and had an elegantly trimmed white beard. While he was driving he put his hand on her leg. This man was older than Ed Cipriano. The smell of the tainted bed came back to her, a phantom odor that made her cringe. From her pocket, she pulled out the little blue box cutter that the old French ladies had given her and sliced open the top of his hand. She did it in one quick, untroubled movement. It took a full minute for the man to even notice the blood. When he did, his eyes snapped wide open in a comical way. He swerved the car into the next lane and crashed into a low cement guardrail. June glanced over at him. He looked unhurt. She, herself, only felt a little sore where the seatbelt had cut into her. But the man was not moving. He just stared ahead blankly.

"Are you okay?" She pushed him a little. His hat, dislodged from the impact, toppled off the back of his head.

"My hat," he mumbled. She reached in the back seat and retrieved it for him, then opened the door and walked off, finding another ride a few yards up the road.

Today, however, no one was stopping. Maybe it was the heat. Cars sped past—strangers that June would never get to meet. Across the field, the farmer emerged from his house, lank and bowed, shuffling past the long-deserted cinderblock chicken house. He walked through his cornfield, talking, touching the young stalks. As he came closer, June saw that he was having a conversation with no one at all. He asked a question and paused, even stopped walking for a moment to listen to the answer. "Well, that's the truth in a hand basket."

"The heat's likely to fry us both," June said to him when he was close upon her. He moved his head about in her direction. His eyes were coated with a blue film. She smiled widely. His face grew stern; he no longer trusted the corporeal. He waved his long, yellow hand dismissively.

"No," he said.

"I said, it's hot as—"

"No. Move on," he ordered.

"I'm June—"

"No, no," he refused her, turned his back to her and began to return to his house. It put her in a bad mood. She paced the side of the road. Sweat stung her skin and the ostrich feathers were making her collarbone itch. In the distance, a silver car appeared and she stood out near the middle of the road and stuck out her arm, her feet planted, her blue eyes burning into the windshield.

The car slowed. Its wheels turned onto the gravel shoulder and passed over the small burial mound of the hummingbird, pressing it into the ground. The driver was an Asian man who looked somewhat bewildered. He reached over to unlock the passenger door and hastily moved clutter from the front seat to the back.

"Where are you going?" he asked. June said nothing but slunk down in the car seat. When June was very angry she tucked herself into a lapse, experienced a sort of vertical fainting spell. The man stared at her for a moment. He had a plain, wide, patient face.

"Excuse me." He reached across her and fastened her seat belt. June sat up and looked at him.

"What's your name?"

"Sunny Taka," he said. He looked like a brand-new sofa pillow.

"Where are you going?" he asked. When he spoke it seemed like he was biting the air.

"Where are *you* going?" June asked.

"Home."

"Okay then." She sat back and stared ahead, waiting. He looked at her a minute, decided that he was amused and interested. They drove only three or four miles out of Loomis when he turned in at a motel. Its sign was a huge, freestanding cow with a blinking yellow neon bell at its throat. THE MILKHOUSE MOTEL was scripted across the cow's side but the motel office had a cardboard sign on its window: "Breesport College Dormitories. NO VACANCIES."

Sunny Taka's dorm room was at the far end of the motel's parking lot. He opened the door for her, swept his hand, and said, "Please." The room was neat and flimsy. The curtains and the bedspread looked as if they had been sewn from little girls' dresses. On the ceiling panels, beige water stains bulged.

June parted the curtains and looked out the back window. Three yards away a herd of Holstein cows grazed behind an electric fence. They seemed particularly inclined toward gravity; their legs lifted off the ground with effort and were replaced gratefully. They didn't play, they didn't quarrel. Each one kept careful distance from every other one.

"Moo," June said.

At his little utility kitchen Sunny had taken out a bag of grapes and was carefully washing the fruit in the tiny sink. June walked around the room, stopped at a steamer trunk on the floor.

"I'm going to open this, okay," she said and lifted the lid. Inside were smaller boxes, mostly cardboard, and in those were Ziploc baggies with rocks inside. Sunny came over, grapes in hand, and knelt by her as she peeled open a baggie and removed a rock. It was oval with furrows running across its middle.

"Bumastus," Sunny said. June traced it with her finger, then put it back in the bag.

"There's loads of junk like this in Loomis Park," June said.

"Fossils?"

"Stuck in the mud. It used to be a pond a few years ago. But the water's gone. Can I hold your hand?" She reached out and pressed his hand into both of hers. She brought it up to her nose and smelled it.

"I like the smell of Chinese."

"Japanese. So." Sunny bit at the air nervously, then took his hand away and clapped his head.

"What is today's date?" he asked.

"July second," June said. Sunny Taka laughed.

"Tomorrow," he said, "I am a married man! This is my joking." He laughed some more, then opened his eyes wide at June. "I am hiding from two ladies which frighten me so badly." He sighed. "Tokyo, so, five years ago. I was at the university. I was not happy. My mother had chosed a career for me and then a girl for me to marry. I met her once. There was nothing so wrong except I did not want her and she did not want me either. I have habits. A wife will disarm me." He broke off a bunch of grapes, put them on a paper towel, and handed them to June.

"But more than that," he said, "I had ambition—big and small together. Like a fossil, a small item, but big consequence. It made me feel lazy and immoral. In Japan I always feel immoral."

"Don't feel that way," June said and patted his back gently. He smiled at her.

"Thank you," he said. June put a grape in her mouth, rolled it around. Then she spit it out and tore off the skin with her front teeth.

"Do you know what a seizure is, Sunny?" she asked.

"Seizure, yes, yes. I know," Sunny said enthusiastically.

"I have seizures sometimes. Right before they come, I see a certain thing. The same thing all the time."

"What thing?"

"I see a pair of arms with no fingers. The arms are wide open, like this, and they are coming at me. When they touch me I have the seizure."

"Frightening!"

"I used to be frightened. But the last time it happened, I looked up. Right before the arms closed around me, I saw its face. Do you know who I think it is, Sunny?" Sunny shook his head.

"I think it's God." She gazed directly at Sunny, who looked up at the ceiling for a moment.

"Ah," he said. He nodded his head slowly. "Such kind of interesting thing. Because it is often the young girls who see this kind thing, a holy vision. We have, in Kyoto, a thirteen-year-old girl who cries tears of small, colorful threads. In any case, what is God like?" He smiled at June.

"Well," she said, "his breath smells of blueberries." She opened her purse and found a tract that had, at the back, two little boxes you could check off. One said, "I have received Jesus Christ as my personal savior," the other said, "I have rejected Jesus Christ as my personal savior." She handed him this tract. Then she folded her paper towel around her grapes and gently opened the door to let herself out, back to the highway for the next ride.

CHAPTER TEN

THE TOWN OF LOOMIS was so nearly exactly the same as Lee had remembered it that any small changes were glaring. The grocery store, with its faded advertisement for Black Bowl Tobacco painted across its brick side, had installed large picture windows, through which the new, computerized cash registers could be seen, as well as a shelf of video rentals. The mingy stone on the post office building had been scoured bright with acid.

The houses remained the same, for the most part—plain, boxy clapboard. The ones closest to the pond were larger, more original, but generally more dilapidated. These once belonged to Loomis's first citizens, farmers who had prospered on dairy or chickens, then plunged back into poverty after the Second World War. Poor management often brought them down, the sons lusting after glittering machinery and taking out impossible loans. In the end, anyhow, they could only afford a back toss of technology's favors as she sped on toward ever-fatter arms. Some of the families recovered, though their farms did not. The old dads took work in the shoe factory in Breesport, their tanned, creased necks growing pasty, bending over rubber soles, while their sons gratefully put aside the stink and squall of farm life for cleaner commerce.

The center of Loomis then slid east, away from those old farmhouses. Here and there, marks of those pioneer merchants remained: an ancient gas pump resting in someone's front yard like a sun-weary cowpoke, houses with double storefront windows and a pair of rusted, dangling chains hanging off the porch roof where a sign used to be.

According to Iris, everyone was to meet up at Loomis Pond. But when they reached the spot where the pond should have been, it wasn't there. Instead, there was an empty basin filled with a veneer of fine grass, sheltered by straw, and evidence of work in progress: a stack of lumber, a series of drainage pipes, a tractor. Iris and Lee stood for a moment, disoriented.

Then they saw the people gathered at the far end, about a dozen of them. They were wearing jeans and bright, cotton dresses—dressed for a picnic. A wave of self-consciousness about her own black dress made Lee's face heat up, but her sense of propriety squelched it quickly; these people had never done what was proper.

They descended a set of stairs into the basin, and right away saw a single figure break from the crowd and come toward them. The woman had long, white-gray hair and wore a loose white dress. She looked like a well-heeled, middle-aged angel, which was exactly what she was. A fallen socialite, a displaced debutante, Carol Ann Enders blew into the commune one year, bringing with her a redheaded child named Wanda, who still had a rasp in her voice from the California sun.

"Lee! Without a doubt, Lee! Wanda will be so happy to see you," Carol Ann cried as she closed in on them. Lee noticed how Carol Ann had aged in opposition to her personality: a loss of weight urged up the severity in her face, her wide lips pinched downward, and two pouches of dissatisfaction formed on either side of her mouth. Her voice, however, was the same—buoyant and sweet.

She reached for Lee first. Lee's muscles clenched automatically, as they always did when people touched her, but she returned the embrace.

"And Iris!" Carol Ann's voice betrayed a small tonal drop of dismay. It was only a moment's lapse—Carol Ann was one of the people who left the commune once Joseph became involved with Iris. But then she took Iris's face between her hands, as though greeting a small child, and kissed her forehead.

"I am so sorry," Carol Ann said, crediting Iris with a widow's grief, a display of generosity typical of her. "It would have made Joseph very happy to know you came. He adored you."

"I doubt that *they* will see it that way," Iris said, staring at the crowd.

"Nonsense," Carol Ann assured her.

"Is Kitty here?" Iris asked.

"Is it *Kitty* you're worried about? Oh, she'll barely notice you. She's fairly overcome, poor thing. She's hardly said a word and hasn't stopped clutching Joseph's urn since she arrived. She says the ashes are to be scattered in the stream up on Mercy Hill, is insisting upon it, as a matter of fact," Carol Ann shrugged and smiled. "Come." She hooked her arm through Iris's. "The service has started already. It does look like rain, though. I hope it holds off a little longer. I'd hate to go slogging through the woods in a storm."

They approached the small gathering. Iris and Carol Ann slid into the thick of the crowd, but Lee remained on the periphery, listening to the man who was giving a sort of eulogy. His name was Ivan Robbins, a slender, game-looking man in his early forties. His face was small and oval. His lips were bowed and chaste. He might have been a priest and then again he might have been an actor, which, in fact, he was. He was well known among a small circle of theatrical pioneers, mostly other actors, who regularly admired his courage for acting in unknown plays staged in murky, unknown theaters. When they told him this, he generally answered, "Here's my secret: I'm the most unmarketable actor in New York." It was spoken with self-deprecating humor but it often left the young actors feeling slightly cheap.

"The first time I saw Joseph," Ivan was saying as he gazed around at the group, "he was sitting on a bench on 86th Street, right outside of Central Park. It was the middle of winter. I had just finished my first semester of university. I was snug as a bug in my declared major and my L.L. Bean parka and here was this man. Sitting alone. All he had to keep him warm was a thin horse blanket and his beard, which was down to here. I dug into my pocket and held a dollar bill out to him.

"'I'll take your dollar,' he said, 'if you'll sit on this bench with me for ten minutes.' So I did. We talked for a long time, or really, he talked and I listened. About love. About God. I realized that I had just spent five months at an institution of higher learning—one of the best in the country—and never once did a professor speak about love or God. When I started to shiver, Joseph took off his blanket and wrapped it around me. Later, he told my wife, Kitty, that he'd netted me like a butterfly that day." Some of the audience laughed appreciatively and turned to look at Kitty.

Lee followed their eyes to a heavyset woman with two pudgy children standing on either side of her. Lee was shocked at the change in Kitty, whom Lee had remembered as a slim, athletic woman. She had been Joseph's first, and most ardent, devotee and shouldered the bulk of the commune's chores. Now Kitty's face was misshapen with added weight, and her skin looked siphoned dry. Her blonde hair, once soft and long, was now so coarse that it tented stiffly around her head. She was crying, and from the raw look of her eyes, had probably been at it for some time. In her hands she clutched what looked to be a beer stein—Joseph's urn.

It seemed impossible that Joseph could be held in someone's hands like that. In life, he had been untouchable, beyond the reach of all of them, save Iris, perhaps. No one knew where he came from, who his family was, what he did for the first thirty-nine years of his life. He simply appeared one day, as Ivan said, on a bench outside of Central Park, and people came to hear him speak. So many people came, in fact, that the police began to chase them away for blocking the sidewalk. It was Ivan who purchased the land on Mercy Hill—in all likelihood, he owned it still—a home for the prophet, and anyone else who wanted to follow him.

Out of the corner of her eye, Lee caught sight of a large, unsavory-looking stranger. He stood apart from the crowd, a sheepish loiterer, and he was staring at her. His hands were stuffed in the pockets of a cheap suit jacket, which was too small for him, and his blond, almost white, hair was slicked back into a greasy ponytail. Lee felt an instant aversion to the man, yet she wondered if he was someone from Mercy Hill whom she simply did not remember. She forced herself to nod at him quickly. His eyes brightened, making Lee sorry she had done it.

"He broke us and we mended stronger at the break …" Ivan was saying, his voice growing louder as if he were approaching a conclusion. Lee edged her way deeper into the crowd, away from the man with the ponytail. Bothered suddenly by the thought that she might have offended him, she glanced back. The man's eyes were still fixed on her, and he pushed his chin out toward her encouragingly. No, he didn't seem at all offended, Lee decided. His type didn't have the sense to know he'd been insulted. If anything, he had the look of a person who wanted something, and who would have no compunction about asking for it at the first opportunity.

CHAPTER ELEVEN

THEY TOOK THE OLD Indian trail. Once in the woods the group grew quiet. Lee noticed that people often did that when they first entered the woods. She wondered if it was the crush of nature that shut them up, the sudden burden of plant oxygen crowding out their own breath and the barometric drop of human confidence. Lee, herself, felt it powerfully, even on this old familiar footpath, overgrown from lack of use.

The path turned steep. As the group ascended, their breaths became heavy, toiling pants. Some of them stopped to crouch against a tree for a moment, to rest and laugh at themselves: "It's been a while, it's been a while." The trail, vague to begin with, had disappeared altogether. Led by Ivan, the procession began to wind about in a halting, roving manner until, finally, Ivan stopped.

"I think we're a little lost, folks," Ivan said.

"Well, there's a fucking epiphany," came a voice from behind Lee and then a hollow thumping. Lee turned to see a young woman with flaming red hair standing barefoot, slapping the soles of her shoes against a tree trunk, trying to dislodge the mud. Wanda Enders, Carol Ann's daughter and Lee's old playmate, nattily dressed in a navy linen suit with a delicate gold chain around her throat. Her expertly cut hair was the same brilliant orange of a stripper's. Lee recognized her old friend instantly, yet Wanda had changed. Her cheeks had grown taut and she gave the impression of being "finished."

Carol Ann took the shoes from her daughter's hand and wiped off the muck with her fingers. Relieved of her cares, the young woman looked around. Her eyes rested on Lee, her expression betraying neither surprise nor pleasure.

"And then, just as they realized that they were hopelessly lost, it began to rain," Wanda said to Lee. The sky had indeed grown dark, and there was an ominous dampness in the air. Wanda looked down at Lee's black dress, and her eyebrows rose derisively.

"That's taking things a little far, don't you think?" Wanda said. "Everything but the armband?"

"I'm dressed properly," Lee answered.

"And the rest of us are very improper, yes, point taken."

"Don't listen to her," Carol Ann said. "Wanda isn't happy unless everyone is squirming." She handed her daughter back her shoes and rubbed the muck from her hands.

"Then I'll be in pure ecstasy when we're all standing in the rubble and rot of whatever it is that's left up there," Wanda said. Her freckled eyelids, coated with pearl shadow, fluttered. "Stay for the summer? We'll be lucky if we can find a dry shrub to sleep under tonight."

"Are you staying up here?" Lee asked Carol Ann.

"Ivan and Kitty are, at least. I brought some extra clothes and whatnot, in case I decide to. Wanda is free to do what she likes, of course."

"Say that louder, please, for the gods to hear," Wanda replied.

The group began to complain about poor planning and someone suggested that they scatter the ashes right there, where they stood, then head back the way they had come.

"Absolutely not!" Kitty said and clutched at the urn as though it were about to be wrested from her fingers.

"It's going to rain any minute," Kitty's son said morosely, slapping at the air. "I'm going to get soaking wet."

"Put your bug cream on," Kitty said distractedly.

"It smells like feet," he said.

"You smell like feet," his younger sister muttered. She was as fat as her brother but had a pretty, round, insolent face and creamy skin.

Iris's spirits, however, appeared to rise in inverse proportion to the falling ones around her. She walked several yards ahead, up the crest of the hill. "Ivan, come look," she called back down over her shoulder. "Isn't that a path up there?"

Ivan rushed up to join her, calling back to the group, "Just sit tight, everyone. I'm going to jog up ahead for a look-see." Iris joined him, and the two of them disappeared into the woods.

"That's what I always admired about your mother, Lee," Wanda said. "She can ferret out the ugly drama in any situation. Poor Kitty. Oh, yes, there's going to be trouble. She doesn't have a lot of time, but your mother's a dervish. She'll manage."

Lee glanced at Kitty. Her face was tight with annoyance.

"I'll tell you a secret," Wanda continued. "I had a little idea about you and your mother. Made a little bet with my mother on our way up here. Didn't I, Mom? I bet that the two of you would have switched places by now. That Iris would have buckled down, gained fifty pounds, and turned into a big old housefly. And that you would have become a fabulous, promiscuous lunatic. Remember I told you that, Mom?"

"I don't know, Wanda. You tell me so many things."

"But I was completely wrong," Wanda continued. "I don't think either one of you has changed at all, have you? Except, you're a little more so, Lee. You remind me of something…what? Yes! You remind me of an eccentric countess, exiled to a crumbling palazzo in Venice. *Self*-exiled for some dark past misdeed. What have you done, Lee Utter? Confess, and you can glide out of purgatory with your dashing gondolier."

A shower of light rain began leaking between the leaves and the odor of the woods deepened. Iris and Ivan returned triumphantly, looking very much the picture of an attractive and intrepid couple, who might as easily be adjusting their crampons in Nepal as leading a hike up Mercy Hill. They found the trail, they said, only a few yards away.

The ground underfoot was moist and mucky. Lee's heels snagged in the soft earth and she stumbled repeatedly, grabbing hold of branches to steady herself. Though she'd grown up in the woods, she'd never developed a knack for it. She generally stayed close to the commune grounds while the other kids gloried in the endless maze of trees. The city suited her more. She liked its fabric of numbers laid out lengthwise and crosswise, ascending and descending; she liked the way the city was nestled in a cradle of phone lines and gas lines and water pipes, which hardly ever failed and were swiftly and mysteriously repaired when they did.

Now she found that if she stepped on the balls of her feet, she could keep her heels from sinking. It was a slow, mincing stride, an awkward tiptoe, which slowed her down until she fell back to the rear of the procession.

"Hello, Iris's daughter." The voice crept up behind Lee as if it had been crawling on its hands and knees the whole way. It was the man with the ponytail in the too-small suit.

"Don't be nervous," he said, which made her very nervous.

"Well, that's fine," he said. "You don't know me. It's normal to be nervous. You're just a normal gal. Nothing unusual. Nothing to be ashamed of. My name's Jack. I'm an old friend of your mother's. She ever mention me? No. Well, that's all right. She's never been one to dwell on the past."

This was so true of Iris that Lee now cut a careful glance at the man beside her. He was not at all Iris's type. There was something deeply unsavory about him, a shade of rough trade. Maybe he did know Iris, but she couldn't imagine in what capacity. Overhead, there were soft ripples of thunder.

"Tell you what," the man continued, "I have a daughter just about your age. Little Junie, she's fourteen. A real pistol. Not too bright, well, I can see my own children for what they are, and I won't lie for pride. You should know that about me right off the bat. Some say it's my worst quality, some say it's my best, but I'll let you be the judge."

"Will you leave me alone. Please." The "please" was an afterthought, tagged on because she didn't like making her contempt for another human being so obvious. It echoed the accusation she had heard all of her life: that she believed herself to be above others, scoring them against her own code of conduct. But this was not so, not true at all, and she rushed ahead of the man with hurried, lurching steps that resisted the pull of the mud, feeling guilty and misunderstood.

As usual Jack missed his mark. He blamed his overdeveloped sense of delicacy when it came to women. He hadn't wanted to come right up to Iris, after all, to accost her. He'd waited and watched. A certain shyness overcame him at the last minute and his courage failed. He waited too long, and Iris had been swallowed up by the others. It was Iris he'd wanted, but he got the girl instead. It had irked him at first. Then he noticed her fingernails.

A feeling of pride warmed his gut. She was a Mayborn, there was no mistaking it. He laughed out loud at her back, and he saw her head heave a bit, but she kept going. The plain, gangling girl snubbed him. He liked her the better for it. She could not touch her mother in looks, but Iris never gave off such an air of superiority as this one. No, Iris could not take the credit for that!

He turned around now and headed back down, out of the woods, his thoughts raging with this unexpected gift: the evidence, finally, of what was possible when a Mayborn chose the proper mate.

The root of the Mayborns' disgrace struck him now—it was so logical that he wondered it hadn't occurred to him sooner. Sure, it could be traced to the first bad marriage that a Mayborn made: some club-headed farm girl, no doubt, with a breeding stock libido and the sperm of every male relative sloshing around inside of her. Then come her infant half-wits to begin the long drag-down of the Mayborn name. Wasn't it true that every so often a Mayborn emerged, fresh from the grimy gene pool, clever and successful. Grandfather Raymond had served a term on the town council, and as a youth invented his own hair tonic, rubbing it on the heads of his own three sisters and parading them at the state fairs. But here, again, leave it to a Mayborn to fall in love with a peanut roaster, dumb as a box of rocks: Granny Sulley, a woman who couldn't find her way back home from the far end of town.

His own Ruby! Jeez, when he thought of it! At twelve years old Ruby couldn't read or write. She lived on the other side of Mercy Hill, her mother dead, she running wild with her older brothers. Ruby's mother had been a school friend of Jack's mother, and when she heard about Ruby's situation, Jack's mother drove straight out to Wellsyville and came back in an hour with Ruby chattering away in the passenger seat, a garbage bag full of her belongings in the trunk. She had a narrow, yellowish face that never reacted the way you'd think it should. The manner in which he and Ruby were thrown together, like brother and sister, even though they barely knew each other—it was unnatural. It wasn't his fault that they wound up all tangled together. His mother never should have brought Ruby in like that. Jack never had a chance.

CHAPTER TWELVE

WEST OF LOOMIS POND, separated from the squeeze of houses by a mile of marshy lowland and a small bridge spanning a brisk stream, was a sizable remnant of the Libargers' original tract. It had been signed over to the Mayborns since the time of Jake's Jake. By merit of its proximity to nothing at all, and containing a decrepit, uninhabitable old farmhouse, it had been leased out for various endeavors over the years, used up, then leased again. Souvenirs of its incarnations were tucked beneath the high grass and thick brambles: in one spot, the shattered lumber from an ancient silo; in another, a grove of fir trees, survivors of a long-ago Christmas harvest.

Cats knew the place, and worked hard at thinning the population of rabbits and field mice and woodchucks. Local kids, forever scavenging for privacy, ransacked the land for rifle shells and rusted saw blades, and snapped their ankles in badger holes.

That past spring, trucks from Ferguson Lumber had rolled through the wild field to the twenty-acre stretch of oaks and maples that grew thick behind it. This land was also owned by the Mayborns, but the hardwood trees growing on it had been under a fifty-year lease by Ferguson. That spring the lease was up, and Miles Ferguson, who had been in his mother's arms, sucking on the ends of her limp, brown hair, when the original deal was struck, had now come to collect his harvest.

The land shook violently as the trees came down. The last remaining panes of glass on the house shattered from the jolting. The animals were long gone, having scrambled off at the approach of the trucks. Only a few of the more daring cats hunkered in the grasses, recoiling at each drop of a tree.

One week later, there was nothing left but a legion of hard stumps and soil that had not felt the full heat of the sun for half a century.

On that day, back in the early throes of May, Frank Mayborn had surveyed the gutted land with profound satisfaction. The sky was dark with the threat of rain that would not come, an atmospheric misstep. It dimmed the horizon and gave Frank the dazzling feeling of having arrived unencumbered with a history.

He was a young man, only twenty-three, but a certain hardness in him kept his features carefully nested in neutrality, even in his present satisfaction. As he and Boulevard walked across the sprawl of stumps, the shadows of passing clouds breaking across them, he resembled a soldier stepping through the spoils.

Boulevard sped ahead of Frank, his long, slippery-jointed limbs paddling through space. Strangled by the umbilical cord while exiting the womb, Boulevard spent the balance of his life trying to regain those pivotal, lost three minutes. He stopped short suddenly and knelt down at a clearing toward the back of the property, then began to wave furiously.

"Fank!" Boulevard called. "Fank, come look come here!" Frank took his time while Boulevard paced, his eyes fixed on Frank.

"What?" Frank asked as he came close.

"Graves." And, in fact, it was a small gravesite, a dozen or so standing headstones, and others that had crumbled to the ground. Frank knelt in front of one of the headstones. The face was worn and the writing barely legible, but Frank could make out the name *Betty Libarger* and the dates *December 1877–December 1877*. As he inspected the other headstones he found that they were mainly Libargers, most of them women, but some Mayborns, too.

"Here you are, Fank! Look what I found. Look over here for yourself!" Boulevard was standing in front of a fallen headstone. Frank approached and gazed down at it: *Frank Mayborn, 1855–1899.*

With the toe of his boot, Frank scraped off the moist layer of moss. To the right of the name was a hand, pointing down. The inscription below said *Husband to Grace Libarger. May his spirit repent his earthly trespasses.*

It made Frank smile.

"We won't put the barns over here, okay?" Boulevard rubbed his hands together in front of his chest.

"This will all be pasture land. Once we clear it."

"But we won't let the cows come near the graves, Fank. It will make the milk go sour."

"We'll see."

"Okay, but we won't do it."

"The land isn't even mine yet, anyway. You always get carried away."

When Frank was a child, he trailed his classmates to the land that he knew was his father's, and stood off while the others ran roughshod through it. Once, his father passed by in his truck at the exact moment that one of the boys had dropped his pants to pee into the silo's debris.

Jack slammed on his brakes, and the boy yanked up his pants and stood poised for flight. But Jack headed directly over to Frank, who was standing alone by the road. He grabbed Frank hard by his shoulders and swiveled him around so that he was facing the land.

"See those boys in my field?" Jack asked. Frank nodded. "One day they're going to be grown men. And they're going to have some money in their pockets. And possibly they'll want to send some of their money my way to buy the property that they're playing on now. But if you stand there all day like a jackass, they're going to associate my land with *you*, and that's going to lower its value. Understand what I'm saying?"

Frank had passed from grade to grade with little incident. But when he turned fifteen and left school for good, his teachers were glad to see him go. Some of them had taught his father as well as Jack's cousins, all of them difficult children. At the time, those teachers complained bitterly about the Mayborn children, returning home with backs pulled from trying to restrain them. As long as there were Mayborns in the school, there was trouble.

By comparison, Frank went through school quietly. But the day he left to start full-time work for Evergreen, a landscape construction company, the teachers breathed a collective sigh of relief. To one another, they said it was best for a boy like Frank to go to work young, that he was an indifferent student and it would be good for his self-esteem to excel in a more "hands-on" field. But in truth, he made them uncomfortable. It was his way of looking right through them, his curiously expressionless face, defying nature and hinting at a frightening numbness in the boy's heart. They wished him well, but they wanted him gone.

For the first six months he mowed lawns. The manager at Evergreen teamed him with Boulevard as a joke. But the two of them worked well together. They were a strange sight: the older man bouncing alongside the younger one, brandishing a line trimmer and caroling in his ceaseless, throaty monologue over the groan of Frank's mower.

All the while, the piece of land by the truss bridge loomed in the back of Frank's mind. He had never been in love. But his consciousness wrapped itself around the land in the same way that other boys his age wrapped their bodies around girls.

His future burrowed deep into the soil. He worked outside each day, at the mercy of the burning summer sun and the early, brute cold of upstate New York. Yet he never minded much for himself, but rather felt how the vicissitudes of weather acted upon the land; how the sun made the greens wax and wane, how the winds shouldered the tangled limbs of the trees being fattened for Ferguson Lumber. How the first freezing rain mortified the earth, its iced grasses shattering under the hooves of hungry deer as their bellies passed over, like cold, white sky.

CHAPTER THIRTEEN

THEY ARRIVED AT THE commune grounds just as the storm reached its peak. The wind thrashed the canopy of leaves and a cold rain spiked down on the group, soaking them all to the skin.

The group's dismal mood matched the condition of the old commune. All around, in various stages of dilapidation, were the little round yurts, their umbrella-shaped roofs mostly caved in. Some had collapsed altogether in small, sad heaps.

The main house—the building in which they had all cooked and eaten together, played games and curled against each other's warmth in the stuttering light of winter evenings—had fared badly. Its roof had rotted and sunk in toward the back. Every glass window cracked as the building adjusted each year to the harsh snows and summer heat. The front door was so severely warped that Ivan had to throw his shoulder against it several times before it opened enough for the rest of them to slip through.

Inside, it smelled of mold and rodent scat. The blankets were still hanging on the wall and several potted plants, now just parched soil, sat in the sunny spots beneath the windows. The long dining table was heaped with debris—discarded clothes, pots and pans, a guitar with no strings, children's toys. A shelf from the huge standing bookcase had toppled, and the books were in a waterlogged huddle on the floor where, even now, the rain was pooling around them, pouring through the battered roof above.

Her prediction fulfilled, Wanda Enders alone seemed pleased. She clapped her hands. *"Quelle horreur!"* she cried cheerfully. But the rest of the group was silenced by the bleak sight.

Joseph's old cabin had fared best of all the structures. It looked as though someone recently lived in it: the stove bore fresh drippings on its surface, and beside it, on a small card table, was a recent issue of *Boxing News*.

Toward the back of the cabin, above a narrow bed, dark forms lined the walls, jutting out from a legion of shelves: animals in various stages of dismemberment—mink, mallard ducks, pheasants, badgers; a turkey head with fine pins stuck in the skin around its eyes, its beak clamped shut. One shelf held a morbid collection of flayed animal bodies, raw and pink, still holding their shape. Ivan picked one of them up, and his son shrieked and stumbled backwards.

"Look, it's not real," he told his son, turning it in his hand. "It's only a foam mold." He tried to get his son to touch it, but the boy cowered away.

The storm upset their plans to scatter the ashes. The wind would blow them all over the woods, Kitty said. They would have to wait until tomorrow.

In the end, nearly everyone left, preferring to brave the mucky, vague trail rather than spend the night. They'd had enough, and now wanted to return to their clean, dry homes; they wished, in fact, that they had not come in the first place, since the image of the decrepit commune would now forever obscure their memories of Mercy Hill in its prime: the flourishing garden; the flocks of hens scratching at the ground; winter evenings in the main house, when Joseph used to read the *Upanishads* to them, while the children played on the floor by the wood stove.

"We should go, too," Lee said to Iris.

"Go *now*?" Iris exclaimed. "We can't go *now*."

It wasn't hard for Lee to guess why Iris wanted to stay. Since the memorial service, Iris's mood had been steadily quickening, and she'd been hovering close to Ivan the entire time. Iris's wet hair was now slicked back off her forehead, and the evening shadows made her eyes more brilliant, nearly feverish, under her long, dark eyebrows. Lee considered— not for the first time—how reckless it was to have such beauty bestowed on a person like Iris.

"You're making Kitty uncomfortable," Lee said. "Or is that the whole idea?"

"The idea of what?" Iris protested. There was an exhilarated, blatantly covert quality to her tone that disturbed Lee. She was hiding something, and furthermore she wanted Lee to understand that she was hiding it. "We came here to scatter the ashes, didn't we?" Iris added. "We can wait one more day."

By nightfall the rain outside had let up and the moon was nearly full. The cabin was too small for all of them to sleep in, so it was decided that Kitty and Ivan should have it, because of their children, and Carol Ann and Wanda, and Iris and Lee went off to find yurts that could be used.

Behind a copse of pine trees Iris and Lee found one that was still in decent shape, its yellow plaid curtains still hanging across the plastic-sheet windows, and with no obvious rents in the roof. Lee pulled open the door. It rubbed against the ground but opened easily enough. Apart from the odor of moldy carpets, the place might have only just been vacated. A large plastic basket filled with a jumble of clothes stood under one window and a dusty collection of candles topped a low night table. One of the table's legs was missing and an end was propped up with carefully stacked shale. There was no mattress. They had always slept on layers of rugs inside the yurts. Lee and Iris pulled the rugs outside and shook the dust from them as best they could.

But when they finally lay down, Lee found that she could not sleep. She lay on her back, her eyes open, staring at the woolen tapestry of a trio of llamas, which was tacked to the ceiling, and listening to the rain pattering down on the green plastic roof from the leaves above.

Iris laughed suddenly.

"What?" Lee asked.

"I feel happy," said Iris.

"Good." Lee shut her eyes.

"Are you happy, Lee?"

"I'm fine."

"Fine isn't happy. I want you to be at *least* as happy as I am. You live your life so small. You hold the reins so tight."

"I consider the consequences."

"Consequences to what?"

"To everything."

Iris had stayed long enough to name her newborn baby Noah. Days after his birth Noah's eyes began to lose their cast and to fidget in their sockets. He would focus momentarily on a face then look away, as if he was not quite sure what he was seeking. Iris was there to see this, too. She tended to him with extravagant affection. She tore apart an expensive silk sari that Joseph had given her and used it to line the swaddling blanket.

She was constantly using Q-tips to swab the crust from his nostrils and the sticky crumbs from the corner of his eyes.

Loath to be separated from him, she let the other women hold him only with great reluctance. Even when Joseph picked him up, Iris hovered beside him, her hands stretched open as if the baby would flop out of his grasp like a fish. Lee, who was seven at the time, wasn't allowed to hold him at all, and her hands had to be scrubbed before she could touch him. This lasted for nearly five weeks.

Then one day, without a word, Iris simply packed her belongings and left, accompanied by a young man who'd arrived at Mercy Hill the month before. She had bothered to write a quick note to Lee, explaining that she was unhappy and that she needed to get away, but she would be back very soon. Iris had pinned the note to Lee's pajama top as she slept, but the pin had not been fastened correctly and it stuck Lee's chest in the morning. She woke from the pain and rubbed her chest, felt the paper under her fingers.

For a while Lee almost forgot that the baby existed. It was relegated to a small group of women, Kitty among them—right before she and Ivan left the commune for good. The women managed to keep the baby alive and away from Joseph, who hated the sight of it. It was his own son, but it reminded him too much of Iris.

After she left him, Joseph changed. He became violent, slapping and kicking people for no reason, then retreating to his cabin for days at a time. If he saw Noah he would tear the child away from the woman who held him, take the baby off to the woods and deposit him there. Occasionally, he slapped at the woman too, who would have to wait until Joseph retreated to his cabin before she could go and fetch the baby back.

In the end, no one wanted Noah. Not Iris, not Joseph. Even the other women began to tire of the baby, since all they received for their trouble were slaps and insults. The baby was shuffled between yurts and occasionally overlooked, often left in a spot and not found again for hours at a time, cast down upon someone's rug, flailing like a bug on its back. His clothes went unwashed; his diapers were left to fester against his skin and he developed a frightening rash that crept up his back in clammy, red tendrils.

It was in this state that Lee noticed him again. In fact, she nearly stepped on him right before she crawled into bed one night. He had been left in a knapsack, apparently tucked away in there while his caretaker that day had cleaned up the children's cabin. She had zipped him in snugly, so that only his head appeared at the top. Then she had propped him up in the plastic milk crate, where the children kept their socks and underwear, and promptly forgot all about him.

Lee didn't love him back then. He was filthy and strange. But she cleaned him up and found out how to mix his formula. When he tried to suckle on her flat chest, she put a twist of her shirt in his mouth and let him tug on it. She hauled him around, wrapped in the silk sari swaddling blanket, parading him past Joseph, who, to everyone's relief, seemed not to notice the baby when it was in Lee's arms. Or maybe it was because Lee had, even as a young girl, an air of being inviolable.

When he grew heavy in her arms, the ache became the ache that she felt for Iris, who showed no sign of ever returning, and Lee bore it with flinty perverseness. Reveled in it, even, because it was pain that was actual, and Iris was pain that was without location.

Lee held him while she ate, and while she did her chores in the garden, and even while she ran about with the other kids, Noah's head bobbing and his mouth open in silent remonstrance. At night, when he lay next to her on the little cot, they stared at each other. He had dark eyes, almost black, shaped like almonds. He played with her hair until his eyelids shut. She never loved anyone or anything that much in her entire life.

When Iris returned two years later, she exclaimed over Lee's height and offered no excuses for her absence, her joy falling away only after she asked to see Noah.

"He's gone," Lee had told her and then she bolted off, not wanting to cry in front of her, not wanting Iris to see how much she hated her, for fear that her hatred would drive Iris away again, and that this time she wouldn't come back.

When Lee woke the next morning, her body was stiff from the hard yurt floor and she felt empty, scooped out. The material of her black mourning dress was slick, still damp against her skin from the rain and cold. Her stomach growled, then cramped. She turned to Iris, but Iris had gone, risen early.

Lee sat up and combed her hair as best she could with her fingers. Her body felt dirty, the surface of her teeth gluey. Outside she heard footsteps approaching and in a minute the door opened and Ivan was standing there, his eyes darting around the yurt.

"Where's your mother?" he asked. He was clearly fighting back distress, his normally imperturbable features were drawn tight, pinching a vertical crease above the bridge of his nose.

"I don't know," Lee answered. "Why?" A sickening, yeasty dread began to form in the pit of Lee's stomach. She got to her feet and wrapped her arms around her middle, pressing hard against her belly.

"*Is she in there?*" Kitty's voice, shrill and panicked, came from behind him, and then she appeared at the door, her face wild, her shirt bunched up and hanging out of the side of her jumper. Her daughter was at her side, the child's mallowy chin lowered, her pretty eyes leveled at Lee.

"Just tell me what kind of car she drives," Ivan said.

Lee went to the window and watched through the cloudy plastic as Kitty and Ivan made their way back down the trail. Kitty started at a run, but when she tripped, Ivan caught her by the arm and slowed her down. Let *them* try and sort it out, she thought. I'm so tired of it, all of it.

Sinking to the floor, Lee pulled up her knees and pressed her cheek to the dress's cold fabric. She thought about the scholarship; if she received it, everything would change. She would move upstate, away from Iris. She imagined college to be a place of rest. Like a nunnery, sober and quiet. She longed for the regulated days of labs and lectures and dining hall hours. The hollow, subterranean silence of library stacks.

The door opened yet again, and this time it was Wanda.

"Hiding from us?" Wanda asked.

"Please, Wanda, leave me alone," Lee said. But Wanda never did what you wanted her to do. She walked into the yurt and shut the door behind her, then sat down on the rug and looked around.

"Fucking Mongols, whatever. A house should have corners." When Lee did not respond, Wanda said, "Don't worry, she'll turn up."

Wanda lay down on the layers of carpet, her arms behind her head. She kicked off her shoes, revealing small, well-formed feet with manicured toenails painted a pale coral.

"Remember I had that stash of *Tiger Beat* magazines. And we used to read them at night in the outhouse, with a candle. All those cute little boys with clean hair and birthstones and hobbies. What trash. Fucking Kitty told Joseph about them, remember? And he tossed them in the stove. Power-hungry Mussolini bastard. They should have given your mother a medal for sleeping with him. Why did she, anyway?"

"Probably because he was supposed to be celibate," Lee answered, and Wanda smiled.

"You see, that's why I've always liked her. She's worth her weight. She cocks things up, but good."

"Joseph never put those magazines in the stove," Lee said.

"No? He said he did."

"Leon got to them before he could do it. He hid them until Joseph calmed down, and he gave them back to me later. You were gone by then, I think."

"Leon." Wanda shook her head "What a strange bird. Always skulking around, not saying anything. You'd think you were alone and there he was, sitting on top of a roof, patching it up. But you could swear he was spying on you, too. He gave me the creeps half the time. But *you* were always tagging along after him, weren't you? Always hauling around that toolbox of his."

God, the toolbox, Lee thought. Suddenly, she could see it so clearly in her mind—red, slippery, cold metal, the steel latch; she could feel the heft of it and hear the clatter of metal within as she carried it for him, helping him to repair doorjambs, and roofs, the chicken coop. She remembered how, when she measured out planks of wood for him to cut, he never rechecked her measurements.

Wanda stayed with Lee—whether out of kindness or boredom, Lee could not tell—regaling Lee with stories about her various boyfriends. Wanda spared neither the men nor herself in her candor, every episode leading into the next one seamlessly, as if she were the only girl in a team of circus acrobats, who one by one dandled her dangerously until she leapt to the next man. It diverted Lee's attention sufficiently to keep her from panic whenever her thoughts drifted back to Iris.

Sometime midmorning, Carol Ann rushed by the yurt's window and Lee and Wanda got up and went outside.

In the clearing the sun was burning. A clean, scouring brightness that made Lee squint. She blinked against a sunspot that hovered on the edge of the grounds, suspended above the thick underbrush. After a minute, Lee's eyes adjusted and the sunspot split and resolved itself into Ivan and Kitty, walking up the trail, accompanied by their son, who broke into tears the moment he saw that everyone was staring at him. He turned his head and slapped his hands toward them to make them stop staring, the way he slapped at the insects that persecuted him. Right behind them, plodding onerously up the trail, was an officer from the Loomis Police Department.

CHAPTER FOURTEEN

"I'D LIKE TO BE a fly on that wall," said Officer Dugger, peering out the window of the police department, watching the street. "He had best sleep with his eyes open tonight."

"Shut up," said Officer Kinnunen. He looked at Lee, who sat very still and erect at his desk chair. If it hadn't been for her fingernails, he'd never have believed it.

"This is ridiculous," Lee said. "I can take a bus back to the city." On her lap was the physics textbook that she had insisted on pulling out of Iris's car.

"We can't let you do that," Officer Kinnunen said. "You're sixteen, so while your mother is in custody, the court is responsible for you." Then he added, with sincerity, "I'm sorry."

"Who is this person who's coming?" Lee asked.

"A relative," Officer Kinnunen said. Officer Dugger laughed.

"Shut up," said Officer Kinnunen.

"I don't have any relatives," Lee said.

"Sure you do," Officer Kinnunen said as though he were reassuring her.

"No, I don't."

Officer Kinnunen sighed. He sat down on the edge of his desk, facing the window, slipped his folded hands between his knees and waited.

To his credit, Jack Mayborn did not expect a warm welcome, and therefore entered the police station with an exaggerated jauntiness. He had dressed carefully, in blue slacks and the pink dress shirt that he wore when he sold cutlery. He greeted the officers loudly, as though he'd just seen them at a card game the night before. They nodded back.

"And I guess this is the young lady?" he said, smiling at Lee. He saw the mortification on her face and his smile diminished somewhat.

"Nice work, Jack," Officer Dugger said, his eyes sliding over toward the door that led to the jail cells. Jack felt Lee's eyes on him, taking him in from head to toe, and he drew himself up.

"Is the mother here then?" Jack asked casually.

"The mother is here," Officer Kinnunen answered dryly. "I guess you'll want to go see her."

"No," Jack said. "No, no." He didn't feel quite ready to face Iris yet. "We'll settle the young lady in first." But Lee still did not rise out of her seat.

"This is the relative?" she asked Officer Kinnunen, her mouth twisting slightly in a tart smile. "Is that what my mother told you?" She looked around at their faces.

"We'll settle her right in," Jack said.

"Forget it. I'm not going," Lee said.

"You don't have a choice in the matter," Officer Kinnunen said. "I'm sorry."

Lee shut her eyes. This was one of her mother's games. In all likelihood, Iris just wanted to make sure that Lee was kept in Loomis, close to her.

"Fine," she said and stood up, her physics book pinched beneath her arm.

As they walked together through the streets, Lee focused her mind elsewhere, fastening her thoughts onto a power line that ran overhead, stringing the town together like a God's-eye. She balanced her mind on the wires, moving with the current from post to post, dipping with the slack, disappearing within the thick depths of a maple, a skittering race. She nearly succeeded in forgetting about the man at her side but he insisted on speaking.

"Did I tell you I have a girl about your age?"

"Yes."

"So what's that book you're reading?"

"Physics." Finally, after trudging up a short hill, Jack stopped in front of a house and said, "Home sweet home." It was a large house but somehow thin-looking. It tipped noticeably to the left, dislodging window casements and clapboards, and looked as though it were about to slide straight down the hill and into the old pond bed.

They walked up the driveway toward the house. A row of peony bushes tumbled over each other in full bloom and a tremendous, barrel-like dog appeared soundlessly from behind them and stood in front of Lee, panting up at her. Jack shoved the dog away with his foot and the dog backed up a little, not far, and followed them into the house.

Sitting at the kitchen table were two men, both caked with dirt, eating out of a saucepan. Three opened cans of beer were in front of the one with glasses, who rose nervously as Jack entered and rubbed his filthy hands together, then wiped them on his chest.

"Boulevard, sit down. Finish your food," the other man at the table said harshly. He was the younger of the two and he had a brutish, bluntly faceted face.

"Having a nice time, Boulevard?" Jack asked as Boulevard took his seat again.

"Yes, sir."

"My son treating you good? Plying you with my beer?"

"Sure thing."

"Yeah. Well, this here," he stepped aside, "is Miss Lee Utter." He said her name as if it should have some significance to the men, which it obviously didn't.

"Nice to meet you," Boulevard said, half-standing, then sat back down when the younger man glared at him.

"That other young man," Jack said, "the one who is ignoring us, is my son, Frank. Don't let it bother you if he won't speak to you. He feels very awkward around pretty young girls." This made Frank look at Lee with a grim, assessing gaze, then let out a derisive snort.

"Did you notice the book she's holding, Frank?" Jack folded his arms across his chest. "It's a book on physics. Do you even know what physics is, Frank?"

"Do you?" Frank retorted.

"She hugging that book up against herself," Boulevard said. "Tight against."

"You shut up," Jack said. Lee was so close to the door she might have, in a single swift movement, run out. But she reminded herself that she could tolerate this, she would make herself tolerate it.

"Now where's Junie?" Jack asked. "Where's my June bug?" His voice grew louder as he headed for the living room. "June baby? I have someone I want you to meet!"

"She's with me!" came a woman's voice. The sound of the voice stopped Jack. He looked back at his son, who had pitched his spoon into the saucepan and pushed his chair away from the table. Boulevard did exactly the same, with great enthusiasm, and both left through the kitchen's screen door, letting it slap back loudly.

"Okay. Well, come on," Jack said to Lee, his lofty mood suddenly flattened. Lee followed him past the stairs and into a small side room, shut off by a pair of swinging green saloon doors. Inside, kneeling on a floor strewn with tangles of fur, a yellow-headed girl was gripping a wild-eyed dog around the neck in a chokehold. At the dog's rump, an older woman with long black hair and wearing blue medical scrubs was yanking at the burr-covered fur with a metal pick comb. The girl at her side looked bored, even though the animal was putting on an impressive show of ferocity, growling with its snout wrinkled high above its yellowed teeth. Now the girl stared up at Lee in a curious way, stretching her neck forward and wrinkling her nose up.

"Who's this?" the woman asked. Her quick eyes flickered over Lee, and she stood suddenly and pressed one long hand to her midsection.

"I don't need any grief about this, Ruby," Jack warned.

Ruby approached Lee, looked carefully at her.

"Who's your mother?" she asked Lee.

"Iris Utter."

"It's only for a few days, Ruby," Jack said quickly. Ruby ignored him.

"You're Iris's girl?"

"Are you a friend of hers?" Lee asked, wondering if she had solved her mother's association with the man.

"She's no friend of mine. I've never met the woman. Heard about her, though." Ruby squinted at Lee. "You're nothing special to look at, are you? I thought your mother was supposed to be so goddamn good-looking."

"I don't look like her," Lee said squarely.

"No?" Ruby said. "Well, you don't look much like your father neither."

"How do you know my father?" Lee asked.

"How do I know your father?" Ruby raised her eyebrows, then snorted.

"Now, Ruby," Jack said, "don't rush things."

"Didn't you think she'd stick two and two together after she met June? No? Didn't think that far ahead?" June had rested her head on top of the dog's, adding to its grievances. The sound from his throat was like metal shearing metal.

"Let him go, June, and get over here," Ruby said. June released the dog, stepping back before his snapping teeth could reach her face. The animal scurried into a corner and crouched down, shaking.

"June, this girl—what's her name, Jack?"

"My name is Lee."

"This girl, Lee, is your sister, June. Half-sister, I guess." She lifted June's wrist. Lee looked at the girl's fingers: the black, withered nails were exactly like her own.

CHAPTER FIFTEEN

L EE NEVER ENTERTAINED HIGH hopes for her father. He existed in her life as a mutual omission, which Iris was only too pleased to accept.

Lee knew her mother's taste in men. It varied, throughout the years, but it was never good. Lately, her taste ran toward cloying young Buddhas; sensualists who called their laziness "detachment" and their greed the "pursuit of transcendent beauty." Iris was part of that pursuit, her own beauty having the accidental quality that these men cherished, and Iris always managed to pluck the highest notes on their sitars, hurling them down the path of longing until finally, spent as devotees, they no longer interested her.

But this man—Jack Mayborn—he was beyond what Lee had ever imagined. For the past two nights, Lee had barely slept, concentrating instead on handling thoughts of Jack Mayborn: he did not smell and his hair was combed, with the comb tracks visible. But he was dirty. He was dirty the way people are secretly dirty and everyone knows it. He was an oaf and he was repulsive and he had always been right behind her, crawling along, unnoticed. By the first night, she accepted that he might well be her father. By the second, Jack Mayborn seemed absolutely inevitable.

She ran her thumb across her fingernails, feeling their rough riffling. Monstrous hands. The nails of an ape. They tagged her for abomination— for something she had done or for something she was going to do. Feeling this, she had always been careful to keep herself above reproach. But deep inside, she felt soiled, as if she had clawed her way out of a swamp. Inside of her there was dirt, an unclean essence, a bad odor with no discernible source. Jack Mayborn. He had caught up with her.

In the lifting darkness, she looked over at the girl, June, whose body lay unfurled on the bed across from her. June's face was open as a slap, her nostrils twitching, her hands flung down and glancing the carpet. Unlooked-for sibling. A thought struck her. If Noah, today, had found out that she was his sister, that Iris was his mother, would he be just as dismayed as she was now?

Noah had been so clean. His nails were perfect, pink opals. Lee had been mesmerized by them, and she checked them regularly, fearful that they might begin to turn black like her own. She polished them with clear nail lacquer, believing that the shell of paint would help protect them from the blackness, and when she fixed his formula, she was careful not to let her fingers touch the milk, lest he catch the disease that was on her nails.

The night he was taken from her, he had been sick. His nose was running and Lee had propped his head up on her hand to quiet his wheezing. She took off one of his socks and used it to wipe his nose.

The next morning, he was gone, a cool spot on the mattress. No one knew a thing. No one had seen a thing. He had simply vanished. Someone suggested that he might have crawled off into the woods. Lee doubted it.

He stayed beside her always. He would not have left her. Still, they scoured the woods, calling for him, each thinking, but not saying, what they really suspected—that Joseph had done something to the baby.

For weeks after Noah had disappeared, Lee felt a phantom weight on her side or pressed against her chest. The smell of him was still on her clothes. Whenever she rose, she felt Noah's small downward pull on her shoulders, as if he were still strapped to her. As that sensation left, her body felt flimsy and insubstantial.

On the morning of Iris's arraignment, Lee awoke to find June standing over her.

"What are you doing?" Lee asked. June backed up and snuffled. She giggled, snuffled again. Lee wondered if the girl was doing drugs.

"Never mind." Lee sat up wearily. She had slept in an oversized pink T-shirt with a giant blue turtle embroidered on the front. June's shirt. On a chair by Lee's cot was a stack of tight-fitting clothes in absurd, piñata colors—a loan from June, just one more indignity.

She leaned down and checked beside the bed to make sure her physics book was still there, letting her fingers rest on its slick, cool cover for a moment. In the room next door, an alarm clock went off. Lee could hear Frank cursing, the sound of a dog's nails against the bare floor.

Bright sunlight poured in through the French doors, thoroughly exposing the shabbiness of the bedroom. Its dented plaster walls were covered with a stale green paint, and there was black mildew filigreeing across one end of the ceiling. The only decorations were a poster of a girl in a bathing suit and a hoop of embroidery. The rug was worn down to the webbing.

"Do you have something I could wear?" Lee forced herself to ask. "Something nice?"

June blinked down at Lee. The edges of her nostrils flexed.

"I've got a yellow dress that's nice."

"All right."

"I'll get it."

"All right." Lee slumped down onto the cot, her head in her hands while June rose and rummaged through her closet. She pulled a bright yellow dress off its hanger and held it up. It had a texture like meringue, with spaghetti straps and a deep, drooping neckline.

"Don't you have anything quieter?"

"Quieter? Nah." June put the dress down on the cot next to Lee, then sat down beside her, close, and inhaled softly.

"Stop doing that, will you," Lee said. She took up the dress, hesitated. "Thanks, for this," she muttered and went down the hallway to the bathroom.

She showered, rinsing the soap off carefully before she used it, dissolving it down to an untouched layer. There was no fresh towel for her. But rather than rub herself with one of theirs, she let herself drip dry in the tub, squeezing out her hair and shaking herself off like a dog.

The dress was too big for her, the hem landing below her shins and the neck hanging low. Still, it was better than nothing. As she came out of the bathroom, Frank's bedroom door opened. His dog barreled out of the room first, its mouth wide open in a heckling grin, its large feet making the floorboards creak beneath the carpet.

Then Frank emerged. She guessed that he knew she was there and had deliberately come out to make her uncomfortable. The hallway was very narrow and he would not move aside. She forced herself to stare straight at him. This was her brother. She looked at his broken, rough face, his sinewy limbs. He was a creature as far removed from her as was physically possible.

"Excuse me," she said.

"Going to a party?" Frank asked, his eyes moving down to her dress.

"No."

"Then why are you dressed for a party?"

"It's your sister's dress," Lee said, feeling unaccountably compelled to give him an explanation.

"It's *your* sister's dress," he retorted, and he walked past her, without turning his body to give her room. She backed up against the wall quickly to let him pass, but his dog managed to swipe his mouth on her dress, leaving a grayish smear.

In all of Loomis, the two most elegant buildings were the courthouse and the funeral parlor. Within winking distance of each other, their heavy stone structures and towering columns added all the gravity that Loomis could afford to the business of petty larceny, parking violations, and death.

Lee climbed the courthouse stairs, the borrowed pair of June's white heels, which were too big for her, clicking hard against the marble. All at once she began to feel the weight of Iris's situation. Here was a fortress less manageable than she had imagined—a spot where dim, bleary-eyed Loomis put its foot down and grew strict.

A security guard in the lobby directed Lee down a long hallway of red-veined marble to the courtroom. Outside, several people were milling about, waiting for their cases to come up. Lee pushed open the heavy wooden doors and quietly took a seat. She looked around the courtroom. There was no sign of Kitty and Ivan.

Up front, another case was being heard. A teenage girl was slouched in a seat on the stand, chin pressed down nearly to her chest, hands clasped over her belly. She looked persecuted, although it gradually became clear to Lee that she was not the one on trial. She was explaining how she had paged a person named Ray with the number sequence 6-7-

8-3. The lawyer, a tall, slender, balding man, walked in uncertain circles around her and asked her what that sequence meant.

"It was a code," the girl said.

"A code. You were sending him a code. What did the code mean?" The lawyer began all his questions with a theatrical flair.

"It meant 'I love you.'" The girl looked at no one. The lawyer said he had no more questions and took his seat beside a man in a suit who was slouched in the same exact way as the girl on the stand. The judge looked at his watch.

The doors flipped open and Iris entered, followed by a uniformed jail matron and an older woman in a flashy red suit with red heels whom Lee presumed was Iris's lawyer. Iris wore a solemn, dark dress, not her own—not too dissimilar from Lee's mourning dress—and her hair was pulled back into a long ponytail.

As they passed her, Iris stretched her hand out toward Lee but the jail matron patted it back down. Barefaced, Iris looked wan and resplendent, like a model for a religious painting. Like a person who had suffered.

Up front, the judge set a date for sentencing. The teenage girl heaved herself up from her seat and glanced briefly at the defendant before silently sitting down next to a man a few benches in front of Lee.

"He don't even look sorry," the man said.

"He ain't," the girl said, lifting her head for the first time. "Neither am I."

There were several more cases: a bell-shaped woman in sweat pants who had written a bad check. A man in tight-fitting low-slung jeans and long, permed hair, who swaggered up and pleaded guilty to attempted rape. He told the court that he was unable to complete the act because "I couldn't rouse myself." Then he started to cry, and it was unclear what he was most upset about—his crime or his inability to fully commit it. The judge asked him this and he answered, "A little of both."

Finally, Iris was called. She walked up front briskly, her eyes fixed on the seat she was about to take, the same seat that the rapist had just vacated. She looked at nothing else, just the seat, and when she sat down, she locked her hands around the edge of the armrests. Iris's lawyer faced the judge and told him that Iris was pleading guilty to the charge of endangering the welfare of a child. She was a petite, narrow-shouldered lady, and when she sat back down, her head barely nudged past Iris's shoulder. One tiny hand rested lightly on Iris's spine.

"Miss Utter," the judge said without looking up from a spread of papers on his desk, "will you please give us your statement." Iris began, explaining that she had come to Loomis for a memorial service. And during that service she encountered a person who had, she believed, stolen something from her.

"And that person is?" the judge asked. He looked at Iris now and bit briefly at his bottom lip.

"Kitty Robbins," Iris said.

"What was it that you believed Mrs. Robbins had, Miss Utter, which originally belonged to you?" he asked. He had a paternal, reasonable manner. Iris frowned.

"I'm a little thirsty. Do you think I could have some water?"

"Certainly," the judge said. He pushed forward a pitcher in front of him and Iris's lawyer clicked over in her red heels. There was no extra cup, so the bailiff scurried off to the back office to find one.

Lee could see Iris's body relax, soothed by these shufflings to make her more comfortable. Her eyes began to skim the courtroom, brushing across Lee, across a couple who were awaiting their own hearing, past the jail matron who escorted her in. Her eyes settled momentarily on someone in the back of the room and she smiled slightly. Lee turned. Sitting way in the back was Jack Mayborn, dressed in the same cheap suit she'd first seen him in.

The bailiff returned with a short stack of paper cups and the lawyer pulled one out and poured a cup of water for Iris.

"Is there anything else you need, Miss Utter?" the judge asked. Iris sipped at the water, then shook her head.

"I'm fine now."

"I'm glad to hear it," the judge said and suddenly Lee felt a ripple of apprehension. She'd seen this sort of moment before: the point where Iris believed she had gained favor but was, in fact, mistaken.

"Please let's finish this thing up. What was it that Mrs. Robbins had that belonged to you?"

"Actually, she's not *Mrs.* Robbins. They're not legally married." Kitty's lawyer stood, but before he could get a word out of his mouth, the judge motioned him to sit down again.

"Just answer my question," the judge said. His voice had turned sharp and Iris looked at him, surprised, as if he had double-crossed her.

"I lost a son nine years ago," Iris explained.

"He passed away?" the judge asked.

"He was stolen from me," she said, her voice rough with anger. "And then he was adopted out. Without my consent."

"The court does not adopt out children illegally, Miss Utter."

"I didn't say it was done legally. It was just done."

"I'll ask you one more time, Miss Utter. What was it that you believed Mrs. Robbins had in her possession that originally belonged to you?"

"My son."

Lee closed her eyes and shook her head. A slow internal trembling started in her body. She squeezed her legs together to stop the shaking, but she could not control it.

"Please state what you did on the morning of July third." The judge didn't even look at her anymore. He was looking down at his papers again but when Iris would not answer, he looked up.

"Did you understand what I just said, Miss Utter?" His voice was cold.

"Did you understand what *I* just said?" Iris replied. There was a perceptible shifting in the courtroom.

"Control your client," said the judge. The diminutive lawyer nodded, without conviction, and pressed her palm fully against Iris's back, looking as if she were about to shove her forward with all her little might. She whispered something to Iris.

June's yellow dress, made of some horrible, cheap material, was making Lee sweat. Her skin felt tacky and she pulled the material away from her body.

"On the morning of July third, I woke up my son—" Her lawyer shook her head. "I woke up *Kitty's* son and told him that I wanted to take him out to breakfast."

"Why?"

"I just wanted some time with him."

"Did he go with you willingly?"

"Yes."

"Then how come he was found at a rest stop, crying and screaming for someone to help him?"

"He's a very nervous boy," Iris replied.

"You drove the child clear to the Pennsylvania border, Miss Utter."

"I was looking for a place to stop and eat. There's the diner just outside Loomis, but I had been there just the other day and had a fight with the waitress, so obviously I couldn't go there. We just kept driving and I didn't see any place to stop—"

"And it seemed right to you to take someone's child without telling them?"

"They did it to me, didn't they?" Iris cried. "Yes, I left my children. Briefly—and I'm sorry, I am really, really sorry, but I was very young and…and when I came back to Mercy Hill, they told me that Noah had been given away. They didn't know who to. It could have been anybody, they said. There were always people coming and going up at Mercy Hill. But the minute I saw that child yesterday, the *second* I saw him, I knew." Iris turned to glance at Lee, as if she could hear her daughter's stifled protest, then turned back to the judge.

"All I wanted was one morning with him. One morning, since I've lost him for the rest of my life." The color on her face was high; her brilliant eyes smacked of archetypal fictions, a bold, biblical righteousness. In truth, the judge was genuinely moved. He remembered quite well the gaggle of hippies that had invaded Loomis over a decade ago. This woman must have been very young at the time, and he had no doubt that a baby could have been passed around up there like a bottle of whiskey. Still, there was something about her that gave him pause. He looked at her levelly.

"Are you pleading guilty, Miss Utter, or aren't you?"

"No. I've changed my mind." She stared back at him as though this was his fault. He returned her stare until he shook his head and looked down at his papers. He picked up a pen and tapped it on the desk a few times, then he looked up again.

"You'll be held until your hearing. You'll be notified of the date. The bail is set at ten thousand dollars."

Lee pulled the breath deep into her lungs, and her muscles sighed and softened. Iris was going to be brought to account. Finally, finally, Iris was going to be made to pay for her offenses. Lee wanted to laugh. And then she did, but quickly bent her head to hide it. She sobered in this position, feeling suddenly like she was on a pew in church, and she felt all at once the delicate, infallible correctness of the world; how it worked with scientific precision in all things—just as she had always suspected—answering moral and natural infractions with the same beautifully impartial strictness. And now it had answered Iris, too, who had for so long and so inexplicably escaped its vengeance.

But the thought that she would now be forced to stay longer with the Mayborns soured her gratification. Lee decided then and there that for the length of Iris's stay in the Loomis County lock-up, she would not visit her. She would not provide her mother with an audience, and without an audience, Iris would simply grow bored. Her whims fluttered like a hummingbird from feeder to feeder. When she was finished, she was finished, and she turned her back on whatever came before, refusing all petitions. This nonsense about Kitty's son would be forgotten within a week, Lee knew, and by the time Iris's hearing rolled around, she would be sufficiently miserable to admit her mistake. As for Lee, it was simply a matter of bearing up, which is what she had been doing all her life anyway.

CHAPTER SIXTEEN

FOR THE FIRST DAY, June kept very still around the house, waiting to catch each fortuitous waft from her new sister. Whenever Lee passed, June's upper lip lifted as she drew the scent up into the damp, fatty recesses of her nostrils and down through the narrow nasal passages, letting it finally rest on the pillow of her thin, pink tongue. She sucked her tongue against the roof of her mouth. Bewildering. Lee was a creature both familiar—June had smelled that she was a Mayborn the moment she'd entered the grooming room—and alien. The Mayborn odor, as June had known it up till now, had resolved itself into the general odor of Loomis itself: thickly dank, reedy. But in Lee, the odor had clarified. Outside of Loomis, June thought, a Mayborn had no definition. Outside of Loomis, a Mayborn smelled of possibilities.

Exhilarated, June became shy. She was afraid she might scare Lee away. She smiled as sweetly as she could when Lee caught her staring. And when Lee noticed her smelling the air, she wiped her nose with the edge of her hand, pretending to have a sniffle.

Out on the highway, June caught a quick ride from the boy with the orange goatee. He saw her and braked hard, backed up on the highway. This time, she had a destination.

They pulled up at the Milkhouse Motel and June told the boy, "Just wait here for a minute." He nodded and his eyes followed her shiny gold skirt as she walked down the driveway toward the rooms. She knocked on the door but there was no answer.

In the distance, she heard a pop pop sound, like pistol shots, and she followed it to the pool. She crouched down on the pool's baby blue edge and called, "Sunny Taka." Sunny looked up. He was standing on the pool's drained bottom, just about ready to serve in a game of handball with another student. Cupping his hand over his eyes, he smiled widely at June.

"Yes! So!" He bounced the ball to his partner and clattered up the pool ladder in a crabwise manner. He held his hand out to June. She extended hers and he shook it enthusiastically.

"Do you remember me?" June asked.

"I always to remember such kind of interesting young lady."

June smiled and pushed her hair behind her ears.

"I brought something for you." She opened her white clutch purse and pulled out a ball of toilet paper. Sunny took it, carefully unraveled it. Inside was a fossil. It was a sea lily stem—a lovely specimen, with a clear imprint of the animal's feathery arms. He bounced a little at the knees.

"Anyways," June said and glanced back at the boy in the pickup truck, who was examining a blemish on his chin in the rearview mirror.

"Where did you find this, please?"

"Loomis Park. My brother found it when he was digging to put in drainage pipes. I thought it looked like something you'd want."

"Yes, so, very much. Thank you. I must to show this to the geology department."

"I got a guy in the car so—" She hooked her thumb backwards to the pickup truck.

"Certainly," he said. June turned and walked away. Sunny looked at the boy in the car. The boy's jaw hung slack. He looked stupid and crude. The girl was probably crude and stupid also. But here, in America, he found he was unable to trust his judgment; things were suspended in an ether of unfamiliarity.

Sunny thought of his fiancée. She was an "office lady" in Tokyo. She was clever and pretended to be foolish. She was formidable and pretended to be pliant. No one was fooled but everyone pretended to be fooled. While he contemplated these things, his thumb never stopped moving across the shallow, feathery imprint.

CHAPTER SEVENTEEN

WHEN LEE RETURNED TO the Mayborn house, Ruby was out front, sitting on the steps, sipping from a tall glass of iced tea. Her long legs were stretched out and her brown belly pillowed unabashedly above her jeans.

"That's Junie's dress, isn't it?" Ruby asked. Lee nodded.

"It's right for June. Not for you. So what happened in court?"

"My mother pled not guilty."

"Not guilty of what?" Ruby asked.

"She took a boy." Lee shook her head ruefully. "She says he's her son."

"Is he?"

"No."

Ruby paused, took a sip from her glass. "I went to see your mother the other day. I never saw her before. Oh, the officers were glad to oblige. Gave those hens something to cackle about for a few days."

"What did she say to you?" Lee asked nervously.

"Nothing. I didn't stop to talk to her. I just walked by and looked at her. That's all. I think she knew who I was." Ruby fished the wedge of lemon from her iced tea and rubbed it across her teeth, then licked her teeth. Lee guessed that Ruby had wanted Iris to see *her*, too.

June walked up the driveway then, on her way home from town. She was wearing a little gold lamé skirt with double-tiered ruffles and a matching gold off-the-shoulder blouse, like a town float of rejected regalia. In her hand was a demure white clutch purse.

"Where were you, June bug? The Ladies League again?" Ruby asked. "What do those old girls want with something like you anyway?"

June smiled, shrugged, and began to walk up the steps. Ruby grabbed her by her ankle.

"What kind of shit are they putting into your head, Junie?"

"Nothing," June said, and she shook her ankle loose and went inside.

"Bunch of sour broads. One of them has a thing for my Jack, big old hypocrite."

The yellow dress had incubated Lee's anxiety in the courthouse. The smell of it hit her freshly in the stagnant house air. She climbed the stairs quickly, already working at the zipper in the back. By the time she'd entered the bedroom, the zipper was halfway down her back

June was sitting on her bed. Waiting. Above her head, tacked to the wall, was the poster of the girl in the bathing suit. It caught Lee's eye particularly, without her knowing why. But then she saw that it was the expression on the girl's golden profile—a bloom of nervous anticipation, a lip-biting greediness for the very next moment as she pulled herself out of the pool. It was the same expression that June now had on her face.

Lee turned her back. June's scrutiny made her feel like a small animal being stalked, with the predator in no particular hurry and capable of unwavering concentration. Shrugging the dress off her shoulders, Lee tugged at the waist until the thing fell off her body and collapsed to the floor in a ring of yellow gauze. The jeans and velvet shirt from the day before were folded beneath her bed and as she put these on, June moved in and gathered the yellow dress up in her arms.

"It's filthy," Lee said and held out her hand, palm up. "Give it to me. I'm going to wash it."

"That's okay," June said. She folded the dress hastily and opened her dresser drawer.

"Don't put it in with your clothes! It stinks." But June shoved it into her drawer and shut it quickly. She turned to Lee and smiled.

"Not to me." The sudden candor on June's face, the sweetness of her admission disgusted Lee. She turned away, sat down on her bed, and opened her physics book.

June sat down next to her, the stiff material of her skirt crackling.

"What's your book about?" she asked, pressing her palms together and tucking them between her thighs.

"Nothing very interesting."

June gazed down at her pointy pink shoes and tapped them together listlessly.

"Do you have a boyfriend?" June asked. Lee sighed and rolled her eyes.

"No."

"Have you ever?"

"No."

"I had one for a while." June's toes stopped tapping, and she used the edge of the bed to pry off one shoe and then the other. "It was nice."

"Did he mind about your hands?" Lee asked the question impulsively, looking up from her book for the first time.

June frowned as though she didn't understand Lee's meaning, but then she said, "Oh, you mean my nails? I don't think so. Why?"

"I don't know," Lee said, now embarrassed that she had brought the subject up. "It just seems that some people wouldn't like it."

"Yours aren't so bad." June reached out and took Lee's hand quickly. Placing it palm down against her own, she scrutinized it like a fortune-teller reading the wrong side. Lee was mortified, and yet, no one else had ever looked at her hands with such open curiosity before.

"Your thumb is nice and smooth, see?" June rubbed her finger against Lee's thumb. "And this nail is not completely black. It has a pinkish spot there. They look strong, too." She flipped Lee's hand over and laid her own on top. So strange, Lee thought, to see those twisted nails on a hand that wasn't her own! So strange to talk about it frankly, like it was any other thing.

"Mine are too weak," June said. "I keep losing bits." She tapped her index finger against Lee's palm. Only a small black shard of nail was left on the finger. The top of it was red, raw skin.

"Does it hurt?" Lee asked.

The door opened and Jack walked in, followed by the dog, who sniffed at the spot on the floor where the yellow dress had lain. Jack stared at them for a moment, frowning.

"What's going on in here?" he demanded. "Why the hell are you touching her, June? Huh? She doesn't want you touching her. Take your goddamn hands off her." He slapped at June's hand, and June pulled it away from Lee's. Then, after staring down suspiciously at them both, he stormed out onto the verandah.

"Frank!" he bellowed out toward the park. "Frank, goddamn it!" Then, having apparently caught his son's attention, he hooked his arm backwards several times. "Now!" he bellowed.

"You!" He pointed at June. "Downstairs!"

"She wasn't doing anything," Lee said when June left.

"That's all right, I'm not mad at you. It's just...I don't like them all pawing at you like they own you." He went out to the verandah again, watching Frank's progress as he climbed the hill to the house.

"Hurry up!" Jack leaned over the railing when Frank was a few yards from the driveway. "And bring your crowbar!"

In another minute, hard slow footsteps sounded on the stairs and Frank appeared at the entrance of the room, a short, rusted crowbar in his hand.

"What do you want?" Frank asked his father.

"From now on, I want Lee to sleep upstairs in the attic."

"It's sealed up."

"Why do you think you're holding a crowbar?"

"I'll do it later."

"Do it now."

It didn't take long. Down the hall there was the sound of nails squealing out of their long-held grip, curses, and then a sharp crack.

Frank appeared at the door again and with a twitch of his head motioned to Lee to follow him. They walked down the hall, past his own bedroom, to a tiny bathroom at the far end of the house. It was less a bathroom than an alcove with a cast-iron, claw-foot tub shoved up against the wall. The drain was stopped up with a small doll, its arms over its head, looking exactly like it was being sucked down the pipes, and the tub itself was half filled with stacks of yellowing magazines and catalogs and, on top of them, a small television set with its cord wrapped around it.

There was a low door to the right of the tub with a crude, wooden handle. Frank pulled it open and a skulking, musty air crept out from behind the door.

Inside was a narrow flight of carpeted stairs. As they walked up, Lee looked at the small, framed paintings that lined the wall, ascending neatly alongside the steps. There were some pastoral scenes: a barn dance lit by torches, ladies bicycling on a narrow country road, their hat ribbons trailing. There was a painting of the Champs Elysées with the crowds of Parisians depicted by egg-shaped drops of paint. Some old photos, mostly of children, but one of a man with the squat, unequivocal features of a monkey, dressed formally with a white collarless shirt and dark jacket. Lee realized that they were the only pictures she'd seen in the entire house, save for June's poster. At the top of the steep flight was a small, very elegant room.

When Lief Mayborn brought home his Finnish bride in the bone-dry August of 1914, he left a vacancy in the center of the feather bed that he shared with his two brothers, one cousin, and his baby sister, Margaret. As a honeymoon present, his mother and aunts had sewn a quilt from the broad skirts of his deceased grandmother and tacked it up in front of his new bed, which sat not three feet away from his old one.

When his bride saw the arrangements she bolted back to her father's house, with Lief at her heels, the vestal hem of her wedding gown gathering dust from the parched roads. Her father told Lief that he and his family were a pack of dogs for living in such a way, especially since they were not poor, and so he could only assume that they enjoyed their debauchery, which made them worse than dogs. He went no further, though he might have. And Lief, who was no fool, knew that the legacy of Jake's Jake's papers was on the tip of his father-in-law's tongue, swallowed back only in deference to the Mayborns' wealth.

Within the space of a few weeks, Lief fixed up the attic room. His wife still remained at her father's house, so his haste was considered a good joke by everyone in Loomis, including his own family. But when the wife was actually installed in the attic, now decorated with fine French furnishings, carpets, and linens purchased in Albany, the Mayborns were deeply perplexed. They had always lived together snugly, tribally. The notion of privacy was as unthinkable as wanting to occasionally detach your own head from your body.

Lief and his wife lived together in their grotto for just a short while before the wife saw another thing that offended her. It was serious enough that she never spoke about it, but a day later she miscarried, a tiny, gelatinous baby boy that slipped out of her and plunged into the toilet. Soon after, Lief and his wife headed for Rochester and disappeared from Mayborn history and thus, effectively, from the face of the earth.

The exquisite room was shut up. It was a brief, experimental sojourn, less embarrassing than just plain foolish.

CHAPTER EIGHTEEN

JACK'S SHOES WERE POLISHED and his face was shaved clean and pink as a baby mouse. Escorted by Officer Dugger, he recognized the auspiciousness of the approach, the renegade spin of his own history.

"You lucked out, Jack old man," Officer Dugger said. "Ordinarily, she would have been kept over in Breesport, in the county jail. But they're doing some renovating, so they threw us their scraps."

They went through a heavy metal door into a small anteroom with a sink. The sink's faucet had a medieval-looking attachment—two metal cups side by side on metal stems.

"To wash out the eyeballs," Dugger said when he saw Jack staring at it. "Sometimes we have to pepper-spray the boys when they get out of hand."

"Is she being kept with men?"

"Relax, Jack. The men are on that side, the women on this side." He gestured to the two doors on opposite sides of the room.

They went through the door on the left and into a room lined with cells. The cells were as spartan as the office upstairs was cluttered: a narrow plank of wood fixed to the wall and topped with a thin mattress served as a bed. A toilet bowl with a push button flush set in the wall. A sink with a morsel of green soap.

They passed a cell that was occupied by a heavy-set woman with glasses, who was sitting on her cot, reading a magazine and eating a hamburger. She looked up expectantly when they approached, then grunted when she saw the visitor wasn't for her and returned to her magazine. They passed two more cells, both of them occupied, and finally came to the last one in the line.

There she was, right in front of him. Leaning against the wall, arms crossed, as if she knew he was coming. Dugger opened the cell's door, let Jack in, and shut the door behind him. For a moment, Jack just stared at her without saying anything, afraid he would ruin it all.

"I must look like shit," she said. "You're shocked at how awful I look, aren't you?" Jack noticed that she didn't run her hands through her hair like a regular woman would when she said something like that.

"Don't say stupid things to me," Jack said. She was nervous, he could see that. Her right thumb and forefinger twitched against each other. She noticed his stare and she pushed off from the wall with her foot and sat down on the cot.

Set on the floor by the cot was a metal tray with a hamburger on a napkin and a paper cup filled with juice, both untouched.

"Is that your lunch? Go ahead and eat it," Jack said.

"I have no appetite."

"You have to eat, Iris." He sat down near her but was afraid to touch her. She shut her eyes, and he gazed at the single blue vein that grazed each eyelid and at the miraculous delicacy of her bones. Then, all of a sudden, he was touching her—stroking her arm, her face, the side of her neck—

and she let him. He remembered that about her suddenly; that when you touched her she always let you.

Suddenly Iris drew back. "You have a wife," she said. It was less of a statement than a challenge.

"*You* should have been my wife." He pulled her in by her waist, close, and kissed her.

"Easy there, Romeo," Officer Dugger said. Jack glared at Dugger quickly, but let go of her. Iris tugged at the orange jumpsuit and glanced up at the window high above her cot.

"I've got the master suite. The only cell with a window, aren't I lucky." She shook her head and frowned. "I frightened him. I keep thinking about that."

"Who?"

"Noah. He was okay at first. But then he started to get scared. He peed in the car, he was so scared." Then she asked, "Why hasn't Lee come to see me?"

"I don't know," Jack said.

"She's probably happy to be rid of me. Does she ever talk to you about me? What does she say?"

"Nothing, Iris." He got up and took both of her hands, pressed them between his own. He couldn't stand to be so close to her without touching her.

"They took Noah away because of *her*, you know," Iris continued. "She'll lay the blame on me, but that's not the truth. The truth was that Lee was too rough with him. That's what everyone told me."

Jack withdrew his hands and squinted at her. "Are you saying that there's something wrong with the girl?"

"With Lee? No," Iris said, "of course not."

"You tell me straight, you tell me right now, because I need to know."

"Is this how you talk to Ruby?" Iris stood up and backed away from him. "And she allows it?"

"I'm sorry, Iris."

"I can make other arrangements for Lee—"

"No, please. Iris." He got up and put his arms around her, feeling the unfamiliar shallowness of her body, the elasticity of her back.

"Hands off!" Officer Dugger kicked at the cell bars.

"Mind your own fucking business," Jack barked back at Officer Dugger.

"That's it, Jack, fun's over. You're out." Dugger opened the cell but he kept his hand hovering near his gun, just as a reminder. He'd seen Jack in a few bar fights, so he wasn't going to be careless about things.

Jack looked at Iris. Her beauty at that moment was so vivid as to alarm him. It had seemed to intensify from even a few moments before, and he suddenly felt foolish and humiliated without knowing why.

"I'll come back again," he muttered, and he walked out of the cell without looking back at her.

Alone, Iris positioned herself under the little window, hunching up and pulling in her extremities so that her whole body could be circumscribed within the patch of sunlight, and no part of it would graze the cell's darker recesses.

CHAPTER NINETEEN

A SLOW, DREARY RAIN began soon after dark and continued through the night. The droplets plucked at the house relentlessly. Sitting on her bed, Lee tried to focus on her book but her mind kept wandering. Overhead, the rain sounded like a person crawling around on the roof, slapping wearily at the shingles to gain admittance. It was a hopeless, melancholy sound, echoing her own mood.

Until today, Lee believed she had seen the full range of her mother's excesses. She believed she had delineated Iris's boundaries, which, though far-reaching and mutable, stopped short of self-ruin. But the courthouse was a new venue for Iris; a new venue for a drama enlisting all the poignancy Iris's life could muster. She relinquished her bottom line of self-preservation. In this drama, she was the good mother, the wronged mother.

Unnatural mother. It was something she'd heard Joseph say about Iris after Iris had left, and it had stuck in Lee's mind. *Unnatural mother.*

Unnatural mother. The rain took on the rhythm of the words and she fell asleep to it, her head leaning against the headboard, then woke again, the same meter strumming in hard, hollow taps. Sitting still, she listened to it for some time until she realized the sound did not come from above. The rain had stopped. But the sound was distinct and regular.

The textbook still lay open on her lap. She closed it and shoved it under the bed, then got up and went to the window. The sound seemed to come from outside.

She opened the window. The air outside was cool from the rain and rushed through the collar of her T-shirt. The sound was louder now, a heavy clopping with a metallic echo at the end. She wondered that it didn't wake the whole house up.

Pushing her hair behind her ears, she bent deeper over the sill. The edge of June's verandah was just visible from her vantage point, and she caught sight of something moving across it. It was human and slight. It appeared, then limped out of her view, its footsteps making that faltering rhythm. Behind her, in her own bedroom, there was a smothered snap, and she withdrew from the window so quickly she hit the back of her head against it. The window slammed shut violently, the noise sounding like a thunderclap.

She stood in the darkness for a moment, breathing in short, hard breaths. The sound outside had stopped. She relaxed a little, only now feeling the pain in the back of her skull where it had hit the window.

She turned to go back to bed, then stopped short. In the dim light, she saw that her bed had been stripped. The blanket and pillow had been thrown to the floor. The edges of the sheet had been unhitched at every corner and lay in a twist on the center of the bed. She stepped back, moved away from it. Her eyes swept across the room. There was nothing moving, no sound.

Then she heard footsteps, different from before. They were muffled and approaching, climbing the steps to her room. She froze where she stood, wrestling against panic, then finally submitting to her own fear because it had already invaded her body. The door opened. A nimbus of light from the downstairs bathroom revealed Frank, standing in the doorway. He entered cautiously, looking around the room as if he suspected Lee of hiding something.

"What was that noise?"

"I don't know," she whispered. Her eyes returned to the bed. "There was something out on the verandah."

"I heard a crash."

"A crash? Oh, the window." She shook her head, turned away from the bed. "The window slammed shut."

"You saw something out on the verandah?" he asked, walking over to her, looking at the plundered bed. It was so quiet that she heard the click of his Adam's apple as he swallowed.

"I thought so. Walking back and forth."

Frank went to the window, lifted it, and leaned out. Then he pulled his head back in and jiggled the window a few times, examined the frame.

"The rope came off the pulley," he said finally.

"Who was out there?" Lee asked.

"June," he said.

"It didn't look like June."

"I'll fix the window tomorrow," he said before he left. "Keep it shut in the meantime."

CHAPTER TWENTY

JUNE HELD THE SHINY, red "u" in her hands, reluctant to place it in the groove on the Fellowship Church sign. Kneeling on the grass beside the carton of plastic letters, she sifted through them again, stopping occasionally to tug up her yellow tube top or tug down her cut-off jeans.

"There may be a black 'u' on the bottom," she said.

"No, June, love," Linnet said. "We're low on black 'u's. You'll have to make do with the red."

"But you said the red letters are only for Jesus' name." June looked up, troubled. Her skin had grown coppery from the sun, making her eyes so blue in contrast that she appeared to be blind. Linnet felt a warm proprietary satisfaction: here was a wild thing that Linnet had managed to subdue. Even the Ladies League marveled at her success. And yet, Linnet admitted, the transformation was next to no trouble at all. The girl was so eager. In fact, June often reminded her of those particular types of Catholic saints whom Linnet had always secretly admired: St. Lucy, St.

Agnes, St. Joan—young girls who straddled divinity, who lived their lives with perverse willfulness, and ended them in rapture.

"We can bend the rules a little, June."

June stood up and, reluctantly, placed the red "u" in the groove. After digging out the remaining letters, she completed the new monthly words of wisdom on the Fellowship Church sign.

"Now stand back and see what you've done," Linnet said, placing her hand on June's bare shoulder. She found herself touching the girl often, like a fetish.

June rose, stepped back, and crossed one leg over the other. The sign read "Exposure to the Son Will Prevent Burning."

"What do you think?" Linnet asked. June nodded uncertainly.

"I'll get Mrs. Trott and show her what a stupendous job you've done," Linnet said and disappeared into the church.

June looked at the sign. Her eyes kept wandering back to the red "u." It struck her as a grievous imperfection. Linnet didn't care. But God would know. Maybe it would anger Him. He might strike at June with a seizure, bearing down on her and slamming her body against the ground. Or He might turn Linnet against her, and June would be shut off from the church, maddeningly isolated once again. For the first time in her life, she felt panic. She could not track it or name its parts, the way she could with odors; rather, it wafered within her chest walls, black and thickening.

She went to the sign, slid the last six letters out from "Burning," and shoved the red "u" in the back pocket of her cut-off jeans. The letter was too big and the tips poked out. Quickly, she replaced the "r," "n," "i," "n," and "g" back on the sign. She read it again without the red letter. She took a deep breath. The panic lifted.

Linnet and Mrs. Trott emerged from the church now, Mrs. Trott squinting against the sun, her shoulders still cupped forward from bending over bookkeeping ledgers in the church's basement. Her gaze went first to June's outfit, but Linnet quickly directed her attention to the sign.

"June labored over it all morning," Linnet said. Mrs. Trott read it, frowned.

"The 'u' is missing," she said. "The 'u' in 'Burning.'"

"Oh. But we had it just a minute ago. Has it fallen? The red letters are a little smaller than the black ones, and they sometimes come loose."

While Linnet examined the grassy patch beneath the sign, a tall woman dressed in pale blue from head to toe made her way up the street toward the church. June saw her first; or perhaps she had simply sensed her approach, because she turned suddenly. Ruby was coming their way, fast, her long legs snapping at the pavement succinctly, beneath a straight hipless body. Ruby's black hair, loose and tucked behind her ears, disappeared behind her back and reemerged between the triangles formed by her swinging arms.

"Well, I don't see it anywhere," Linnet said, turning her attention away from the lawn, and then she, too, saw Ruby approaching. For a moment, Linnet felt the urge to flee; Ruby had such an aspect of an angry bear coming for her cub. Even Mrs. Trott retreated back into the church, wordlessly, implying that June was Linnet's problem, after all was said and done.

"Good morning, Ruby," Linnet said brightly when Ruby came close. But Ruby ignored her and addressed herself to June.

"Dammit, June, you were supposed to help with that Rottie. I can't handle that animal on my own, you know that. He's crashing around in the goddamn crate right now, and his owner's coming for him in half an hour."

Linnet cringed inwardly at Ruby's swearing but kept her face neutral.

"June has just finished putting up our monthly words of wisdom," Linnet motioned to the sign. Ruby stared at it blankly. "It's missing a 'u,'" Linnet added.

"It doesn't matter," June said. "She can't read it anyway."

Ruby raised her eyebrows, stared at her youngest child. June lowered her eyes, but without fear, just a simple refusal to engage.

"If June forgot her chores, I'm sure I'm partly to blame," Linnet said pleasantly.

"Why don't you let her alone, Linnet?" Ruby faced Linnet full on now, her arms crossed against her thin scrubs, her black eyes furious. "Why don't you stop poking and prying at her, and let her be."

Linnet took a minute before she answered, and when she did she whispered her response, trying as best she could to keep June from hearing: "Because she hates what she is."

"*She* told you that?"

"Isn't it obvious?"

"No," Ruby said. Linnet was silent for a moment, weighing what she would like to say against the anger it would generate.

"Does this mean you're going to prevent June from coming to church?" Linnet asked finally, her courage failing against Ruby's glare.

"She can do what she wants," Ruby replied. "But right now she's going home."

"You're welcome to come to church too, Ruby," Linnet said, but the offer sounded insincere, even to Linnet's own ears, and she blushed, knowing that Ruby would detect it as well.

Ruby's hand shot out and grabbed at June's back pocket. She drew out the red plastic "u" and looked at it for a moment, then tossed it back toward Linnet, so that it landed on the grass like a horseshoe.

CHAPTER TWENTY-ONE

THE FOLLOWING MORNING, WHEN Lee went downstairs she found the house to be absolutely silent. Everyone, it appeared, was out. Alone for the first time, Lee looked around carefully. The place was in ruins, yet there was something about it that defied ruination. It was as if the house had turned on its heels and stubbornly welcomed its devolution of plaster and beam and civility. The old oilcloth on the kitchen floor crackled underfoot, and the floorboards were so rotten that, here and there, they dipped into long, shallow depressions. Some walls were laid open in spots, exposing wires snared in spider webs, which were themselves in a husk of dust. Upstairs, all the ceilings had brown water stains, the dark edges continuously spreading, groping toward each other. Everywhere, there were cracks and blisters and missing parts. Nothing was repaired. The house and its occupants turned their defeat by attrition into an obstinate backward march.

Outside, the day was quintessential summer. The warm, green air had a lift, an expansiveness. She headed down the block, away from the center of town. In the opposite direction from the police station.

She followed a road that led through the back end of Loomis, where the houses thinned and the woods grew denser. She wore a pair of June's shorts, thankful that June was taller and the shorts reached the middle of her thighs. The shirt was snug, but she had pulled at it until the material creaked and gave. On her feet she wore a pair of flip-flops that Ruby had dug up for her. They were too big for her and kept slipping off her feet. After a while she removed them altogether and let her feet scrape against the rough pavement. It amazed her that the bottoms of her feet were so tender. Her body had always been embarrassingly strong. Her muscles kept their stringy resilience though she did nothing to encourage it. By the end of the day, her feet would be raw, but afterward she might grow a callus or two. She remembered Leon, who had such thick calluses on his hands that he let the kids on the commune stick pins into his palms.

After some time, she reached a slender, steel truss bridge that passed over a creek. She remembered the spot with sudden vividness, the creek having been a source of fascination for her as a child with its innumerable schools of thin, silvery fish that darted along the edges. Once, when she was young, she and Wanda had crouched beneath the bridge, the water skimming their thighs, and waited for a car to pass over. When it did, it made the sound of a hundred dishes clattering against each other.

She dipped her hands in the creek and poured the cool water over her head several times, then she followed the creek as it passed into the darkness of the woods. Without the play of sunlight on its surface, the water grew secretive and hushed in the manner of all isolated things. It meandered, thinned and thickened. The air was still.

She stopped short when she spotted a man peeing against a tree. His back was partially turned to her and he appeared to be in pain as one hand clutched at his belly. Finally, he zipped himself up, still with his one hand holding his stomach, and craned his head about a few times. Then his other hand shot up underneath his shirt and he extracted a can of beer and quickly snapped off the top.

"Boulevard," Lee said. He turned so quickly that his body seemed to have lifted up slightly in the air and flipped around. He held the beer behind his back. It was tipped and the liquid was trickling out.

"You're spilling it," she said.

"Oh, shit," he said and righted the can. He smiled at her. She noticed the fine lines fishtailing beneath his eyes, the salt-puckered dryness of his lips. He was older than she had first thought, forty at least. His skin was the brown of old lemons. An angry, pink sunburn crept around from the back of his neck.

"Don't tell Fank, okay?" he said.

"I won't. What are you doing here?"

There was a rustling footfall and Boulevard shoved the beer beneath his shirt again. Frank appeared at the crest of a hill where the land sloped up sharply. He was approaching briskly and his face was a mask of suspicion, fixed on the two of them. When he reached Boulevard he lifted the man's shirt up and grabbed the beer out of his hand.

"I told you not yet," Frank said. Then he added to Lee, "You're trespassing."

"On whose property?"

"My father's," he said after a slight hesitation.

"In that case, so are you," she answered.

"We buying it," Boulevard said.

"Quiet," Frank said.

"You want to see it?" Boulevard asked her. "Come on, Fank, let's show her."

As they walked through the woods, up the sharp slope, dead pine needles pricked her bare soles and small stones pressed painfully into the pads of her feet. At the top of the slope, she found herself at the edge of a vast clearing. The land was pocked with hesitant new growth. Here and there were stumps of trees, and a yellow backhoe had its shovel poised by the base of one of the stumps. The soil was soft against her feet, and rutted. As they walked, Lee could see that the creek had miraculously reappeared, cutting through the back edge of the property, once more immersed in sunlight. The water was shallower here, traversing the glassy bed of gray stones in a slow, circumspect flow. Ahead of them was a wide green field with a small, ancient farmhouse floating in the midst of it.

"It's beautiful."

"I know it," Frank said. She looked at him carefully, searching for the elements in him that tied them together, a temperamental essence more than a resemblance, a winking fragment of familiarity. But it was a stranger's face.

"Fank!" Boulevard called over to them. He was sitting on the backhoe and reaching down into a pail by his feet. He pulled out a can of beer and held it up. "Okay?!" he asked. Frank nodded and Boulevard snapped the top off.

"He drinks a lot," Lee said.

"That's right."

"Then why do you bring beer for him?"

"He'll do it anyway." He watched Boulevard for a minute as he drank greedily from the can. "When June was little, she had fits. She'd scream and shake and bash her head against the wall till it opened up and bled. No one knew why. I used to grab the back of her neck." He put a hand on the nape of Lee's neck and squeezed lightly. "Hard. By her scruff, like a dog. It calmed her right down. After that, she'd go right to sleep. Ruby didn't like it. Said it made June out to be some kind of animal. So I stopped."

His hand lifted from her neck and he grabbed up a hank of Lee's wet hair and wrapped it in his fist. He squeezed it and the water trickled down her back.

She took a quick step backward, disengaging his hold.

"But June *is* an animal," he said. "And Boulevard's an alcoholic. We are what we are."

"I don't believe that," Lee said, disarmed by his touching her and needing to hear the sound of her own voice.

"I don't care."

No sooner had Lee walked away than a car pulled up to the land, driving directly onto the front field. It stopped near the old farmhouse, and a heavyset man came out and moseyed across the field. He wore a white, short-sleeved dress shirt, open at the collar and tucked sloppily into his pants. His hips pushed from side to side as he walked, an almost womanly way of walking, except that he kept a stick in one fist, like a boy. Pausing at the house, he shaded a hand over a window and peered in through the glass. Then he continued on his way, his shins disappearing within the high grass. Spotting Frank in the distance, he waved in a friendly manner.

"That's the dowser, Fank." Boulevard had dropped down off the backhoe and took his place beside Frank.

"I know it."

"Did you tell him to come here?"

"No, I did not." Frank made no movement toward the man, who was clearly headed for them. It was a long approach and on the way he smiled at Frank and Boulevard, then pretended to be fascinated by the ground, then the sky. The stick that he held had a forked end. When he was within a few feet of the two men, he turned his smile on them again and called, "Boys!" He was a little out of breath from the walk and his happy, ham-jawed face was flushed.

"Hello, Ben," Frank said.

"First-rate job you two done on the farmhouse. I never would have thunk you could make that old coop livable. Geena's been saying someone ought to burn it down for safety's sake what with all the kids that play out here and now look what. It just goes to show."

"It still needs work," Frank said carefully.

"Don't we all though."

"You picking up some business here and there?" Frank nodded toward the stick in Ben's hand.

"Here and there. Not a lot these days. This job's a favor for your dad," he winked. "If you can't sponge off your relatives, who can you sponge off, right?" Ben was not a Mayborn but he was related, a cousin, twice removed.

"What's my dad want with a dowser?"

"Well …" Ben looked confused. "You know. He wants a new well to be dug. For the ladies."

"Whose ladies?" Frank asked.

"For them two…the mother and the daughter. From down New York City." He was trying to be tactful about it, but for heaven's sake the whole goddamn town knew. "He's planning on moving them in here, just as soon as the situation allows, as they say."

"No fucking way for that!" Boulevard said.

"Watch your mouth, son," Ben pointed his stick at Boulevard.

"Is that what my father told you?"

"You bet he did. Told me just yesterday." Ben frowned at Boulevard, who had begun to stalk around in a circle, muttering angrily. "Now you just calm down, son," he ordered Boulevard.

"He's not your business," Frank said to Ben.

"No offense meant to *you*, of course," Ben held up his hand. He had no intention of ticking Frank off. He'd always said to Geena, "When Frank screws up, he won't nickel-and-dime it like the rest of the Mayborns. He'll screw up big time, Riker's Island style." Ben smiled. Waved his stick.

"I'm off to walk the dog." He turned, making his way slowly through the billowing grasses. As he went, he held the stick out loosely in the palm of his hand, feeling for the miraculous, satisfying drag of gravity as the miserly earth gave itself away.

CHAPTER TWENTY-TWO

THE SECOND TIME JACK entered the police station, he walked taller and held a bundle of yellow carnations in a paper cone.

"Nice flowers," said Officer Dugger. Jack nodded pleasantly.

"I hope she's being treated properly," Jack said.

"Oh, like a queen, Jack. Like the Queen of England."

This time it was Officer Kinnunen who led Jack to Iris's cell.

She sat on the corner of her cot, her legs splayed out in front of her and her head leaned against the wall. She didn't look up, even when her cell door opened.

"Hi, Iris." He held the flowers out to her. She looked at them briefly, then looked away.

"What took you so long to come?" she asked.

"I'm only allowed to come on visiting days, Iris. You know that."

"You're avoiding me."

"I brought you some flowers." He went to her and sat beside her on the thin cot. He put the flowers on her lap.

"What am I going to do with them here, in the dark?" She dropped her arm onto his thigh in an easy, careless manner. Jack felt, extraordinarily, that he was entitled to her. A swell of resentment rose up for all the years he did not have her, did not feel he had a right to her. He smoothed down the fine hair on her arm, rubbed her narrow wrist.

"Why hasn't Lee come?" she asked.

"I don't know."

"She hates me." Iris picked the flowers up from her lap and smelled them absently. Her brow softened, and she lifted her eyes to his. She snaked her hand up to his cheek, her thumb nestled between his lips. He felt the heat of her thumb, the slip of dampness as it brushed the inside of his lower lip. Drawing back abruptly, she leaned her head against the wall. She held the flowers loosely against her chest, closed her eyes, and shook her head.

"What's wrong?" Jack asked, a lump of panic forming. She was quiet for some time. He took her wrist between his fingers. His thumb circled the nubby bone.

"Someone has been coming to my window at night," she said finally.

"Who?" Jack asked. Iris shrugged.

"Is it a man?" his voice slipping toward anger.

"Yes, a man. I don't know who. I just hear the voice, but I can't see. The window is too high. You're pinching." She twisted her wrist out of his hand, then said, "Each time he comes, the strangest idea pops into my head: I wonder if it's Joseph. I wonder if he's fooled us and didn't really die in that fire after all." Her chin strummed across the top of the bouquet, back and forth, like a cat against an indifferent hand.

"Well? What does he say?" Jack asked. Iris sighed, shook her head.

"Different things. The first time he came, he said he was sorry. I asked him for what, but he didn't answer. Maybe he couldn't hear. He might have walked away. Last night, he told me I should stop saying that Kitty's boy is my son. For Lee's sake, he said."

"Goddamn! Goddamn, is he threatening you?"

Jack shot up and went to the cell's bars, so that he could see Officer Kinnunen, who had stationed himself on a stool a few yards away.

"You hear that, Kinnunen?" Jack said. "She says someone is standing outside at night, harassing her. Did you know that? Where the hell are you all when this is happening? Drinking coffee and scratching your balls?"

"Careful, Jack," Kinnunen said offhandedly. Then he added, "We know about the situation. She's told us."

"So what are you going to do about it?"

"Do? Nothing. I don't know what she thinks she's hearing, but whenever we check, there's no one out there."

"Do you think he's going to wait around for you?" Iris screamed from her cot, her body suddenly snapping to attention, the carnations toppling to the floor.

On his way out Kinnunen turned to Jack and said, "It's none of my business, but I'll say it anyway. The lady is not worth the trouble. She's minus some buttons, I mean it Jack. First this whole thing with that kid, now she's hearing voices. She ain't well, and she's getting worse by the day."

Jack should have been furious. Even Kinnunen had braced himself for an outburst, but the words defeated Jack, hitting him like every other twist of misfortune in his life—an internal, bitter nod at the way things never went right for him, the way the universe seemed hell-bent on keeping him chained to his birthright. Just as Iris became his, people were saying that she was crazy. Of course. Why else would she want him? Ruby would laugh at him. Inside, to herself, she would laugh. And Frank, too. And goddamn everyone else in Loomis, because there wasn't a soul who didn't know his business, was there?

He left the police station and stepped out into the blinding voltage of midday. The sun branded everything, taking its inventory of the bits and pieces of Loomis. Nothing escaped its scrutiny: the mildewed porches, the scrappy yards, the siphoned spirits of landowners, even the salt-pocked cars on the street whose owners Jack could tick off, in succession. And Jack, too, standing in front of the police station received a backward glance from the elderly Celia Brace, her kerneled face satisfied as she coupled Jack and the police. He felt the familiar low ebb of his own life begin to consume him once more as he effortlessly calibrated himself to Celia Brace's assessment.

But he stopped himself. Maybe Kinnunen was wrong. Iris was high-strung, always had been. That didn't prove that she was crazy. He walked back to the police station, turning down the strip of grass that lay between the side of the station and Dubert's Insurance next door. There were only two small windows, set toward the back of the building. The first one was frosted—probably a bathroom window. The second one was almost at the very back of the building and was set high up, too high for him to see into, and braced with iron bars.

That night, he told Ruby he was going out to the Casablanca, then skirted the edge of the park toward the police station. He came up from the back way, along the periphery of Loomis Park, where thick bushes marked the edge of the basin's drop-off. The moon was slivered and a damp haze hung in the air. A thin fog levitated over the park's basin, bobbing and shifting cunningly. The streets were so silent that Jack had to take care with his footsteps, particularly as he approached the police station.

When the brick building was just a few yards away, he slowed his pace, keeping close to the bushes. Once or twice he stopped short and listened, heard nothing. When the alleyway between the station and the insurance building came into view, Jack crouched down. Across the street, the alley was so dark that Jack had to stare at it for a minute before he could discern that the blackness was uniform. The alley was empty. He squatted down by the bushes, a position that made him feel old and clumsy. He'd wait out the night here, if he had to.

The next moment he heard screaming, muffled and frantic. The darkness in the alley had changed, and a darker shape emerged as if it had passed through the very walls of the station and stepped out into the night. Jack stood so fast that he overbalanced and stumbled, then regained himself and ran out across the street, toward the station. The screaming grew louder—it was Iris, he could hear her now—and Jack rushed by her window, following the fast-moving shape in the distance. It was a man, tall and slim, putting distance between himself and Jack, then pivoting sharply and darting down a side street. Jack was breathing hard; he knew he couldn't catch the man, but he kept his eyes glued to him until the man ran beneath a streetlight and Jack could see his profile, briefly but plainly illuminated.

CHAPTER TWENTY-THREE

THE DAY WAS HOT, so June forsook her customary position in front of the cornfield and moved to a spot further up the highway. Here, the road narrowed to two lanes and the landscape became close with pockets of woods interspersed with fields and houses. The shade was thick in many spots and June selected a fat elm tree to stand beneath.

More and more, she found that things kept getting away from her. The day was always too short, she thought, and the people she met once were never met again. She left her scent in cars that traveled on without her, shedding the cells of her skin through the open windows. Against her will.

The bear smelled it before she saw it—faint; perhaps human. But she was distinguished by her imprudence and continued on nevertheless, swaggering and flatfooted. Her head hung close to the ground. She stopped at a large rock and flipped it over. A colony of ants scattered, and a startled field mouse, taking shelter from the heat of the day, froze, its tiny muscles contracting. She dropped her paw on top of the mouse, then lifted it again. It lay still, a droplet of blood beaded under its nose. She scooped it up, careful not to pierce its flesh, and put it in her mouth.

Again, the odor assaulted her nose, stronger, translated as impulse. She lifted her body and waved her snout into the heated breeze. Hanks of fur hung off her belly and thighs. The odor was unfinished. Human only in fragments. She might have turned and gone in the other direction then. But she had lived a reckless life, had ranged across the Pennsylvania Appalachians to western New York, much further than the others.

The breeze shifted, the odor vanished. Plunging into a bushy thicket, she allowed the branches to catch on the loosened strips of fur and tear at them. Pushing through, she emerged into a grassy clearing at the edge of the highway. There it was. The odor. Human. Almost hidden beneath a tree, looking directly at her as if it were expecting her. Human but throbbing in and out of potency, a miasma rising and vanishing so that the bear, with her weak vision, became confused. Stood up on her hind legs.

"Man oh man," June said. She had known it was coming but did not know what it was. She had leaned against the tree, no longer looking for passing cars, and waited expectantly, demurely, with her hands pressing her pocketbook up against her belly. Like she was waiting for a date in front of the movie theater.

The bear moaned softly. June did not move an inch and so the bear felt no desire to restrain her. She stepped closer, homing in on June's winking odor, her snout pushed forward and twitching. June felt the bear's scrutiny like a blind hand roaming across her body. It was heavenly. She blew out puffs of air for the bear to savor.

The bear drew in June's breath. She had a taste for the untried, for the anomaly. Extending her arm, June offered up the inside of her wrist. Here, the scent was pure coquette. The bear pressed her nose against the wrist and June groaned at the touch of its rough dampness.

With her incisors, she picked delicately at the watchband, like extracting berries from a slender twig, until it tore from June's arm and fell to the ground with a soft thump. June pressed herself against the bear in a paroxysm of relief, of love, plunging her hand into the thick, dry, molting fur. The hanks came up in her grasp so she pushed her fingertips deeper into the undercoat, clinging, listening to the muffled heartbeat and the liquidy internal workings. The berry breath warmed her skull, and June felt her spirit come unhitched, the loosely tethered ghost that always occupied her body so ineffectually.

There was a squeal of brakes and then the warble of tires as a car frantically steeled itself against motion. The two-tone Buick swerved one way and then the other before it came to a stop, whereupon the bear drew back and dropped down to all fours. Her brashness was instantly humbled, her eccentricities admonished. She had gone too far this time.

She lowered her head and ran, scrambling past the car and out onto the highway. Again, the screech of brakes and a dry, nauseating thud. She flew into the air, crying out in a bellow of pain, and dropped back down to the pavement. Lying on her back, her great thighs spread, she rolled her head in resistance.

The man who drove the tractor-trailer took a moment to realize what had happened. He sat very still, blinking through his windshield at the massive black animal on the ground in front of his truck. He turned his cap backwards and said, "No way, no way," over and over.

The Buick's door opened, and Mrs. Cipriano jumped out, stumbling in her excitement. She ran toward June, her arms extended helplessly but full of the intention to help.

"Did he hurt you? ..." She wanted to call the girl by her name but she could not quite remember it. Sue or Jean, something only one syllable long. Instead, she said, "Did he hurt you, Mayborn?" because she was sure of that, at least.

The truck driver was still in his cab, talking to someone on his radio. The bear's head lolled back. She took one more breath. Her belly rose and fell and that was all.

June's mouth stayed open. A damp oval of despair. She kept still as Mrs. Cipriano pawed her all over, looking for *something*—an ugly gash in her flesh or for blood, at least. Mrs. Cipriano's face was the color and texture of a freshly peeled potato. Her breath was tainted by a lunch of cold, greasy ribs and orange-flavored diet soda.

"Jeez, when I saw that thing I nearly peed my pants! I ain't never seen a bear around here. Jeez, you must be the bravest kid I've ever heard of, wrestling with that thing. You sure you're okay? People are never going to believe this. I wish I had a camera."

The truck driver was standing beside the bear now, running his hand through his thin hair. He kicked the bear in her ribs. She didn't move.

"It's dead, honey," said Mrs. Cipriano. "It's all over. I'll take you back home. Get in the car, honey, I'll take you home."

The state troopers arrived, two cars and a pickup truck. They set down orange cones on the highway and shot the bear several times in her torso with their revolvers. Then they lifted her into the back of the pickup truck, leaving a long, dark stain on the pavement.

CHAPTER TWENTY-FOUR

WHILE THEY WERE IN the car, Mrs. Cipriano fussed over June, replaying the drama in her gusty, inflectionless voice, the sound of steadily escaping steam. June stared ahead in a fixed manner, but her breathing was quick and audible. Mrs. Cipriano wondered if the girl was in shock and pushed at June's arm with her index finger. June's head reared back.

"I'm sorry, oops," Mrs. Cipriano said. "We're almost home." In a minute Mrs. Cipriano rolled down the Mayborn driveway. She had never been inside the Mayborn house before. Her bland, prosaic life was marked with brief, spectacular excursions. Like her recent affair with the furnace repairman. Like today, with the bear. She was not changed by these events in the slightest way and resumed her former life in exactly the same way as always. But she cherished small doses of excitement. Entering the Mayborn house for the first time would nicely cap off a run-in with a bear.

Mrs. Cipriano opened the car door for June, taking hold of the girl's upper arm to lead her out. June got up, her head ducked down. Her upper arm shuddered against Mrs. Cipriano's hand in the oddest way, as if her skin twitched independently of her muscles.

The house was clean, which surprised and disappointed Mrs. Cipriano. Still, there was a low-slung gloom about the place and a curious background humming and not a soul around.

"Hello?" Mrs. Cipriano called but softly, suddenly not sure she wanted to summon anyone. "Where are your people, honey?" she asked June.

"It's coming on," June said, then turned and ran up the stairs.

Mrs. Cipriano followed her. She tried to take in the details of the house, but it was all she could do to watch June's slim, straight back and follow her, ending up in her bedroom where the girl faced her and said, "The bear was a she. You keep saying 'he.' The bear was a she."

"Don't think about it, honey. Just put it out of your mind. God spared you." At that, June's eyes rolled up in her head. Her limbs stiffened and she collapsed to the floor. Her mouth opened wide, as if she was going to scream, but no sound came out. Then her head began to slam against the wall. It seemed to have a magnetic pull on her and just as she lifted herself away, she was propelled back against it. A strand of pink saliva dripped from her bottom lip.

Mrs. Cipriano watched, horrified, then in the faintest voice that gradually grew louder and louder into a shriek, she called for help. June's face was paper white, her eyes were wide. On the floor, her head continued to slam against the wall as her body spasmed. A tapered, blade-like shadow cut across her face, appearing and disappearing rhythmically, and Mrs. Cipriano fixed her eyes on the pulsing shadow.

"Thank God," she said when a woman came to the door, dressed in doctor's scrubs, and for a moment Mrs. Cipriano thought that she must have called an ambulance without realizing that she had.

"Is she dying?" Mrs. Cipriano asked the doctor. The doctor knelt beside June and cupped her hand behind the girl's head to soften the impact of each spasm.

"Oh, June bug. Oh, little June." Then Mrs. Cipriano realized that she was no doctor, she was the Mayborn woman, the mother. June began to grow quieter. Her body grew limp, her eyes shifted around blindly.

"There's matches there, in her nightstand drawer," Ruby said. "Bring it here. Strike one, will you? Then blow it out and hold it under her nose."

Mrs. Cipriano did as she was told, crouching unsteadily beside June. The thin smoke wafted up. June's nostrils responded in small fidgets.

"What is she doing?"

"After fits, her sense of smell gets too sharp. The matches help, Mrs. Cipriano." The sound of her name recalled Mrs. Cipriano to her own part in the day's drama and she told Ruby everything. When she finished, she dropped her buttocks to the ground. The girl looked to be peacefully resting, her eyes open but soft and limpid.

The long, rapier shadow still crossed the girl's face, and Mrs. Cipriano glanced up to see what it was that was casting it. It took her a few moments to fix upon it—the shadow had been so elongated and distorted. But when she found it, on the wall above June's head, her mouth opened in surprise. She recognized her own unfinished embroidery. The needle, which was the cause of the shadow, was still poised in the same cluster of grapes, just as she had left it.

Her thoughts struggled around this discovery: the embroidery had been in her room right before the fire. She had noticed it that very morning and thought that she would hang it in the boarder's room when it was done to cheer him up. That was the last time she'd seen it. When she returned, after the fire, it was gone. She had assumed it had burned with the rest of her things.

Now June turned her spent blue eyes on Mrs. Cipriano. Her neck was encased in Ruby's arms, her face appeared purged. It was an astonishing face, Mrs. Cipriano realized. Stripped, amoral. The face of indescribable piety.

"You can take it back," June said. "I don't want it any more."

The bear's legs were tethered and she was hung upside down on a tree behind the police station. They named her Francine and they had big plans for her. She would be kept right in the station, next to the Pepsi machine, standing tall on her hind legs. They'd put a sheriff's hat on her head. They might even have a uniform custom-made for her. But they wanted her done right. There were two or three fellows they might have called upon to stuff her. But in the end, they decided on Leon. They knew he could probably do the best job on her. Plus, they could name their price and were pretty sure he'd take it.

"It took five bullets to do her in," Officer Kinnunen told Leon. Leon approached the carcass and ran his hands through its coat. He found each bullet wound with his fingertips, spreading the fur to reveal them.

"She's not very big," Leon said.

"No?" Officer Kinnunen said and folded his arms across his chest the way he did when he questioning a suspect. "She looked big enough when she was mauling that little girl."

Officer Kinnunen, and everyone else at the station, took a great personal interest in the bear and the circumstances surrounding her capture. If the actual events did not quite add up to heroics, there was, at least, the potential for the eventual erosion of truth. She was certainly the most interesting collar they'd ever made and had the added advantage of being suitable for display. The officers were already champing at the bit to show her off to the other troopers in Harnass County and Breesport, and all fully expected that, in time, with the addition of the sheriff's hat on her head, she would become a symbol and a warning of their competence.

Leon nodded.

"All right," he said. "I'll do it."

From inside the police station, Leon heard faint wails, pitched and wordless. It sounded like the cry of fox pups at night. But awful. Human. It reminded him of the crying that he'd heard up on Mercy Hill. But it was different, too. Officer Kinnunen did not appear to hear it, or else he had heard it so often that he no longer paid it any mind.

"We'll haul her over to Edie's today," Kinnunen said and slapped the bear's bottom. It swung lightly from its rope. Leon nodded but didn't leave. Officer Kinnunen waited. He didn't think that Leon was dim-witted. Plenty did, but he didn't. He preferred to think that most deviant behaviors were willful. Leon was staring off toward the police station.

"What is that sound?" Leon asked. Kinnunen listened, noticed the wailing.

"That? That's nothing, a woman in the lock-up," Kinnunen said dismissively. "Now remember. Teeth bared. Claws out."

CHAPTER TWENTY-FIVE

LEON SAT AT THE Casablanca bar, whittling away at a chunk of white foam. On the overhead television, Tuesday night fights was featuring a bout between a very dark-skinned black man and a thick-waisted white man; the black man was backed against the ropes, his forearms lifted in front of his body to fend off the other fighter's blows.

"The African will take him out by the fourth round," said Phil Mason, who sat a few stools down from Leon. "Remember I said that."

"Are we watching the same fight?" said Tom Alve, who sat next to him.

"Morrison is a bonehead," said Phil. "Plus he doesn't train. Plus he's hook-happy. He'll punch himself out."

"Morrison is John Wayne's grandson," said Shane Eskeli.

"Where did you hear that hogwash?"

"It's well known. Everyone knows it."

The door opened and Jack Mayborn came in. By his side was a thin, severe-looking girl dressed in clothes that were too big for her. She looked reluctant to enter, but Jack herded her to a table and pulled out a chair for her. She looked down at it, pressed her mouth into a thin line, and then sat on the edge of the chair, her back to the bar.

Jack went up to the bar and sat down heavily beside Leon. Without looking at over him, Leon obligingly brushed the scattered white shavings on the bar counter into a little pile in front of him.

"Hey, Leon, what you got there?" Jack asked. Leon stopped the movement of his knife and flattened his hand out for Jack to see. It was small and oblong like a potato.

"A mold for a squirrel," Leon said.

"Someone's paying you to stuff a goddamn squirrel?"

Behind the bar, Edie lit up a cigarette.

"It's for Jeannie down at the Pick-A-Part," she said. "She tamed it. He'd sit in her lap. She took it for rides in her car."

"So why's she stuffing it?"

"The cat got to it."

"Well," Jack said, "that's what happens when people take wild things into their homes." He winked at Edie, slid his eyes toward Leon. Leon's knife had slowed its chiseling and Jack considered him again.

"Say, Leon," Jack said, "I hear you're sewing up the teddy bear that nearly ate my June a few days ago."

"The police hired him to do it," Edie said, putting her hands on her hips, her cigarette pointing at the ceiling, and eyeing Jack warily.

"Nice. Good, good. Good that's someone's profiting from the whole misfortune. Hey, I got my daughter here. Not June, my other daughter, from down in the city. You remember Lee, don't you, Leon? She's sitting at the table there. Right over there. Go on and say hello," Jack said.

"That's all right," Leon said, his face dipped down, and he started chiseling more intently.

"Are you so delicate you can't even say hello?"

"Leave him be, Jack," Edie said.

"I mean, you *definitely* know Lee's mother," Jack continued. "Iris Utter. Ring a bell? Should do. You been hanging outside her goddamn jail cell every goddamn night, tormenting the shit out of her."

"I swear it, Jack, I will chuck you right out of here…" Edie crushed out her cigarette in a Saranac Ale ashtray.

"There's people who are saying that Iris is crazy, because she hears voices outside her window and because she thinks that kid is hers," Jack said, lowering his voice so that only Leon could hear. "Well, we know where the voices are coming from, don't we? And, I'll be honest, I don't give a shit if that kid is hers or not. But I *will* not have people saying she's crazy. So if you know something about what's what with that kid, you had better tell me now."

"No," Leon said.

"No? No, you won't?" Jack's eyebrows were raised up so high that the creases on his forehead formed numerous, shallow striations.

"No, I won't," Leon confirmed. Jack grabbed up the squirrel mold and threw it hard against the wall. It bounced back and skidded along the floor and under the piano.

"Get the hell out of my bar, Jack!" Edie yelled.

Leon rose from the stool, head ducked, and moved to retrieve it.

At the sound of the raised voices, Lee turned. She recognized Leon immediately. He had changed a little. He looked thinner, his face had narrowed, and his eyes were deeply mantled under a lowered brow. But it was Leon, so vividly Leon that she nearly expected to see him gripping the red toolbox. She stood up and walked over to him, smiling so widely that she had to bite her lip.

"Leon!" She reached out to hug him—a thing she rarely did—and he turned his back to her, leaving her arms stretched aloft, reaching for him. Her arms dropped down, a stuttering and ugly movement. She swallowed back the aching constriction in her throat, but felt the muscles in her lips slacken anyway and her eyes begin to sting. A man at the bar snickered and Lee felt her face grow hot.

Jack came at Leon then in full fury, grabbing a fistful of Leon's shirt, right at the collarbone, and pushing him backward, both of them stumbling between table and chairs. With a single, powerful shove, he threw Leon up against the wall, so hard that the television quivered on its stand. Jack's fist slammed against the side of Leon's head, making a popping noise.

Edie screamed and ran out from behind the bar, but one of the other customers restrained her from throwing herself in the midst of the fight. No one else was willing to try to separate the men.

Lee watched as blood branched across Leon's face and his body curled up around each punch, like a worm being prodded at with a stick. Brutal and disgusting. Yet she was conscious of nursing a feverish free-floating anger that made her muscles jump in sync with each vicious blow, until, finally, several men worked up the courage to interfere and pull Jack off Leon, pinning him against the opposite wall. Still Jack struggled to return to his victim, his legs kicking out furiously, his neck and shoulders heaving forward against the restraining hands.

Lee slipped out of the bar, the sound of her Jack's curses still ringing out on the street. She walked off swiftly, strangely ebullient and without direction, through a darkened tangle of streets. She was suddenly very aware of her bones scissoring as she walked, the pain in her bruised feet, the forging of her cells, and her body's constant and relentless needs winding through her.

She passed a huddle of teenagers, perched on the steps and railing of a porch. They looked sleepy and coiled but as Lee approached, they grew alert. All heads turned in unison, and a cigarette lighter was poised, its flame straining for something to light.

"How's the bear?" asked one of the boys. He had the crude, round face and puny features that had been commonly seen around Loomis for the past one hundred years. "That's the first thing I said when my dad told me June Mayborn met up with a bear. 'How's the bear?' I said. 'I hope she was gentle with him. It was probably his first time.'"

The other kids burst out laughing and Lee walked by without looking back. They know I'm a Mayborn, she thought.

At length, she found that she had wound her way in a circle and was now at the head of Loomis Park. She walked down the steps. There was no one else around, except a dog pawing at the ground at the other end of the park. She could see the Mayborn house across the way. June's light was on, throwing the twisted ironwork on the verandah into relief.

"I am walking on the bottom of a pond," she thought. How quickly things were capable of changing! How easily history could be snuffed out.

As she got closer, the dog sat back on its haunches. It stayed perfectly still with its forelegs off the ground as though someone were commanding it to perform a trick, but there was no one there. Its back was thick and she wondered if it was Keeper, Frank's dog. But it was too far and too dark to tell. Only when it stood up completely did Lee realized that it was not a dog at all, but a man. He moved across the park and stopped again, dropped to his knees and began to work at the ground. This time he knelt in a spot that was dimly illuminated by a streetlight above. She could see he held a trowel that he was shoving into the ground, turning up the lawn that Frank and Boulevard had recently laid.

"Hey!" Lee screamed. The man stopped. He looked around. When he saw Lee, he stood and waved enthusiastically.

"Sorry, so. My fault, my fault."

"The grass was just planted," Lee said angrily, walking toward the man. The violence was still so fresh in her mind that she felt an urge to slap him.

"I was being careful. So. Not to hurt anything. Just to dig." He turned on a flashlight and pointed it at the ground. A small edge of turf was turned up. The man was Asian, short and chubby, with a sagging knapsack on his back.

"Why are you digging?"

"Yes, exactly," he said as if she had finally understood a point that he was trying to explain. "A friend told me that there are many kind interesting fossil in this area. I came to see."

"You can't dig up a park."

"No, this is true. My apologies." He slipped his knapsack off his shoulder, unzipped it, and dropped the trowel inside. "Good night." He began to walk away, a short-legged, carefree stride.

"If you want fossils," Lee called after him, "you should go up there." She pointed toward the shadowy rise of Mercy Hill on her left.

"Ah, thank you very much, I will do so. Up there? Good, good."

CHAPTER TWENTY-SIX

LEE SLEPT LATE INTO the next day. She might have slept on but the hammering down below, in Loomis Park, woke her and kept her awake. Still, she did not want to rise. The soles of her feet burned, the bones felt bruised. The sound of the hammer pressed into her like a prodding fingertip, then slipped along the roof of her mouth. She swallowed and the sound drummed against her throat and made her cough. Everything was jumbled up, a tangled filigree of sentience as if parts of her brain were shutting down while other parts were beginning to stir.

She dressed herself in June's bright blue tank top and a pair of shorts and descended the stairs. Her body felt odd, weightless, existing without relevance to anything else. She passed June's bedroom and peered in. She could see June through the French doors, standing out on the verandah, staring off as if she were on the deck of a ship in the middle of the ocean.

Downstairs, the mudroom door was open and Ruby was working on a small gray schnauzer that was standing on the metal grooming table, his neck in a noose attached to the table's raised arm. Ruby held his front paw out, pressing against its pad with her thumb to expose the webbing, and clipped the hair between the dog's toes. The clipper's droning pitch dropped an octave, then ceased. Ruby hit the clippers with the heel of her hand and blew against the edge of the blade before noticing Lee standing in the doorway.

"Do you need something?"

"No," Lee said.

"Well, come in and or stay out." She turned the clippers back on and picked up the dog's paw again while Lee stepped inside. "Is June still out on the verandah?" Ruby asked. Lee nodded.

"It's those church women," Ruby shook her head angrily.

"What did they do?" Lee asked.

"Turned their backs on her, like I knew they would."

"Why?"

Ruby shrugged. "Mrs. Cipriano told them something about June."

"What?"

Ruby hesitated. "I don't know. Something about June and Ed. It was a lie, of course." Ruby shut off the clippers, snapped off the blade, and replaced it with another one lying on the edge of the table. She turned the clippers back on, tapping it against her hand a few times before it started up, and began to shear off strips of fur, starting at the base of the dog's head and moving in a straight line, right back to the nubby tail. Lee watched as the dog's dingy gray fur dropped to the floor, revealing a small, neat torso.

"Ruby," Lee asked shyly, "would you cut my hair?" Ruby glanced over at Lee.

"Why? It's getting nice and long. Oh, all right. Go wet it." Ruby nodded toward the sink.

The sink smelled of dog—brackish and overlaid with some kind of floral shampoo. Lee wet her hair and wrung it out, then sat down on a tall stool and waited as Ruby scooped the schnauzer up in one hand and put it in a crate.

Standing behind Lee, Ruby drew her wet hair back, away from her face, and combed it through, smoothing it down with her raw-boned hand.

"Cut it straight across," Lee said. "As straight as you can." The sound of the blade tearing through her hair was like fabric ripping. The air Ruby stirred as she moved smelled vampish, and the feel of Ruby's hands against her skull made Lee feel sleepy and drugged.

"You're a little bit like Frank, aren't you," Ruby said suddenly. "Quiet, the both of you. Hard to guess at. He seems to like you." Then she added, "Jack won't be happy about that."

"Why not?" Lee asked. Ruby combed Lee's hair down and stepped back to check if it was straight. Then she snipped at the ends carefully with the tips of her scissors.

"The problem with Jack is he's proud," Ruby said. "That's a bad quality in a Mayborn. It makes them mean. You know when I like him best? I like him when he's down. I like him when his spirits are low. That's when he's most like a Mayborn. And I love Mayborns, I have since I was this high."

"Why do you stand for it?" Lee asked. It was a question she had wanted to ask Ruby for so long, but only now, with her back to her, did she dare to.

"You mean about Jack and Iris?" There was a pause, during which Ruby's hand raked Lee's hair back from her temple and tucked it behind her ears. "I do, until I don't," Ruby said simply. "That was what Jack's dad said at his own wedding. Well, that's what he told everyone he said. Might have been true."

Frank came up to her room that night. Lee heard nothing, no sound to puncture the house's stillness, but she felt a galvanic intent, and there he was.

She had opened her eyes but lay still, watching his approach to the bed. She gauged how fast she could make it to the door and down the stairs. The room was very dark—there was hardly any moonlight coming through the window—and his eyes would not be fully adjusted for another moment or two.

He sat down on the edge of the bed with his back to her. Her muscles contracted, ready to bolt, yet she kept still. He said nothing; just sat there with his elbows resting on his knees and his head dipped down, like a man at an impasse.

The house creaked gently, rearranging itself. At that moment she perceived the house itself in a burst of unannexed intelligence—the same way in which she occasionally understood physics. The house carried a horizontal vastness, like a field or the ocean, containing immeasurable strata, efforts and incidents, leaky toilets and cobbed marriages. Infants who lived one day, then expired, and infants who sprouted man-sized limbs but maintained the callow urges of infants. The deposits of sun and ceaseless rain, frigid nights passed in unbroken sleep. Now she felt that she had also been acquired by the house; that it had shifted and created a space for her to slip easily into.

Suddenly, Frank reached across the thin blanket and found her hand, which was pressed against her stomach beneath the blanket. He covered it with his own for a moment, the blanket between their skin, the cool fabric growing instantly warm.

She tried to slow her breathing so that he wouldn't feel the quickness of it against the rise and fall of her hand, but she couldn't manage it. She forced herself to sound out the word "incest" within her mind, and when it had no effect, she grasped at scraps of biology: it was a dangerous ferment of genes, whose monstrousness was so indisputable that it even produced monsters—babies with malformed skulls and twisted limbs, or whose very blood refused to cooperate in keeping them alive.

Then, slowly, Frank's fingertips described the shape of her hand, pressing the cloth down around it and between each finger, raking his own fingers between hers. "He doesn't want to touch my nails with his bare hand," she thought suddenly, and the pain and force of the insult made her own hand fist up and she drew back.

But Frank leaned forward. His hands closed on either side of Lee's neck and he kissed her; first her lips, which would not respond for shock, then the bone beneath her eye. He kissed every hard place on her face—the slope of her jaw, the wide bone of her nose, the veined indentation of her temple, which was now pulsing quickly, and she felt his lips linger against the pulse, as if he were timing it. After that it wasn't far to go; just a small nudge, and the tender conscience snapped in two.

After that he came up to her room every night, his footsteps silenced by the thickly carpeted stairs, her senses primed for him. As they made love she watched his face very closely, astonished at the transformation. His guardedness was overthrown. The bones of his face came undone. He explored her with impunity—the furrows alongside her spine and the white halo of her belly—as if he were rooting through her, and the places that he touched left her skin feeling branded. They barely spoke, contracted by secrecy, the current of their offense brokering between them, driving them against each other roughly.

If he slept while he was with her she never caught him at it. When she opened her eyes, she met his, open and watching.

"What are you doing?"

"Keeping an eye on you." As if there were any chance that she would leave. As the room lost darkness, his composure was reclaimed. The daylight separated them ruthlessly; the bones in his face would set against her again and, for her part, she would notice their mortifying resemblance. Once she had seen it, she wondered how she could have missed it before. Each day it was different. Sometimes it was the flat disk of cheekbone they shared or the way they both shifted their eyes away before speaking. Other times it was the quick-twitch retraction of muscle against muscle, an ionic repulsion of like to like.

Once, as they lay tangled together, his hand splayed out against her collarbone, she thought of Noah; how he had slept against her every night, his hands fisted up, his coiled mouth parted, night after night. Night after night. Frank and Noah were her brothers at opposite ends—one lost as an infant, the other recovered as a man. In her mind, they juxtaposed, overlapped. What was *this,* then? An attempt to regain one brother by cleaving to another? She panicked at the thought that her feelings might be dissected and, therefore, fraudulent. Refusing this, she gladly accepted another option: that there was a kink in her moral codes, a depravity that followed her throughout her whole life. It was the dirtiness she had always felt within her. It grew on the tips of her fingers.

CHAPTER TWENTY-SEVEN

A T AGE EIGHTEEN, WANDA Enders still had another year and a half to
live. It should have been enough time to learn that, in her case,
serendipity never turned out well. A cab pilfered in the rain always had a
driver who stank. The chance encounter with a film star, né teen idol,
whose fold-out poster Wanda had once pulled from the binding of *Tiger
Beat*, and who had a penchant for redheads, had resulted in a botched
abortion that left her sterile. She fared better when she governed her own
life, which she generally did ferociously. But every so often, serendipity
was difficult to resist.

Right before she heard that Joseph was dead, Wanda had found herself
in some awkward romantic troubles with two brothers. The trip to
Loomis seemed like a perfect way to extricate herself from the whole
situation. After Loomis, she and Carol Ann would take a trip up to Maine
and by the time she returned home, Wanda hoped, things with the
brothers would have sorted themselves out.

But Loomis was a failure. Handling the angry brothers would have probably been easier in the long run. Carol Ann decided to stay on at Mercy Hill for the summer, and ditched their plans for Maine. And there they were, holed up in the shambles of a commune, with Ivan and Kitty and their two unpleasant children.

Ivan had momentarily interested her when she learned he was now an actor, but he turned out to be one of those no-name gas bags with absolutely *no* celebrity friends. Useless, pointless. Just like the entire trip. For a while she amused herself with the children, providing them with as much misinformation about the adult world as possible until their poor, fat melonheads were thoroughly rattled. That having been done, Wanda had nothing else to do.

On her way down the trail, Wanda congratulated herself on her choice of footwear—a pair of knee-high brown leather boots with a very moderate heel. Even though she had to take mincing steps through the undergrowth, her legs were completely shielded from the scratching shrubbery. She held her freckled arms out in defense of an olive green dress, palms up as if warding off paparazzi. Despite all this, Wanda moved fairly nimbly. She had a knack for adapting. Having skipped around to far-flung places since she was a child, she had an aversion to appearing ill at ease, ever.

But it was all, nearly, for naught, as she was startled by the disembodied face of Ivan, floating midair in a thicket. She lost her footing and skidded slightly on a bed of slick pine needles, catching herself deftly with one hand before she toppled. It took her a moment to piece out Ivan's situation. He was deeply cupped within a hammock that was strung between two hemlock trees, swinging lightly. He watched her with a serene expression on his face that didn't change one iota when she slipped. She hated that. He had stopped shaving since he'd arrived at the commune and now had a very unattractive beard that crept up too far along his cheeks, consuming half his face. She imagined he'd keep it until he returned to the city and could parade it around his ensemble of rarified actor chums as a souvenir from the wilderness.

"There's a nest of starlings right above my head," he whispered.

"Kitty was looking for you," Wanda said, failing to lower her voice. "Your kids need batteries." His reverie was deliberately, and aggressively, broken. He pressed his lips together—she could tell by the way his beard and mustache closed up into one unbroken patch—and stared at her. She remembered that same look on his face from when she was a child and laughed when Joseph whirled about like a top in the prayer meetings. There was no anger in his face at all, just a pointed benevolence that was unbearable. No wonder his kids were all screwy.

"Don't you think you're making those birds nervous? Swinging under them like that, Ivan." To his credit, Ivan did rise slightly to stop the hammock's movement. He was like that—dutiful without appearing subservient. He was born to be a right-hand man to people who looked inferior beside him. He raised himself by debasing himself. The two brothers who were in love with Wanda would have despised him. To them, power was a simple, pugnacious ascent—another reason she did not want either of them.

"Where are you going?" he asked, no longer whispering. He combed his hair back off his forehead with his fingers and Wanda guessed that he was as anxious for diversion as she was. But Ivan did not figure into her plans for the day, so she pretended not to have heard him and scurried off, her boots hashing at the ground.

When she reached the town, she headed directly for her destination, hastily noting the sudden blare of full sunlight and the gawk of a local man who saw the brilliant redhead emerge from the woods, dressed for cocktails. She passed the schoolyard and was momentarily startled to see the charred remains of Cipriano's. She knew, of course, it had burnt down. But as a kid, her magazine runs to Cipriano's were a weekly bright spot. The sight of the blackened, vacant hull made her mad. She never liked returning to places where she'd been. There was always some bit that curdled her memories.

The Casablanca Bar, however, was exactly as she remembered. The same cheap, sequestered atmosphere. The same shingled faux-roof over the bar area, the studded vinyl chairs by Formica tables, the laminated paneled walls, the piercing odor of cigarettes and conditioned air. The smell of meat cooking. But no smell of booze, oddly. Two men, laborers by the look of their mucky clothes, sat at the bar with beers. The bartender was nowhere in sight.

"Is it self-serve today, gentlemen?" She sat at a stool and leaned across the bar to get a better look at the bottles. The men looked at her and one called out, "Edie!"

"Coming," a woman's voice called from the back. The man turned back to his beer, and the other one followed suit. He'd done his duty.

Wanda didn't know how New York City had gotten such a reputation for being unfriendly. You get New Yorkers in a bar and they became a bunch of Chatty Cathys. It was in these little towns that people guarded their lives, as if they had lives worth guarding.

Edie emerged from the back, a cigarette hanging between her lips. When she saw Wanda, she removed her cigarette and wiped her hands on her apron.

"Can I help you?" she asked. She had a pleasant little face and a neat, organized look about her. Wanda guessed she might be pretty sharp. She hoped she wouldn't give her trouble about her age.

"A Cosmopolitan, please," Wanda said. "In a martini glass if you've got one." The two laborers glanced her way again. One of them looked like he was actually quite good-looking if you were willing to scrape the dirt off him.

"I have no idea what that is, honey," Edie said. "But if you can describe it to me, and if it doesn't have alcohol in it, I'll make it for you."

"I'm perfectly legal," Wanda said. "Would you like to see my ID?" Wanda opened her bag but Edie held up her hand.

"I'm sure you've got one. And I'm sure it's fake. But damned if I can tell. This is why I hate all you girls. You hit puberty and you all look twenty-five. How old does she look to you, Frank?"

Frank sighed. He was the handsome one and it annoyed Wanda that he took so little interest in her that he was reluctant even to turn his head. He did, however, and she met his eyes and smiled lightly. He looked away.

"Twenty-five," he said.

"All right, what's a Cosmopolitan?"

"Triple Sec, vodka, and cranberry juice. In a martini glass, please."

"No martini glass. And consider yourself lucky you get anything at all."

Edie mixed the drink and pushed it at her. Wanda tilted the glass dubiously this way and that, stuck her pinky in it and put the pinky in her mouth. She was very aware that the two men were watching her. The handsome one lifted his hip off the stool to dig inside his back pocket. He put some bills down on the counter, tapped the other man's back, and said, "Let's go."

"One more, Fank," the other one pleaded like a child even though he had at least fifteen years on Frank and a voice like an old bullfrog. "I don't even got a buzz on. One more and I'll get my buzz on."

Frank deliberated for a moment. Wanda hated that.

"Another beer for the gentleman," Wanda said, opening her purse and counting out some singles. She turned to Frank and said, "Just because he's retarded doesn't mean you have to treat him like a moron."

Edie put the beer in front of the retarded man, who stared at it eagerly but kept his hands in his lap. He turned to Frank.

"Don't look at *me,* Boulevard," Frank said. "It's *your* drink. She bought it for you." Wanda should have been flattered. But she wasn't. It only meant that Frank didn't even care enough to argue with her. There was an uneven, malcontented break in the space between his lips. She noticed that he had a blue cast beneath his eyes, as if he hadn't slept well for a while.

Wanda poured the rest of her Cosmopolitan down her throat and ordered another. When Edie hesitated, Wanda rolled her eyes.

"I don't even have the tiniest little buzz on," Wanda said and smiled over at Boulevard, whose eyes slid toward her above the rim of his beer glass.

Wanda looked at Frank. She had radar for minds that were all bungled up. Frank's mind was most definitely bungled. Probably some girl. A current of jealousy passed through her—ridiculous, she knew. She had made her share of men miserable. But their misery grew legs in a short period of time and they all made full recoveries and occasionally rang her up just to say hi. Frank's distress was of a different type. It had gravity. He was in love and bitter as hell and the combination was likely to result in some dramatic fabulousness. Wanda sighed.

"Have you ever had two men in love with you simultaneously?" she asked Edie as her second Cosmopolitan was placed in front of her.

"Never been so lucky," Edie said. She filled a beer glass with water and began to dribble it into the baskets of ferns behind the bar.

"Not lucky! It *seems* lucky, but it's awful. And not just two men, but two brothers! Twins. Fraternal, not identical. Everyone asks that. But let's be honest, ladies and gentlemen. It's the easiest thing in the world to make people fall in love with you, don't we all agree? Laughably easy!" She looked at them all, then laughed, suddenly wishing she hadn't cut her hair so short. It looked better when you laughed with long hair.

"If you can have it that easily," Frank said, "then it must be pretty goddamn worthless."

Instead of looking offended, as Wanda had hoped, Frank now appeared earnestly, almost clinically interested. It made her uncomfortable. But he really was a very good-looking guy, a thuggish sort of beauty, and now she had his full attention. Wanda swiveled her chair toward him. It signaled to Edie that her patrons were fully engaged with each other and she could leave them. Slipping out from behind the bar, Edie went back into the kitchen to shred cabbage for the coleslaw.

"Oh, completely worthless," Wanda said, blinking a little at her own audacity. He was shaping up to be a possibility. She might have an interesting few days in Loomis after all. She tucked back the rest of her drink. With Edie gone, Wanda took the opportunity to go behind the bar to fix her next drink, allowing Frank to get a better look at her. Her eyes were widely spaced, like Jackie O's some people said. He could see that better if she faced him full on.

"Except for the pleasure," Wanda said. She positioned herself directly opposite him. "Which has its worth, I think we'll all admit."

The retarded man pushed his empty beer glass toward her to refill. Wanda turned to Frank; *now* she'd ask his permission. Lost in his own reckonings, Frank's head bowed without response, then lifted. After a moment, he asked, "And after you're finished with them—the men—do they forget about you?" Wanda frowned at this.

"They *hate* me," she said emphatically. "Then, after, they forget. Don't worry, Frank. You won't hate her forever."

"*She* who's going to hate *him*," Boulevard poked his thumb toward Frank. Wanda looked at the two of them.

"Oh," she said. "I see." She rearranged her conclusions, faced Frank's calibrating gaze. She felt that he was testing himself against her boldness, that he was both stimulated and repelled. Thoughts of her hapless fling with the movie star invaded. She snatched up Boulevard's empty glass, the cardboard coaster still clinging to its bottom, and filled it from the beer tap. Her hand felt small and sloppy and the beer spilled, splashing against the toe of her boot. The Cosmopolitans were kicking in now. Her anger was already being replaced by a mellower dislike of people in general. She smiled ruefully at Frank, then laughed, opening her mouth as she did so that he could see the small beauty mark on her tongue. What did she care? She slapped the glass in front of Boulevard, sloshed the froth over the bar counter. Boulevard reached for it but Frank grabbed his arm.

"Enough." Frank stood up. After a moment's hesitation, Boulevard stood too, with one regretful back glance at the overfull glass.

"I'd never laugh at her," Frank said before he left.

"Goody for you."

By the time she was on her fifth Cosmopolitan, Wanda had considerably more company in the bar. People trickled in after work and sat down for a beer and a burger with a side of coleslaw, which seemed to be the only thing on the menu that night.

Wanda had positioned herself at a table dead center, her blazing red hair the first thing that people noticed on entering. They stared at her shamelessly with their flat, gluey eyes, the way people look when they open their front door to a stranger and are wondering what that person requires from their lives. After a minute, they all, with the exception of a few, absorbed Wanda into their consciousness. Tucked her behind their ears.

One summer, Wanda had sailed the coast of California with her father and they saw a beach covered with tumors. Then she realized that the tumors were a multitude of sea lions clapped against the sands. By six o'clock, Casablanca reminded Wanda of that beach—a sprawl of lusterless, static bulk. There was noise, talk, but it was tired, with stretched-out upstate vowels concluded with the refrain, "I know it," like the final, truncated plash of dirty tidewater before it slides back into the ocean.

Wanda swayed a little bit as she stood up, but caught herself. There were a few more drinks in her still, and she did not intend to stop just yet. Edie now appeared to be waitressing, a cigarette still dangling from her mouth. She had relinquished her bartending to a squat man with a fat, black mustache. When he'd handed Wanda her last drink, he warned her to slow down. She gave him the thumbs up.

Now, she went over to the dusty piano in the corner and parked herself on the bench. On the wall above was a cluster of old photos. They were different buildings, before and after some calamity. One was a rudimentary wooden structure, little more than a shack, which appeared in the next picture as a charred heap of timber, a family milling around the ruins. Another was a more attractive building with fine scrollwork on the doorframe and a plaque reading "Town Hall." This too, in the next photo, was destroyed by fire. It was only after seeing the third structure in the series that Wanda recognized the short rise of the first floor above street level and the edge of a curving sidewalk. All the buildings were on the same site—this site.

There was a victorious feeling to the last photo of the Casablanca, in full color and flaunting its triumph over the monochrome Fates. This seemed like a bad omen to Wanda, who had secretly preoccupied herself with doom and its harbingers since she was a child. And whose own doom, on Park Avenue in a January frost, would take the form of a serendipitous run of green lights, from 52nd Street to 78th Street, where, at the intersection after the final green light, a westbound truck would lose its brakes, and Wanda's car would go under it, slicing her in two. One paramedic would say that she looked like a doll someone had pulled apart at its articulated waist, a comparison that occurred to him because he had seen his own daughter pull apart her doll that very morning. It seemed to him like an omen. A useless omen.

Wanda put her drink on top of the piano, lifted the lid, and fingered the keys. It was out of tune—no surprise. Although the groan of conversation was certainly louder than the notes, everyone heard it and looked toward her. She was making trouble for them. Poor things.

She began to play a Mozart piece that her mother had taught her. She played it badly to begin with, and the alcohol made it worse. But it was good enough for the company she was in at the moment. It was pretty, flirtatious; she always imagined astounding some imperious mother-in-law with it one day. Why wait? With all eyes glaring at her, she played until she forgot about them. She played until she forgot she was playing and might have even been asleep without knowing it.

A man took a seat beside her on the bench, and she felt suddenly fatigued, sorry for the company. At first, she tried to ignore him. She kept playing, but the man's continued gesticulations distracted her. He pawed at his head, patting it or tapping it, she couldn't quite tell without actually turning and acknowledging his presence. Finally, she lost her place in the music and dropped her hands, folded them onto her thighs. She turned fully to her benchmate and saw what he was gesturing about. His hair was nearly the same dazzling red as her own, though far thinner. He was tall, with a lean jaw and a strong chin, and he wore thick, wire-rimmed glasses that made him look slightly cross-eyed.

"Us redheads have to stick together," he asserted. His voice was loud and confident, but nasal, as if the glasses were pinching his nose.

"Why's that?" Wanda asked. The man looked confused. He clearly had not completely worked out his theory. But he recovered quickly, stuck out his large flat hand, and introduced himself as Shane Eskeli.

"Town maverick," Wanda murmured. She was pretty loaded now. She'd have to watch her mouth. She told the man her name, which he took as a coup. He smiled, shut the lid of the piano, and rested his elbow against it.

"You from the city?" he asked.

"Yup."

"I knew it. I could tell. I spent a little time down there myself." There was a swagger in his voice, so she guessed this was supposed to impress her.

"Drove a cab for a little while," he continued, "saw a lot of things I wouldn't repeat in polite company. But," he sighed, "in the end I came back for the fishing." He nodded and she nodded.

"Shane," Wanda said. "The reason redheads *shouldn't* stick together is that one redhead is a novelty, but two redheads are a spectacle."

"Yeah, people are real superstitious about redheads. Because of Judas. He was supposed to be a redhead. Although how you going to prove that I don't know. And then you got those Salem witches. No, ever since I went to the city, people treat me different. Like some kind of snob. I don't know." He sighed again, knocked his fist against the piano lid. "City people got a bad name around here because of all the hippies. We had a lot of the hippies come up this way. Nice enough folks," he said, his hand raised against any possible objection, "but you know, they were doing some weird stuff up in the woods. Drugs and sex."

"Weird," Wanda said.

"Then they used to come down here and swim naked in the pond. It went dry a few years ago and people said it had something to do with the hippies swimming naked." He sighed. He was a robust-looking man, but the simple act of conversing appeared to exhaust him.

"Sounds like witchcraft," Wanda said. "Maybe there were some naked redheaded hippies swimming in the pond."

"Could be." He laughed and nodded. They were getting along fine.

"Did you ever see any?"

"Can't say that I did." He kept smiling.

"No? Are you sure? When you and your cheesy little friends were crouched down in the bushes with your tiny little hard-ons," she was on a roll now and could not stop herself, "while your daddies were peering out of their windows with their slightly bigger hard-ons, at all the nasty, naked hippies… didn't you see just one little naked redhead? Looking right back at you. And yours." Her voice was raised, and Shane was frowning, narrowing his eyes. He stood up, and his lips popped against each other knowingly. As soon as he got back to his barstool, the sea lions flopped over to him to find out what they could. Even the drooping bartender was riveted and he motioned over Edie.

"You're no maverick, Shane!" Wanda yelled at him even as he was telling the others who she was. "You're just a foot soldier! Send over the regiment! I want to see the big guns, folks! I know you've got them! Root around in your corn cribs, check under your Lawn-Boys!" She stood up and wobbled but she didn't care. They'd toss her out in any case. And sure enough, Edie was approaching her. A couple of the men trailed behind Edie, for backup Wanda guessed. But Edie whipped around and told them to get lost. That calmed Wanda down somewhat, though she was still breathing hard and was shaking a little bit. She drained her glass and held it out.

"Yes, another one would be lovely," she said. Edie took the glass and looked carefully into Wanda's face.

"One more drink and you'll pass out," Edie said.

"I never pass out."

"Good. I need you to be conscious."

"For what?" Wanda asked. The words plopped out of her mouth. Edie put her arm around Wanda's shoulders. Wanda let her. She had a nice touch, sort of motherly. She let Edie lead her back to a little table in a dim corner.

"Put your head down," Edie said, stroking Wanda's head until it bent and rested on the table, cradled in her folded arms. It was like being back at grade school, after you'd cried your heart out in class and had embarrassed and exhausted yourself and there was nothing left to do but shut your eyes and hide your head.

Edie stood beside the girl for a moment. Serendipity could be a funny thing, Edie thought. It could offer itself up and at the same time demand a small token. Exact a chunk out of your scruples. Still, Edie made her decision swiftly. Marching back to the kitchen, she kicked the little rubber stopper from under the door and let the door swing shut. Then she picked up the phone and called Jack Mayborn.

CHAPTER TWENTY-EIGHT

W HEN JACK ARRIVED AT the Casablanca, Edie was waiting outside for him. She was leaning against the building, her arms folded and the fingers on one hand pressing into the meat of her biceps. When he came close, she unfolded her arms and took a drag from a cigarette, then refolded her arms.

"So," Jack said. He still had no idea why she had summoned him to the bar. He clapped his hands. "What are we doing?"

"You're not going to let Leon be, are you? You're going to plague him about this business with Iris until he tells you what you want to hear, aren't you?" Edie didn't wait for his answer. In fact, these were not questions. She was simply stating her case. "I won't allow it."

"He's a grown man."

"I know that!" Her good face kindled quickly, then mastered its anger. "I've got something to offer you. It's better than Leon."

"I don't want your money," Jack said and to his own surprise, he found that this was true. He thought of Iris ceaselessly. Possessing her was his only concern.

"I'm not giving you my money," Edie said, wondering that the thought of bribing him had never occurred to her. She began to reconsider. Perhaps, since he had suggested money, it was a possibility. Maybe if the amount was large enough and if she pressed him hard enough. But in the end, she thought, Jack is a Mayborn and Mayborns are unpredictable at best. She could not hold him to his word.

"There is a young woman inside," Edie said. "She lived up at Mercy Hill. She knew Iris."

"That's what you called me here for? That's nothing. There are dozens of people who were in and out of that place and know nothing. But Leon knows. He was thick as thieves with Joseph."

"No, I remember this girl. I had a little run-in with her mother, years ago, over Leon. She brought in some fancy lawyer from New York to come to my house and explain why I had no legal right to Leon. It was all done very nicely. Professionally. If Joseph needed help, especially legal help—like for an adoption—he would have gone to her. And her daughter, in there, is sharp as a tack and probably had her nose in everything since she was old enough to wipe her own ass. Plus, she's very drunk."

"All right," Jack said after a moment. "I'll give her a try. No promises." He started for the stairs but Edie caught him by the arm.

"Talk to her somewhere else. Leon's going to be here any minute. I don't need the two of you at it again."

The girl was a shadowy heap at the far end of the bar, her head collapsed in her arms. The chair she was sitting on was pushed away from the table so that her back was stretched nearly perpendicular to the floor, her booted feet splayed to either side.

"Help her up," Edie said impatiently. Jack hesitated.

"Where the hell am I supposed to take her?" he asked. Edie crushed her cigarette out in the red plastic ashtray beside the girl's ear and, shoving her arms beneath Wanda's armpits, lifted her off the chair. Wanda cursed briefly before Jack moved in and gathered her up. She looked around at Jack, his pink and white mottled thick-skinned cheek, his crow's-feet tumbling from narrow, pale eyes. Wanda's freckled lips turned down.

"If you're planning on doing anything disgusting to me, pal," Wanda said, "just stop and look around you." Jack looked and saw every eye in the bar fixed on him and the girl.

"There," said Edie. "I told you. If there's something to know, she'll know it." Jack nodded soberly. He put his arm around the girl's waist and hauled her through the bar and out the door. In the distance, a few blocks off, a slim figure was fast approaching, the telltale wild hair identifying him as Leon. Jack turned in the opposite direction, toward Loomis Park.

"Where's that fellow?" Wanda said as they made their way down the park steps.

"What fellow?"

"The one in the bar, with the dirt on his hands."

"That could be anybody. Watch your step."

Frank and Boulevard had just installed a small gazebo in the center of the park and now Jack guided Wanda up the gazebo steps.

The summer sky had finally darkened. The night contained a tranquility that provoked human collision; had Iris been beside him, they would have shattered it with teeth against tongue, lips against skin. He looked down at the girl, her arms spread over the back of the gazebo seat, her head tipped back, exposing her throat.

It was possible, Jack considered, that she might actually know the truth. And the truth might be that Kitty's son was simply Kitty's son. That Iris was mistaken, or worse, that she was crazy, like everyone said, and her love for him was only a symptom of her madness. Could he stand it? Could he stand one more disappointment in his disappointing life?

He looked at the girl's limp body. His gaze drifted to her breasts. He could give it all up now. The whole thing. It would take no effort at all; a brief scuffle that would surprise no one, not even Ruby. He could surrender to his birthright of periodic jail terms, of pride in nothing and hope for nothing. Right now, here, he could crush out the fragile promise of Iris, follow his bitter path rather than tear out his heart in continuously trying to avoid it.

"Fuck you, in advance," Wanda said, lifting her head with difficulty.

Jack grabbed the bottom of Wanda's dress, closed his hand around the material. She launched the heel of her hand into his face and slammed it against the bone beneath his nose, sending a torrent of pain into his skull. For a moment he could not see, and he pawed at his eyes while Wanda buried her face in her hands, dizzied from her sudden effort. Had someone walked by at that moment, they might have taken Jack and Wanda for a couple in the last, miserable stage of separation, when reconciliation is still a possibility.

When his vision began to clear, Jack saw that there was blood on his hands. He touched the sticky wetness dribbling from his nostrils and looked at his hands again. He reached toward Wanda and she recoiled, her hands raised.

"Next, I scream," she said.

"I'm bleeding, damn it! I need a tissue." He grabbed her handbag but she snatched it back.

"Use your shirt." She watched as he raised his shirt to his face and wiped the blood on the underside of the hem.

"A tidy rapist. Very nice. Now you can go back to your wife and kids who I'm sure worship the ground you walk on." Buried in the cloth of his shirt, Jack's face crumpled. A small, involuntary sound escaped from his lips, which he instantly swallowed back. His body felt like it would rupture from despair; but even now he could feel the perverse strength in his limbs, the native hardiness that was also his birthright, demanding that he press on. He lifted his head from his shirt, sniffed the blood back into his nose and spat a bloody gob off the side of the gazebo.

"My wife is in jail," Jack said. His voice wavered slightly. The momentum of violence had ceased and sidled off, browbeaten. Wanda opened her mouth to say something nasty but didn't. She simply nodded and stood up, steadied herself to walk down the steps.

"Her name is Iris Utter," Jack said. Wanda stopped and looked at him to see if he were serious.

"I know Iris. She's not your wife."

"Not yet."

Wanda considered this. She decided that the man was deceived in some way. Iris may well have led him on the way she led everyone on, and this one was dumb enough to be led pretty far.

"What are you, one of the jail guards?" Wanda asked. "And fuck you, by the way, I have nothing more to say to you." She walked down the steps heavily. Jack stayed with her as she reeled across Loomis Park, her body profoundly drunk while her mind stayed relatively lucid.

"Just tell me straight out," Jack persisted. "What happened to Iris's son?"

"Wipe your nose. Oh, for God's sake." She reached into her bag, pulled out a pack of tissues, and tossed it at him. He caught it but stood there looking at her without opening it, the blood leaking from his nostril.

"Please," he said. "Did Kitty and Ivan take him?"

"Probably."

The answer shocked him so much that he repeated it in a stupor of relief before he asked, "How do you know?" She snorted at this.

"How? Because Ivan and Kitty came to our house one night with a baby that wasn't theirs. Because they sat on our living room couch and had a long chat with my mother's lawyers, signed some papers, and carried that baby out."

"And you recognized Iris's baby?"

"I never saw the kid before. We left the commune right after Joseph took up with Iris. My mother thought it defiled him, whatever. All I know is that the way they got hold of that baby didn't seem kosher, and later, when I heard about Iris's kid suddenly disappearing, I had my suspicions. And the only goddamn reason I'm telling you this is because I'm guessing Iris had to dirty herself up pretty bad in order to get you to crusade for her. And that's a fucking shame, pal." She turned and walked off again, veering this way and that but heading, essentially, in the right direction.

Chapter Twenty-Nine

Lee awoke with a sharp intake of breath. Lying on her side with Frank pressed tightly against her back, she stared into the granular, predawn darkness, listening. At first she only heard Frank's slow, regular breathing. He was sleeping. It was the first time she had ever caught him sleeping while he was with her. His arm rested across her waist and his hand scooped beneath her rib cage. In a few hours, he'd slip downstairs and she'd wake up alone. She shut her eyes again, tucked her body more tightly against his.

A few moments later, she heard a soft, metallic chinking. She recognized it instantly as the mysterious pacing on the verandah that she'd heard weeks ago. Since then, she had put it out of her mind. In fact, she had all but forgotten about that strange night until now. She eased herself from Frank's grasp, waking him in the process. He grabbed her back again, muttering for her to stay. She didn't bother answering him, his voice was coming from the ether of sleep, and pulled his hand off.

Frank had long ago fixed the window's rope and now the window was wide open to let the night air cool the attic room. She put her head out and leaned across the sill. Below her, and to the right, June was pacing back and forth on the verandah, her hand dragging listlessly across the balcony railing. She was speaking to herself in low, sibilant tones. The view of such private unhappiness that expected no pity was all the more pitiful.

Lee dressed and went downstairs. June's bedroom was dark and cool from the open French doors. It looked different to Lee, more spacious; it took her a minute to see that the walls were bare, both the poster and the embroidery hoop removed.

Out on the verandah, June stopped and turned, although Lee had not made a sound.

"I thought you were a ghost," Lee said, smiling. June looked at her for a moment, then turned and leaned across the railing, one sinewy, freckled hand stretched out to work indifferently at a thin branch of the pear tree. She wore a pink tube top and yellow shorts, the gaudy colors fighting through the half-light.

"The water's draining from the park," June said.

"How do you know?"

"I can smell it." Her profile was silvery from the moonlight.

"What does it smell like?" Lee asked and walked up beside her. The motion seemed to startle June and she turned sharply to Lee and smelled the air. Then she shut her lips, her chin pulsing as her tongue pressed up against the roof of her mouth.

"I can't explain," June said finally. The frustration lilted in her voice but was crushed immediately by a more general defeat. She slumped back against the house's clapboard siding. She might have been any fourteen-year-old, but she was not.

"Don't you have any friends, June?" Lee asked.

"They come and go," June said lightly. The dawn was breaking through the sky, and the shadows cast themselves oddly against June's face. Lee went to her and put her hand on June's bare upper arm. It was cold to the touch. She heard the sound of June's small, discreet inhalations.

"Don't do that," Lee said, pulling back. June looked baffled, her nose still squeezing in the air in front of Lee. It was compulsive, Lee saw. She could not control herself.

"At least try not to let other people see."

"There *is* a ghost in this house, you know," June said. Her thin, young voice was suddenly incongruous against her darkling face. "Jake's Jake. He walks on the verandah."

"You've seen him?" Lee asked.

"Not me. Other Mayborns. They say he comes to people before they commit the sin."

"What do you mean?"

"Mayborn sin. Sex. Kin to kin. 'If there is a man who takes his sister so that he sees her nakedness and she sees his, they shall be cut off in the sight of the sons of their people.' Leviticus. Our family is cursed by it. They say so and I believe it."

She realized suddenly that the girl might be able to scent Frank on her skin and she stepped away from her.

"I must have heard the rain against the verandah," Lee said and left quickly, going back upstairs to her room. She looked out the window one final time before closing it. June had resumed her pacing, her hair luminous in the darkness, lighter than the moon.

CHAPTER THIRTY

RUBY HAD WARNED HER about chows. "Nasty, the whole bunch of them." The animal was stocky with a round, lioness face and an abundance of orange fur that was clearly in need of attention. Burrs and small twigs were trapped within the thick mats on her backside and on the outer edge of her flanks. Her owner, a stout, elderly woman, handed the rope lead to Ruby and said, "She may give a growl or two. Just pinch her snout and she'll go sweet on you."

After the woman left, Ruby clapped a muzzle on the dog, barely escaping its teeth. The dog raged even more at this indignity, rearing up and frothing at the mouth until it looked like it would die in a paroxysm of outrage. Her black tongue was panting against the plastic grate of the muzzle and her body was straining to fulfill its threat of violence.

Ruby kept a chokehold on the animal while she raked through the mats below its ribs with a flat wire brush. Lee struggled to snip out some of the worst burrs in the back as the dog's hind legs stomped and kicked, so that she nearly stabbed herself in the hand several times.

"I'd ask June for help," Ruby said. "She's good with the ones like this, scares the bejesus out of them. But I can't get the child out of her room. She's holed up there night and day. Typical teenager. I was the same way at fourteen." She looked at Lee, her eyes searching for confirmation.

"So was I," Lee said. But then they were silent, each one knowing that June's problem was of a different sort. June paced the verandah constantly, talking to herself. Down in the park, people were beginning to watch her. She was becoming a daily spectacle, a curiosity that fell short of amusing. Frank was at pains to keep his temper, scattering the younger kids and occasionally yelling at the others to mind their own business. June herself was impervious to them. She looked as if she were waiting for someone to pluck her up off the verandah and, in fact, even the onlookers suspected that something would happen, if they would only be patient and wait.

The tub was not large, and Ruby and Lee found their arms pressed together as they worked or their hands meshing momentarily as they rubbed the shampoo into the thick coat. They were strangely compatible yet Iris was always between them, keeping them at a wary distance from each other.

They rubbed the dog down with towels, Ruby's hand clutching its nape to stop it from shaking off the water. Once released, the chow circled the room, rubbing her body in the corners, bumping into the table, rattling the shelf, trying to exorcise the liquids and lotions that had been slathered onto her.

After they were done, Lee went outside and headed toward the park. The rains of the past few days had left a dampness in the air. It had turned cool. The yard grasses stagnated. A small breeze brought in the odor of cow manure from an outlying farm.

Lee's body had changed. Her muscles' ceaseless bracing had

unraveled. She felt soft. She had been tired for a long time and had never even realized it. She could not understand why Frank would ever have wanted to touch her sharp, spare body.

Lee ascended the gazebo steps and sat down, watching Frank and Boulevard carry a sapling, its roots bundled in canvas. They dropped it into a wide hole and Frank carefully nudged it into position. Up on the verandah, June was walking back and forth, back and forth.

Lee thought about her mother. Her rancor toward Iris had vanished. She wondered, now, if she had always judged her mother too harshly, and felt somewhat ashamed. I'll go and visit her, Lee thought. But not today, I feel too strange today. Dopey, careless. Iris will notice it, she'll wonder, she'll ask Jack. Maybe Tuesday. She imagined Iris alone in her cell, tried to summon a clear picture of her mother's face. But the picture kept collapsing on itself, crowded out by the movement of the shovel slicing through the mound of soil, of the tottering sapling and the hands that steadied it. She closed her eyes and felt the air pass across her skin, watched the unbidden, lunar images appear beneath her eyelids; they seemed to each take their turn, approaching her like supplicants, people she did not recognize, sometimes animals, flashing before her for a moment, then vanishing the second she became aware of them.

"What are you doing?" she heard Frank ask from the bottom of the steps.

"Waiting for you," she said.

They walked side by side without touching, out of the park and through the ugly wasteland that extended the length of the railroad tracks. She took his hand. She felt a mild resistance and saw his head turn back a little, surveying the streets. But then his hand gripped hers and they listed toward the woods of Mercy Hill.

They made love on the forest bed, the fractured daylight adding an unfamiliar coarseness to their movements. She felt the space of the world extending out beyond them. They were hidden and yet could be found if someone cared to look.

She felt his muscles seize up, ready to come. She imagined her body yielding to a baby, her tensile hips shifting involuntarily, an irreversible consummation. For years she had steeled herself against shame, always careful to keep clean, proper, decent. It was a fight against dissolution and now she simply didn't mind.

What will become of you? She forced herself to consider the question but could not sustain concern. She pressed her hand down on his lower back to pin him within her, to stop him from withdrawing. His breath beside her ear paused and she felt his eyelash tic against her temple. He seemed to be making some subtle calculation, so different from the whiplash in her own heart. At the last second, she reconsidered and rolled out from under him, letting his semen spill to the ground.

CHAPTER THIRTY-ONE

SUMMER WAS REACHING ITS crest. The air grew vaporous, the heat etched an ambient clarity around all objects. People noticed one another a little more, concocted new theories about each other to stockpile in their cellars for the winter months. Children grew visibly taller in a week and the palms of their hands hardened, their fortune lines deepened. The town turned a degree on its axis, quietly altering its view.

Evenings arrived just ahead of darkness, a gradual refurling. The Mayborn house cooled and Ruby exchanged her baby blue scrubs for a pair of jeans and a man's white undershirt, so thin with age that the circle of beauty marks around her navel could be made out through the material. She sat with her ankles crossed against the coffee table and a glass of iced tea squeezed between her legs. Lee sat next to her, reading from the *Loomis Observer*.

"In the process of demolishing the outhouse, a sack of Civil War gold was discovered beneath the floorboards."

"Is there a picture?" Ruby asked. Lee turned the paper to show Ruby a grainy photo of a woman standing on a heap of rubble and holding something up in the air.

"Is that a rabbit?" Ruby squinted at it. Lee looked at the photo.

"That's the sack of gold, I guess. Looks like a rabbit."

Across from them, leaning over the coffee table, Frank was fixing Ruby's grooming clippers, unscrewing the black casing with a stubby, narrow screwdriver. All together, they formed a comfortable, sociable group; people who had no other place they needed or wanted to be. Only a sharp observer would have noticed the fleeting, compulsive exchange of glances between the two younger ones.

Lee finished the article and moved on to Ruby's favorite section, "The Reader's Column," a roster of gossip couched in the form of anonymous complaints: "Some of our neighbors are so loud, they keep us awake night and day with their fighting and other things, too." "Burning garbage while your neighbor is trying to dry her clothes on the line is very rude, in my opinion. So is sunbathing on the front lawn." Ruby took great pleasure in this formal bickering, and tried to guess at the authors. Sipping at her iced tea, she took sides, offered solutions, and was fully engaged in the problems of her neighbors, many of whom would have been unwilling even to nod hello to her on the street.

"'One child in our town is causing a daily disturbance in full view of Loomis Park. This is sad, sad, sad. Something should be done.'" Lee read it, stupidly, not realizing, until she'd finished, that the child was of course June. She looked up at Ruby.

"I'll seal off the verandah," Frank said. "She won't be able to get out onto it."

"I won't have her caged in," Ruby said in a way that made Lee wonder if Ruby had already considered this option, then guiltily dismissed it.

Lee had her own reasons to feel guilty. She had taken great pains to avoid June ever since she had realized that June might be able to detect her indiscretions by scent.

"When does she eat?" Frank said, his anger barely contained. He had stopped his work but was hunched forward still. Although his questions were directed at Ruby, his eyes were on Lee. "When does she sleep? She can't just do whatever she likes."

"I bring her food," Ruby said. "She eats some of it. I can't force her. And she went out the other day."

"I know it," Frank said. "I followed her."

"Where did she go?" Lee asked.

"She went down by the highway," Frank said. "The spot where the bear was killed. She was kneeling on the pavement, sniffing at the old blood stain on the road."

They were all silent for a few moments. Outside, the cicadas were beginning to clamor insistently, so loud and close to the house it seemed they might swarm in through an open window and cover the walls.

"What is she doing out there on the verandah?" Ruby asked, rolling her hands around the half-drained glass of tea. "I don't understand it."

"She's praying," Lee said, and both Frank and Ruby looked at her. Lee had heard June, each night, before Frank slipped upstairs and into her bed. She sat on the floor beside her window and listened as June recited the prayers, in a quick, urgent chant: "Bless the Lord, O my soul and all that is within me, praised be He..." She could not quite make out all the words. At times, Lee felt they were meant for her—a lonely, whispered dirge that frightened her, but still she kept listening.

After a moment, Ruby sighed, recrossed her ankles.

"Read the notices," she said. Lee folded back a page of the paper.

"Born to Dan and Kimberly Taylor, a daughter six pounds, eleven ounces… " She read through the birth notices slowly, rhythmically, until she felt Ruby's body relaxing back into the sofa, though her hands still played distractedly around her glass of tea. After the births came the engagements, then the weddings, then the obituaries, a vulgar, ironic progression.

When she finished, she put the paper down and saw that Ruby had fallen asleep. It had finally grown dark outside. The grasshoppers were whining. She looked over at Frank. His skin had turned very dark from the sun. The small, weary ridges beneath his eyes were more prominent. She hadn't noticed them so much before, she was so accustomed to seeing him in the shadows of her room.

She wondered, suddenly, what he might have made of himself if he had been born in different circumstances. She was pondering this when he looked up at her. It was a rare, warm sensation to be able to scrutinize each other in the presence of someone else. He met her eyes steadily, leaned across the table, and took her hand.

Beside her, Ruby still slept, her head bent toward Lee so that, peripherally, it seemed as if she were watching them. It struck Lee how little she really wanted to be caught, how pained she would be at Ruby's disapproval. The muscles along Lee's shoulder blades steeled spontaneously and she felt her body welcome the familiar bracing. She pulled her hand out of his, but he grabbed it again quickly and held it tight, as if he'd caught her before a precipitous fall. His callused fingers wrapped around her hand like rope, cinching it imploringly.

"Do you think," Lee whispered, "that June can smell you on me?"

"I don't know." He considered this now, his eyes drifting away from hers, then back. "Maybe she can."

They heard the sound of the kitchen's screen door bouncing back against its frame. Frank loosened his grip. Lee retracted her hand and snapped open the newspaper.

"Well," Jack said when he came in the room. "We all look nice and cozy." He stank of alcohol. His nose had been bloodied mysteriously the night before and was swollen and red now.

Ruby lifted her head. "Jack?" she said blearily, intimately.

Jack backed away from them and leaned against the wall, knocking over a floor lamp. He caught it before it hit the ground, lifted it in the air, and brought it down hard, like a gavel.

"Well, folks," Jack said. "Ladies, gentleman. We have a winner! And that would be me."

"Go upstairs, Jack," Ruby said, "you're drunk."

"You've had a nice ride with me, Ruby." Jack's hair had come out of his ponytail and was plastered against his face. The rubber band was still snagged in a small tuft that lifted high on the back of his scalp. "Got yourself a fine house, got yourself a litter of kids. And you have succeeded in bringing me down to your small and puny level. Well, I am starting fresh now." He went to Lee and hauled her up by her arm, wrapped his hammy forearm around her. The booze on his breath was so strong Lee could taste it on her own tongue.

"This one is mine," he said to Ruby. "You can keep yours, I don't want 'em." He kissed Lee on her cheek with damp, sloppy lips and whispered to her, "Do you know a little redhead named Wanda Enders?"

"Yes," Lee said and maneuvered out of Jack's arms.

"Well, now we both do." And he told them about his conversation with Wanda the night before.

Lee wanted to say that Wanda was lying. But whatever else she was, Wanda had never been a liar. Lee searched for the fault in Wanda's story, but even as she probed it she felt a sickening conviction that it held together, that it was probably true. She tried to reconcile Noah's infant face with that of Kitty's son. It was impossible. She felt nothing for that child. He was a blank, a numb spot.

Lee slipped out then, walked up the attic stairs, and shut the door of her room. Kneeling down on the floor, she fished beneath the bed and pulled out her physics book. She'd shoved it under there weeks ago and hadn't looked at it since. It was covered with dust, and when she opened it small particles floated up in the air. She looked at the pages of hieroglyphics, idle scratchings on the ground with a stick. She could not remember their significance. It had all been washed away.

CHAPTER THIRTY-TWO

T HE FOLLOWING MORNING JACK was in a dark mood, making the entire house a battlefield with his insults and threats.

"He always gets like this after drinking hard," Ruby told Lee. Lee longed to escape, but she hung around, not wanting to leave Ruby alone with him.

"Why are you shadowing me, Lee?" Ruby said.

"What about *him?*"

"He's none of your business," she said severely. The worse Jack behaved, the more formidable Ruby grew. Her swarthy face stiffened, warding off disapproval, shunning anyone who dared to shun. Her loyalty was fixed and preposterous, and Lee recognized the monumental effort it must have required of Ruby, an intelligent and practical woman. It was an effort Lee had sometimes made on Iris's behalf, but never with half as much success as Ruby. Never with such conviction.

Ruby reached into her back pocket, pulled out a dollar bill, and handed it to Lee. "Go buy me a lottery ticket. And stay out of the house."

At midday the grocery store was crowded. One elderly woman worked the checkout register while the owner slapped together lunch meat sandwiches behind the greasy glass of the deli counter. Many of the customers were men, arriving in pairs, their boots leaving clods of dirt in the aisles. They all seemed to know each other, so the store was as loud and sociable as an outdoor market. It was a pleasant change, the bustle reminding Lee of the city. She bought Ruby's lottery ticket but lingered afterward, wandering the aisles and listening to scraps of conversations about people she didn't know.

"Pick one or the other, my friends." Lee heard the voice, its slightly nasal resonance, the volume that welcomed strangers' input. "You have your entire lives ahead of you, and there will be hundreds more Twizzlers in your future. Black or red, black or red? May they never have any greater dilemmas!" This last was said to a passerby, because Lee immediately heard a solemn grunt of assent. "Amen," the voice said, reacting to that clerical quality that Ivan radiated.

Lee turned the corner and saw them halfway down the next aisle. Ivan was holding a large bag of Twizzlers in each hand, and the two children were looking put out.

"You're cheap," the girl said. "You should just buy both." The passerby, a sun-browned man in a greasy cap and Carhartt pants, looked back at the little girl sternly.

"Your daddy deserves more respect than that," he said. The girl turned on him with her fat, pretty face and gave him a hateful look.

"I wasn't talking to you," she said. Her round eyes bore down on the poor man who, though he spent his days battling heat and ornery livestock and the pain of bursitis, backed off from this particular challenge.

The boy spotted Lee first. His expression showed no sign of enmity, only a wariness, an expectation of trouble. She looked at him carefully now. She saw that he resembled his sister only in the most superficial ways: the roundness of his body and the whiteness of his skin. That was all. Their features were entirely dissimilar. Although the girl was more attractive on the whole, he had a fineness to his face, a sharpness. His lips were wide and precise and could have been said to resemble Iris's. His eyes, which Lee now noticed distinctly and wondered how she had not before, were a dark brown and shaped like almonds. She smiled awkwardly at him and he smiled back tightly. She walked right up to them, and he looked away, as if he would not be held responsible. His hair was clipped short and neat. Twin ridges of soft stubble trailed a little below his hairline. She felt an urge to stroke his head.

"It's that girl," his sister said. Ivan turned and smiled, not unnaturally.

"Lee! What a nice surprise. How is Iris holding up?" Under the circumstances, it was an audacious question and it shocked Lee so much that she answered, without resentment, "She's been better."

"Mmmm," he lowered his eyes as though he were considering a possible remedy. When he raised his eyes again there was a blue blankness, a vacuity that people often mistook for depth. Joseph would have said something, Lee thought. He would have had an answer to this misfortune, even if he had caused it himself. He would have told her some small thing of great scope that would have stuck in her mind, maddened her with its hypocrisy and its truth. Joseph had a brilliance. Ivan could only ever produce a rising, thin-skinned bubble that burst just as it gained form.

"Oh, a bit of sad news," Ivan said, gathering the two bags of candy in a single grip in front of him. "The commune's been sold."

"You sold it!" Lee cried in disbelief.

Ivan was adverse to such direct implication. "It's been purchased," he said. "By the college in Breesport. They plan to turn it into a field station for their geology department. They'll tear everything down, of course. They're up there now, as a matter of fact, going over plans. The carnage, I call it. Kitty volunteered to stay and talk to them. She's not as sentimental as I am." His blue eyes sought Lee's appreciation of this fact, but finding her unmoved, he gave her a sad, sagacious smile. "After all, we can't resurrect Mercy Hill, can we? And would we want to, even if we could?"

The boy stood nearby, his back still turned to her. His arms had begun to swing back and forth, in a stiff, pendulum motion. A nervous child. She guessed he had earned his nerves but saw, too, that he must be considered odd by people; an innate weirdness, impossible to conceal. Much like June.

"We'll miss the movie because of you," the little girl said, and it was unclear if she meant her father or Lee.

"Very right," Ivan said. "We should go." He cocked his head at Lee and smiled again. "Well," he said. She nearly said good-bye, but she did not want to leave them. She wanted something more.

"I'll go with you," she said.

"It's a kid's movie," the boy said. His dark eyes were on her and once again, she longed to put out her hand and touch his face, to span the distance between them.

"I don't mind."

Lee was careful to position herself in the seat next to him. His sister flanked Lee's right side, an unfriendly sentry. Her clear, wide, suspicious eyes took in everything that might pertain to her, including Lee. A large package of Twizzlers, the red ones, was mashed against her belly. She slid each stick directly up and shot it into her mouth in one straight line.

The lights went down, and Lee took advantage of the darkness to gaze at him. He was conscious of her, too; she could tell by his breathing and a buttressing around his shoulders. He toyed with the ribs of his black licorice, nibbling on the candy self-consciously. After a few moments, the movie began to engage his attention and he forgot about Lee.

She stole glances at his darkened profile, wanting to gather him against her. He placed his hand on the wooden armrest and she reached toward it, without allowing thought to prevent her. She saw her own black fingernails, rotted and grotesque, reaching for him—the same hand that had reached for Frank, night after night. His small, plump fist, his mouth agape in the shape of bird's wing. The impossibility of what she had done with Frank, the abomination of it, froze her system so that her heart stopped for a second. She died briefly and returned, without any knowledge of it. She was only aware of a small insect that had penetrated her ear canal and was humming in her head with no inflections and no pauses. She reached for her ear to hit it but the movement was simply an urge with no power to command itself, and her hand never moved. Suddenly the noise did not seem to be a bug, but a motor with a whine that flooded the theater and smothered all other noises. Her vision was blinded by a staticy, monochrome cast. But she could smell. She could smell a tartness, human and complex. She pressed into it. A meaty sweetness. A small undulation of fear, muscles shifting. Her vision cleared and she saw, first, the candy spilled from the package, splayed across bare legs, black, shiny sticks on the floor.

"Dad, Dad." She had made the shoulder of his shirt soaking wet on the spot where her cheek had lain. He harbored the side of her skull against his soft, fleshy neck. He was paralyzed by his astonishment. She had just dipped to one side and landed on him. She must be sick. He didn't want to catch what she had. She had stared at him in a strange way. No one had ever looked at him like that before. She had made him spill his candy, and his sister would not want to share the red ones.

CHAPTER THIRTY-THREE

LEE FOUND IRIS IN the small courtyard, sitting comfortably on a bench beside the jail matron. Walled in by the same pale orange bricks of the police station's exterior, the courtyard looked like a room that had been built and abandoned before the ceiling was assembled. An attempt to create a basketball court was corrected by the heaving pavement, a dune of concrete riffles and crumbling divots; it was a very rare prisoner who ever defied common sense and played there, although the Rotary Club donated a new basketball to the jail every year. On one side, there was a small rectangle of bare earth where a smattering of grass grew, a spot just large enough for the bench bolted to the ground and the bird feeder squeezed in beside it, which was kept scrupulously full of black, oily sunflower seeds.

An officer escorted Lee to the courtyard and left her there. She stood, unnoticed in the recess of the doorway, and watched Iris and the matron sitting together on the bench. To a stranger, it would have appeared that the matron was the prisoner and Iris was there to keep an eye on her. Both jittery and sluggish at the same time, the matron was occupied with her mouth and nose—sticking a cigarette into one, blowing the other into a handful of yellow tissues. Her skin was colorless and her hair was badly in need of dying, the top half of it dark brown while the bottom was cuffed red. Under her blue uniform dress, her biceps bulged out in odd, uneven lumps.

"Why don't you just call in sick, Joanne," Iris was saying.

"If I'm home, my ex will see my car and pester me." She coughed deeply, turning her head so as not to shoot the smoke out into Iris's face. "He wouldn't dare come around here, that's the one good thing. Scared of cops. He's a decent guy, he's never done nothing criminal, it's just like a… a… phobia."

"They're all decent when they want something," Iris said. A cardinal landed on the feeder, nervously grabbed up some seed, spit the hulls out. They landed in soft ticks against the pavement.

The matron spotted Lee at the doorway. "Who are you?"

Iris turned, then smiled broadly. "Lee!"

"Oh. Your kid, huh?" Joanne muttered, clearly put out by the intrusion. She lobbed her cigarette butt, frightening off the cardinal. She rose crankily and walked off a few paces, her body hunched with soft, staccato coughing.

The change in Iris was shocking. In the past month, Iris had grown heavy. Her beauty was too delicate to withstand such a change and her fine lips slouched under the new slabs of cheek. The added flesh had aged her. Her small features closed in on themselves so that she gave the appearance of being nearsighted and prim. She had softened, not only her body, which pulled her orange jumpsuit taut across her belly and hips, but her entire demeanor. It should have been a relief, but instead it struck Lee as disappointing. A painful, irrevocable waning of spirit.

"Give me a hug, Lee, and don't tell me why you haven't come to visit me, I don't want to know." She held Lee for a moment, then let her go. Lee sat beside her and shook her head.

"You got so heavy."

"It's all the hamburgers they feed me—burgers for lunch, cheeseburgers for dinner and suddenly I'm as big as a backyard. My hearing is in three days, did you know that?"

"I knew it was soon."

"My lawyer says that if I plead guilty, the judge will release me on time served plus one year probation."

"Then do it, Mom. Please. I can't stay here any longer. I can't. Things have happened…" Iris stared at her daughter for a moment, the sunlight pinching her pupils.

"Are they after you, too?" Iris whispered.

"Who?"

"I never told them where to find you, I swear it."

"Told who?"

"I'm so sorry, Lee, I'm so sorry." Iris's face crumpled, racked with a guilt that Lee had never before seen, and she began to cry heavily, grunting from the strain.

Joanne shuffled over, alarmed at Iris's crying, but Iris waved her away.

"What's the matter with you, Mom?" Lee whispered.

"Noah's dead." Iris swiped at her eyes, glancing cautiously toward Joanne, who was now leaning against a far wall, extracting a wad of tissues from her sleeve.

"No, he's not, Mom. No. Wanda told Jack—"

"I know what she told him, Jack was just here. But Wanda is wrong. Noah is dead."

"Who told you that?" Lee clenched her toes tightly, tried to bear down and slow her breathing.

"I don't know his name. He comes at night and stands outside my window. I call him Honey, because his voice is so smooth."

"What are you doing, Mom? What is this?"

"Honey didn't want me to tell you about it."

"He knows me?"

"He called you by name," Iris said.

"How does he know me?" asked Lee, struggling to stay calm.

"He knows *everything*," Iris whispered. "Honey said…Honey said…" Iris curled her hand between her breasts and looked at her daughter carefully. "He said that you came to him late one night, holding Noah, who was wrapped in his swaddling blanket, dead. You told him the baby had been sick and was crying and crying, and you had tried to stop the crying with your hand over his mouth, and God knows, Lee, you were just a little kid yourself. God knows. You can't blame yourself."

Lee stared at her mother but her vision, involuntarily, drew a broader sweep. Lee saw, all at once, Joanne burying her nose in a tissue, the dry, cold blue of the sky, the bottom half of her own body. Her mind was calm and precise. Saber hard. Her mother's accusation left Lee untouched. She felt spare and strong, like Frank. How much of her was Mayborn? She felt as though her own nervous system resonated differently, was tuned to new impulses.

"I don't blame myself," Lee said, "because it never happened."

"It's all right. No one knows, so you don't have to worry," Iris whispered, taking Lee's hand and kissing it. "Honey told Joseph that it was his fault. Honey took the blame for you. He buried Noah himself, up on Mercy Hill. That was the last thing he told me. He goes to a lot of trouble to visit with me. The atmosphere is so bad for him. He fades in and out.

Earth is so cumbersome—it depresses him. " Iris's voice broke a little so that Lee's vision narrowed to meet her mother's eyes. "I haven't heard from him since. That was the same night that Kitty and Ivan turned on their bathroom light and it came directly through my cell window and burned right through my eye sockets. Awful, awful. They make a habit of it now, every night, just to cause me pain. Then they send Jack along to confuse me. Now they're starting to work on Joanne. That's why she's sick all the time, poor thing."

Lee understood now. Iris's mind had committed treason against itself and was whispering lies. Strange, but her mother's madness failed to surprise Lee. In truth, Lee felt she'd always known it was coming, a lingering fear that she had never wanted to name.

"If I plead guilty," Iris asked, "what will happen to me afterward?" She was suddenly lucid again. It was a young, flickering madness, Lee noted.

"We'll go home. I'll take care of you," Lee said.

"You'll go away to college."

"I won't," Lee said.

"You're lying. Never mind," Iris smiled.

The officer entered the courtyard, caught Lee's eye, and tapped his watch.

"I've got to go," Lee said. As she hugged Iris she glimpsed, above the courtyard wall, the undulating, blue-green rim of Mercy Hill.

Chapter Thirty-Four

OUTSIDE THE HOUSE, LEE sat on the stone remains of the ancient Mayborn barn. There was an intimation of autumn in the air, a dry, premature coldness. It lent an anxious mood to the yard, as if it were in the final throes of bloom and waiting to be stricken by an evening's frost. Tomorrow, it would pass. A brilliant August sun would restore the hallucination of perpetual summer.

Lee's feet straddled clutches of wildflowers. They grew with crazy bounty, thick and healthy. The soil must be rich, she thought. Primed for growth. She could imagine the vast, brindled fields of decades ago, idly clipped by slow-moving cows; the way the land would have sloped down toward Loomis Pond with the rest of the world expanding off into a netherworld beyond Mercy Hill. A great, autonomous estate of Mayborns. Living closely with each other, so nearly an organism that they barely noticed their own desires apart from the others, or rather their desires grew out of the clamor of familiar limbs and the exclusive hum of

Mayborn sounds. It was, Lee realized, what Mercy Hill had once aspired to be. And, at times, it was how they were—relative to nothing and no one.

What had broken Iris, Lee wondered? Was it chemicals in her brain? Had the madness been inside of her all along, like a storm quietly gathering? There would be pills. Maybe there would be stretches of sanity. But once the mind had turned on itself, it would always scheme to deceive.

Lee abruptly lifted her head and listened. Something had changed. She strained to detect what it was, and realized that June stopped praying. The house felt stalled. The end of the prayers signaled the start of something else. Lee felt a cold, sickening fear and looked up at the visible edge of the verandah, watching for June to reappear as she paced. But there was no movement.

Lee jumped up and ran to the house, through the kitchen where Jack sat at the table, working his way through a bottle of whiskey.

"What's wrong?" he asked as Lee rushed past him. "Is it Iris?" he called after her. Lee climbed the stairs, an anger roiling within her. June's pacing should have been stopped. Her praying should have been stopped. There were so many things in June that should have been stopped, but here, in this house, nothing ever was.

June's bedroom door was open. One curtained French door was shut while the other was only slightly ajar.

"June?" she called, advancing toward the verandah. There was no answer. Lee pushed open the door, just enough to pass through. She stepped out furtively, her eyes fixed on the grates of the railing toward the ground below. A movement to her left, the fidget of a badly chafed boot, flagged her attention and she saw Frank, sitting in the deep wicker chair. He was looking out, toward the park.

"Where's June?"

"She had a seizure," he said. "I calmed her down. She's sleeping now."

He kept his gaze toward the park, his right hand spread against his chest and his head thrown back, like a man on a hard-earned vacation. This aspect of repose struck Lee as odd, an impression that deepened when he turned to her. His flat features looked thick and barbaric, his eyes as dull as Boulevard's. Why hadn't she noticed it before?

He shifted in the chair, the wicker creaking loudly, and reached for her, missing her body and ending with a handful of her shirt instead. In a man whose movements were always clean and exact, this small miscalculation somehow disturbed Lee.

"We need to stop what we've been doing," Lee said, backing away from him.

"You have that look again," he said.

"What look?"

"The same look you had when you first came here—as if we all disgusted you."

This accusation struck her hard. She felt she'd come so far, that she had surfaced from the murky brew of these past few weeks, humbled. Improved. She had been brought low, and, by that, she supposed she had paid her debt for always feeling above things.

"You don't disgust me—" she began.

"Then come here."

She did and he pulled her back against him, fitting her in the space between his legs. She didn't pull away, anxious to prove him wrong, but she kept her body rigid to let him know that she had meant what she said. He did not seem to care. He leaned back and held her, loosely, as if she crowned his mood of contentment—or, at least, did nothing to detract from it.

The green vista of Loomis Park spread out below them. Already the grass was coming in thick over the bare, mucky patches. Frank had altered the land—an impressive feat, and Lee guessed he must feel the pride of it now. But she wished the pond was still there, with its mysterious, complicated suppleness, its quiet surface and serpentine weeds a poor camouflage for the vigorous life beneath. Like a mesmerist, it had summoned water nymphs and blackbirds and people. Now, with the battalion of pipes and shovels gone, the park looked evacuated.

"People will get used to it," Frank said as if responding to her thoughts. He slipped his hand beneath Lee's shirt and covered her belly. A warm vortex of touch, seeking and tentative. She felt the accelerated movement of blood through her veins, as if his system had leaked into her own. She glimpsed into her future, understood that every other touch she experienced after this would be appraised against his touch; unfairly, because she was wedded to Frank through the cells of her body.

"The water wasn't going to come back anyway," he added. He released her completely and she might have stood up and left him. But the spot on her belly where his hand had been already felt barren without his touch, dry as the pond bed below. She'd be leaving Loomis in a few days, she reasoned. Why not take the time they had left to be with each other, then end it finally and neatly by distance.

She twisted around and looked at him. The brutishness had vanished so thoroughly that she wondered if it was simply a trick of shadows. She kissed him at the corner of his mouth, where his lips drooped slightly and formed a soft, perpendicular ridge in his cheek. The smell of his skin was suppressed in the cool afternoon air. It was a shame. She loved the smell, the way it slipped out in the heat of her room until she felt its full admission.

"I put June in your bed," he said, his breath grazing her ear.

Lee drew back. "But she'll smell us on the sheets."

"I know it," said Frank.

Right after that, the bellowing started. It continued as Jack tramped down the attic stairs so forcefully that the verandah vibrated. They could hear Jack in Frank's bedroom down the hall, his words now distinct.

"Oh my God, he knows," Lee said. She jumped up and shut the verandah door. She tried to work the handle and, seeing that there was no outside lock, she pressed her weight against the doors, but Frank took hold of her shirt collar and yanked her backwards.

"Don't get in his way," he said.

So they waited for him to come. They heard him at June's bedroom door, his breathing audible, and then the French door opened and Jack stood in front of them, his skin clotted pink and white, in the full chemistry of rage.

"Did he force you?" he roared at Lee.

"No."

He grabbed her arm and shook her, repeating his question.

"No!" Lee cried. "I told you no!"

"I don't believe you!" He released her and turned to Frank, his muscles bundled up, ready to strike, needing to strike.

"How did you make her do it? Tell me now before I rip your throat out, you son of a bitch! How?"

"It wasn't difficult," Frank said. He turned and spit over the verandah.

"Frank?" Lee said, her voice low and ragged with shock. It unnerved him, nearly smothering his objective. He turned away from her and reminded himself of the land, *his* land, not hers or her mother's. He thought of the stumps, now almost completely cleared; of the farmhouse that he had labored over, patched and painted, and of the herd that he could see so clearly, in his mind's eye.

"She's polished up nice on the outside," Frank said, "but she's Mayborn trash straight to the bone. Worse. June would never have let her own brother touch her like that."

Lee cried out, a sound of physical pain. Her face twisted and crumpled in anguish. Frank could see that she was coming apart bit by bit, the way that a tree is pried up from the ground; the tensile struggle to remain woven to the soil, to keep the connection even as it was being torn from it. The gradual exposure of its hidden clew of roots, a tangled history of its grip on life.

Jack turned on Lee now. He grabbed her jaw between his fingers, pinching hard. His eyes bore down on her, wet with disgust.

"You've ruined everything for me," he said and shoved her backward, into the railing. He hovered over her for a moment, then smacked her hard across her face. As he left, he pounded his fist into the glass door but failed to shatter it.

Frank felt Lee's eyes on him, but he would not meet them. Instead, his gaze followed the blue-green corridor of veins on her forearms, down to her wrists where the warm junction pulsed in its narrow channel. He looked at her fingers laced into the curls of the railing and then through the railing itself, all the way down to the basin of Loomis Park, cupped and empty, like an outstretched hand demanding recompense.

CHAPTER THIRTY-FIVE

JUNE AWOKE IN THE heart of sin, swaddled in the simmering bed. She smelled the stink of her brother's ardor, so different from Ed's, and the balmy sharpness of Lee's skin, mingled and macerating the sheets. Mayborn sin. She said this to her father, whose sudden entrance had woken her. She repeated it, told him, "It's on the sheets, I can smell them both on the sheets," until Jack understood what she was saying. Then he began to bellow.

The smell was washing the air, like the dry grave of the pond where the long-ago misbegotten Mayborn babies were pitched to their deaths, poor sweet babies. Jesus' angels. They haunted the night air with their violet scent. They pulsed between the words of June's ceaseless prayers, demanding and selfish as babies always are. A world of desires.

June rolled on her side and buried her nose in the sheets. She had detected a small leak of beauty. Like a novice before her final renunciation, she allowed herself to inhale deeply, once, in the spirit of soon-to-beforsworn sensuality. It urged up an ache, suppressed and driven off by prayer. A gush of loss spilled through the leak hole—an odor of pelt, thick and black and fatty. A communion, a love, a heartache.

Then it vanished. All odors, all at once. June could smell nothing. The world went silent. She lifted her head and drew in air until her rib cage swelled tight. The air was merely a sensation of pressure through her nasal cavities carrying no messages.

"Daddy?" she said even though she knew he had already left the room, just to see if all her faculties had left her. She felt as if she were floating in black space without depth. She wondered if she had died. If this stripped existence was the realm of spirits, an ashen ether where Jake's Jake wandered and scolded. Instinctively, she fumbled in her pocket for the soothing pulpy square, pulling out the well-used book of matches. No, she was not dead. She was alive but locked out, evicted from the rich, pungent world. God had punished her for her relapse.

Standing up, she ripped the sheets from the offending bed, as well as the woven summer blanket and the single, wrinkled pillow. She tossed them to the floor. Tearing a match from the book, she struck it and dropped it on the heap of bedding. It rested on the sheet, the flame still burning but not catching, before it sputtered out. Her eyes raced around the room, looking for kindling. She tore clothes from the drawers, drawers from the dresser. She grabbed up Lee's physics textbook that was splayed open and shoved halfway under the bed. The pages were glassy slick and fine. For a moment, she considered that Ruby might like it; though she couldn't read, she liked fine things to put on the shelf in the grooming room. But then June remembered that a sacrifice to God required fine things, too, a cherished goat or a precious bundle of wheat gathered in a time of drought. She pulled pages from the book and tucked them under her altar.

The fire went well after that. It blazed up in the center of the room and rose to June's own height, facing her like a Doppelgänger. Without odor, the heat seemed not to cremate objects but to absorb them in its brilliant vortex; the bedding, the blue and red dye of the rug's fibers, then the fibers themselves. All the while, the pillar of fire oscillated and re-created itself again and again—to a fat cactus plant, to a dense school of goldfish swimming toward the ceiling, to a pair of lungs, and, once, to a beloved bear that reached for June with its berry-stained paws and drew her in, too.

CHAPTER THIRTY-SIX

E
D CIPRIANO PAUSED AT the threshold of their door. In one hand was a plain business envelope, folded in half. He held it as though he was trying to palm it like a magician, or had begun to crumple it and had stopped himself. Lowering his head, he cleared his throat, three little clicks like a frog, and then skimmed his dark hair with his free hand. He knocked on the door rather softly and looked down at his shoelaces while he waited.

"Good morning, Ed." It was Ruby who came to the door. He was glad it was Ruby and not Jack. She was not in mourning clothes—just a plain man's T-shirt and white sweat pants. Her long hair hung in two dark plaits down the front of her shirt, which gave him the fleeting impression of having some particular significance, like a tribal symbol to mark her loss.

"Is Jack around?" he asked, not because he wanted to speak with him, but as a bit of caution before he proceeded.

"He's on the road," Ruby said. "Since last Tuesday. It's county fair season. Knives always sell at the fairs."

"Well. First of all, I want to give you my sympathy. A girl that young has got no business dying."

"Thank you, Ed," Ruby said with dignity.

Ed looked at her carefully. Did she know about him and June? His wife had blathered about the affair to the church biddies, he knew that much. But had it gone any further? He couldn't tell; Ruby was unreadable. Or maybe she knew, and just didn't care. That would be like a Mayborn.

"I guess the damage to your house wasn't too bad," he continued, his nervousness subsiding. "I know firsthand how a fire can spread. You have to be thankful for what you have. That's good, solid advice and we'd all be better off for keeping that in mind."

"I guess the second-of-all," Ruby said, leaning her head against the doorframe wearily, "is the thing you're holding in your hand."

"Yes." He brought the envelope out from behind his palm. As he pulled out the document and unfolded it, it crackled loudly in the chastening silence.

"My wife found this after the fire," he said, looking at the paper. "It belonged to my great-great-grandfather." He didn't mention that Mrs. Cipriano had only just found it, after discovering her own embroidery hoop in June's bedroom. She went back to the candy store, looking to confirm her suspicions about June and Ed, when she'd come across a little metal box that was hidden behind their bedroom wall. The wall had been burned and the box was exposed, resting on a wall joint.

He handed Ruby the paper. "It's a photocopy, of course. We have the original." He didn't mean this to sound like a warning, but it was. "It's a land deed," he said, then added, "I'm sorry."

"For what?" Ruby said, pinching the paper between her thumb and forefinger without looking at it.

"A land deed for your land," Ed replied. "Well, for *my* land, so it seems." Ruby handed the paper back to Ed.

"I can't read this," she said. "You'll have to read it out loud to me."

"On the fourth day of May one thousand eight hundred and seventy-seven, Jake's Jake Libarger delivers and confirms unto Enzo Cipriano and his heirs and assigns forever all that tract or parcel of land situate lying and being in the county and state aforesaid and bounded as follows..." And after that he read an exhaustive description of a plot of land, delineating its borders by the red oak saplings and maple stumps, the winding margin of a creek. He read until Ruby interrupted him, saying, "That's our land by the truss bridge—Frank's land."

"That's right."

"That land has been in the Mayborn family for a hundred years at least. Jack just sold it to our son."

"Well, he may have a deed but it ain't legit. My lawyer went down to the county clerk and dug up a copy of Jack's deed. Libarger's signature was forged. The county clerk looked up other documents with Jake's Jake Libarger's signature on it and they don't agree with the one on Jack's deed. Looks like one of your people wanted that land for themselves, and, from what I hear, the Mayborns had some influence way back when."

"You got yourself a lawyer already? Mmmm," Ruby said. "But I have to ask myself why a Libarger, who was nearly the same exact thing as a Mayborn, would have gone and given his land over to your great-great-grandfather. Enzo Cipriano? It seems like I know the name."

"Enzo Cipriano was *not* my great-great-grandfather," Ed retorted forcefully, making Ruby's black eyes wander in thought. After a moment, she nodded her head slowly.

"Enzo Cipriano. He was that Italian boy, that railroad worker they hanged for murdering a man. I remember that drawing in the police station. I used to look at it all the time when I was a kid and we had to pull Jack's dad out of some trouble. Poor boy, with his eyes rolled up in his head and his scrawny legs dangling in the air."

"Well, what he did was his own business and I guess he paid for it. Anyway the deed's made out to him but he signed it over to his cousin—my great-great-grandfather. It's all legal and right. You can contest it if you want, but it won't do any good."

"You must be in a pitiful state to come to me with this *now*," Ruby observed.

"The fire done us in," Ed admitted. "Plus my mother and my wife are fighting like cats over every tiny thing—the shower pressure, which movie stars got the plastic surgery, anything at all. When I was growing up, we lived with two sets of grandparents and a handful of cousins and still we all got along somehow."

From the interior of the house, a girl appeared. She had a raw, guarded face that blurred her age. She came up behind Ruby and slipped her hand around Ruby's waist. The girl's fingernails were black, just like June's had been. Ed felt a sudden stab of sadness, and said June's name out loud, despite himself. Both Ruby and the girl looked into his face expectantly, with the lust of grief for grief. He realized that, in their case, it must be a lonely mourning. Even after she died, people still said bad things about June. Some of them he knew himself to be untrue. For one, they talked about June being with her brother. But she had been a virgin. She didn't know a goddamn thing, but of course that wasn't something he could mention.

Ruby and the girl waited for him to say more, and he might have. He had known June probably better than any other person besides her own family. He had once even thought that he might be in love with her.

"My wife heard that she had a real knack for the church," he said.

Ruby's face registered a disappointment, or really, sank back into her customary wariness. The girl, however, glowered at him.

"What good did it do *her?*" the girl snapped arrogantly. She was a Mayborn, all right. He could have told that without seeing her fingers. She had the flat, unfinished features and the same wild look about her. But this girl topped them all. She held herself like a rude, young queen. He realized right then who she was. Jack's bastard daughter, of course. The one whose mother had, just two days before, tried to hang herself in the jail cell and was transferred over to the psychiatric ward in the Breesport Hospital. There was no end of trouble that these Mayborns brought into the community. Lord knows *he* had been a victim. Lord knows he had lost everything because of a Mayborn.

Now he looked down at this girl, the way he'd once looked at children he suspected might steal from him.

"It turned June into a citizen Loomis could be proud of, young lady," he said.

"How proud could they have been? No one came to her funeral," she replied. "Including you."

"I barely knew the girl," he said sharply.

"I'd wager you knew her well enough," Ruby said, her eyes leveled at his own, then drifting down to the paper. "You'll want to show that deed to Frank, and he doesn't live here anymore." The young girl at Ruby's side suddenly turned and disappeared back into the house. "You can find him at Boulevard's."

Ed walked back down the driveway. A police car crawled past the house, the officer inside craning his neck to see who had come to the Mayborn door. When he saw it was Ed, he waved and drove on.

Ed spat on the lawn, disgusted with the lot of them. A large, black-jowled dog appeared out of nowhere and, without a sound, walked beside

Ed for a little ways. At the end of the driveway, the dog pressed his nose against Ed's hand. Ed once again thought of June with a lingering ache, offered his hand to the animal, who probed its odor with damp, short whiffs until he had exhausted his fascination, come to some understanding, then withdrew.

CHAPTER THIRTY-SEVEN

SUNNY TAKA'S SKIN WAS very delicate. Though the heat seeped through the canopy of leaves, Sunny kept his shirt sleeves rolled down to his wrists and his pants tucked into his socks, guarding against poisonous plants and prickles.

The heat was made worse by the load that he carried—a knapsack with a little hammer and chisel, a trowel and a magnifying lens, several brushes, some snacks and a thermos of cold tea. By the time he reached the college's new field station, he was red and feverish with exertion.

The college had begun to demolish the old structures—little cabins and huts that had once been part of a commune. Scattered about were piles of debris where the structures once stood. The piles were small, like the remains of campfires. The large cabin was kept standing and used for the main office, but a small lab was being constructed in the central clearing. They had knocked down a huge stone piling that stood in the way and the foundation was already poured.

The college had padlocked the cabin, and as Sunny had neglected to procure a key from his advisor, he rested on the lab's flat stretch of cement foundation. He felt a bit like he was on the edge of a stage in a leafy amphitheater, and he sang a silly tune he'd learned as a child—a song about an old woman who caught a fish and found a tiny golden key in its belly. It amused him to hear the Japanese words pierce the foreign air.

He unsnapped his thermos from the side of the knapsack and took a long drink of the sweet tea. The drink slipped down his throat, almost painfully cool. Refreshed, he let his gaze take in the deep maze of trees surrounding him. He found the American wilderness to be much like the American character—both impressive and disappointing; seemingly boundless and then suddenly you hit commonplace pavement.

He stood and listened for the sound of water. A stream or a creek would likely be close by, but except for the sound of birds and the secret rustling in the trees, he heard nothing.

So he began to meander, following a sloping, rocky hill until the stones gave way to the soft forest floor of leaves. He dipped his head back to follow the ascension of a warbler as it flew from limb to limb toward the deep green ceiling. The leaves riffled like water. He had the sensation that he was strolling on the bottom of the ocean, and at just that moment his shoe sank into wetness that oozed into his socks. He stepped back quickly and looked down to see that the ground here was saturated and the carpeting leaves were dark and soggy. It was a curious trail of dampness, since the forest bed had been otherwise quite dry, and he noted that it traveled down the hill, branching sharply away from the commune.

"Such kind of interesting thing," he said aloud in English. He enjoyed peculiarities of all kinds and was never so happy as when he came across a thing that was unexpected. The young hitchhiker had delighted him in this way, and he thought of her now. It had been her gift of the fossil that had kindled his interest in Loomis and led him to this beautiful spot, where he, in turn, had led the geology department. He wished he had gotten her full name, so that he might find her and speak with her again.

He clasped his hands behind his back, casually, as if he were trying to disguise his interest, and walked in vague circles around the side of the hill. He stopped when he came upon a strange little hump, quite close to the area of dampness. He prodded at the hump with his shoe, then, kneeling beside it, he considered it for a moment. He opened his knapsack and extracted the trowel. With the trowel's edge, he sliced into the knoll. Little by little, he scooped out dirt. It was a tedious business, the trowel making for a poor shovel, but he managed to dig down nearly a foot when he hit something hard. He stuck his hand down the hole and pushed aside the dirt enough to uncover a patch of bright red. Excited now, he began to work the trowel into the dirt more vigorously until he had cleared a hole big enough to see that the object was a large, red toolbox.

Sunny took hold of the handle on top and worked the box out of the ground. It was very light and he thought it must be empty, but when one end tilted up there was a scuttling inside as its contents shifted. The back end of the box was badly rusted but the front of it was perfectly clean. It made Sunny wonder, and he put his hand in the hole, felt the light flow of water as it trickled through the soil. An underground spring. It occurred to Sunny that the toolbox had blocked its flow—the one rusted side indicated it—and perhaps diverted the water down another route.

He unclasped the twin fasteners and lifted the lid. It was disappointing—simply the bones of a small animal, one of the cats from the commune perhaps. The skeleton was partially covered with a folded piece of embroidered silk. Sunny lifted the cloth out to look at it more closely and a small flurry of hair dropped from between its folds. The hair was fine and dark. Clearly human.

He looked again at the little skeleton. Now uncovered, he could see that it was a child's skull. The head, with its perfect, high-domed crown, was resting on its side, in profile. The small bones of its hands splayed near the empty nose cavity and its legs were deeply bent. A sleeping child X-rayed. He'd always disliked the look of X-rays, felt that they revealed too crassly the substructure of life. Now he, too, felt in violation, and he chastised himself for his perpetual curiosity. It must be a child from the commune. One tiny sock was underneath its foot. He wondered how it had died. He'd heard the group had kept to themselves and he supposed that they had shunned vaccines and doctors. Foolish, he thought. But he guessed the mother had suffered for her loss.

Still, it seemed a lonely grave, and the toolbox was such an indecorous coffin. He wrapped the silk cloth over the tiny bones and gathered them up out of the box as carefully as he could. Its frame threatened to collapse in his hands, but he managed to lay the body down in the excavated hole without doing too much harm. Let the bones mingle with the earth. Maybe the water would flow again too, and the child would one day become a fossil. The average human remade into a singular prodigy of existence.

CHAPTER THIRTY-EIGHT

THE BEAST STOOD JUST inside the entrance of the Casablanca. A little under five feet tall, she would have been taller still if not for the droop of her massive, black shoulders and the inquisitive jut of her head. Customers patted her rump as they entered or pinched her snout. She looked as if she'd been caught at the precise moment between inquest and discovery and, despite her bulk and wild black coat, she failed to look savage in any way. For this reason, the Loomis Police Department rejected the bear as their mascot.

They told Leon that he had posed her all wrong. They had wanted her fully upright with her great forelegs coiled for attack and her mouth open to expose her fearsome yellow incisors. This unimposing animal was all wrong for their image. They paid Leon for materials only and told him they'd let him keep the animal as compensation for his labor.

Rain drummed against the Casablanca's roof and plucked at the windows. The bar was crowded tight with folks who'd been sequestered all week by the wet weather, looking for gossip and noise.

"Where's Leon?" Shane Eskeli checked the clock on the wall. "He said he'd be here along eight." Edie's hand felt between the rum bottles for cigarettes that were no longer there. Vestigial nerves.

"I'm sure he'll be along soon," Edie said.

"Hey Edie," Shane said, "did you get a look at that bowfin I caught?"

"Big fish," Edie said.

"A bowfin!" Phil Mason leaned across the bar. "Ugliest fish in God's creation, useless to boot and hard as heck to kill. My brother and I once fished out a pond of them—they were eating all the good game fish. We caught a couple dozen of them and tossed them in a gully. Next day, wouldn't you know it, the damn fish were still alive in the muck, breathing out their swim bladders. It's unnatural. I wouldn't set one on my table for love or money. You know why they call them bowfins, Shane? Comes from Po' Finn. Only a goddamn Po' Finn like yourself would eat that thing!"

"This coming from a man who was conceived in a sauna," his wife beside him said to Edie.

"I'm not going to eat the damn thing," Shane objected, "I'm going to mount it!" He said this loud enough so that half the bar turned to him and laughed.

"Better eat her first or you won't get to mount her at all!" Barb Kinney called from the pool table, which brought another round of laughter.

"That's all right!" Shane said, smiling with a set of very even, white teeth. He had the fatalistic confidence of a much-bullied boy who'd grown into a strong adult. "Laugh away. It doesn't cost me a dime. But when I laugh at you, my friend, I'll be a hundred dollars richer for it."

"Why's that?" Phil asked.

"The hundred we bet with."

"You mean about Loomis Park?" Phil snorted.

"Loomis *Pond,* my friend. The water's coming back, like I told you it would."

"That's mud," Phil said and turned back to his drink.

"It isn't mud either. The water's found a way back in. By next summer, I'll be hanging my fishing pole over the bank."

The door opened and Leon came in carrying a package swaddled in plastic bags under one arm. His wet clothes were plastered against him and his hair dripped like beach weeds. He passed the bear so closely that her muzzle grazed his shoulder and his free hand raked fondly at her belly.

Edie smiled; her pride in him had no proper claim or even, at times she thought, merit. Yet he seemed to her more extraordinary than anyone. Her fingers rubbed together for a cigarette she did not want. Well, she thought, it takes a body time to catch up with change. Desire sometimes lingers past need.

"Come on. Let's see what you've done with her," Shane said and pushed aside glasses and a bowl of pretzels on the bar to make room. Carefully, Leon took the fish from its wrappings and set it down. Mounted on a piece of scrolled oak, it was a strange, prehistoric-looking creature with needle teeth, a fin that circled most of its olive-green body, and a dark, sham eye on its lifted tail. Its real eye, beady and hard, had an insolent, warlike stare. It was a trophy that defied human gloating.

"It looks like it's cursing us all," Edie said and immediately felt sorry she'd said it. After all, it was Leon's own handiwork. But Leon himself seemed relieved to be rid of it. He left it with its new owner and sidled off behind the bar to pour himself a beer.

"Tell you what though," Phil Mason said, picking up where the conversation left off, "if the water is coming back I got a theory on why."

"No one wants to hear your theories," his wife said, but apparently quite a few did and some folks stopped talking to hear what Phil had to say.

"Has anyone else noticed," Phil said, "that the park started getting mucky not long after Frank Mayborn finished the job."

"Well, I guess I did," Shane agreed, and some of the others nodded.

"My theory is," Phil looked about at his audience significantly, "the Mayborns stopped up the pond themselves, then cashed in on the renovations."

"How the heck could they have stopped up the pond? They're not beavers," Edie said.

"Frank's a clever guy," Shane Eskeli assured Edie. His thumb was absently stroking the gleaming bowfin.

"That's what I'm saying," Phil said with satisfaction, raising an eyebrow for his audience's benefit. They promptly picked up the cue and furthered Phil's theory for him. Some wondered if Frank had groped through the woods until he'd found the spring that fed the pond and dammed it up with stones. Then Barb drifted over, seeing the eager huddle.

"It's June Mayborn *I* felt bad for," Barb said. "Shut up in her room. Walking back and forth on the balcony like a caged animal."

"Maybe they shut her up because she knew about the pond…"

"I always wondered about the way she died…"

"I know it."

"Just her. No one else. Makes you think."

"Better that she died!" Barb declared firmly. "A girl born in that family!"

"He's here," Leon said to Edie. His head still sagged a little, a sad remnant of his former days. Edie wondered if it would always sag.

"Who's here?" she asked

"Frank. Near the piano with Boulevard."

"They left hours ago," Edie said, craning her neck over the crush of bodies. But then she spotted them, partially obscured by the piano. They were close enough to have heard everything, yet Frank's back remained stoically turned to the crowd.

"All right!" Edie slapped at the bar counter. "Break it up, this isn't the laundromat!"

Frank stood up then. He leaned toward Boulevard, knuckles resting on the table, and said a few words to him. Boulevard shook his head, clutching his glass of beer jealously. After a moment Frank simply withdrew, alone. He grabbed his jacket from the back of his chair and made his way through the crowd, leaving a trail of silenced gossipers.

Their words hadn't angered him. On the contrary, they had revived him, providing him with the familiar, grim tonic of scorn.

His campaign was over; the land won, then lost again by brute chance and a sheet of musty paper, stained brown with the old blood of a murder. In the end, Frank discovered the soldier's secret: that the outcome of war is swallowed by the details of battle; details which rage on with such luster that it seems decisions can be unmade. Even in his sleep he labored against his own senses, which confessed to him, in a series of garbled bulletins, the times he might simply have retreated, and he woke with an assault of longing in Boulevard's darkened room. Sometimes he reached out to pull Lee closer to him, to press his face into her neck, before he realized that she wasn't there.

Outside, a heavy fog choked the moonlight and clotted the air into soggy shreds. The rain had tapered off to a light drizzle. Sound traveled strangely in this weather, and Frank was able to make out the whistling crescendo of cars passing across the distant highway.

He turned up Willow Street and started to walk back to Boulevard's apartment on the far end of town. As he passed the Fellowship Church he glanced briefly at its billboard, "God Grades on the Cross, Not on the Curve," then descended the stairs to Loomis Park—a shortcut to the north end of town.

As he walked across the width of the park his boots sank deep into the mucky grass. Everywhere were shallow indentations filled with dark water, seeping upwards, rising more each day, drowning the grass and making the gazebo lean to one side like a buoy in the sea. And rising with the water was the thick, briny smell of life: of earthworms and plankton and tiny, hatching eggs.

ACKNOWLEDGMENTS

My most heartfelt thanks to Alice Tasman, a brilliant agent and an extraordinary human being; Laura Moore, who made me try harder; Adam Robersmith, for his tremendous help in editing this book and for his friendship; Daryl Weinstein, my touchstone; Adam, for his unflagging faith; my brothers, Will and Joey; and my friends Mae Beatty, Jillian Bergeron, Heyltje Bond, Ron Campbell, Gabe Lucas Boscana, Todd Herron, Carla Lovas, George Sapio, Marieanne Schlachterman, Maura Stephens, and Jony Weiss. Special thanks to my editor, Pat Walsh, and copyeditor, John Gray, as well as Steger's Taxidermy Studio and the Paleontological Research Institute of Ithaca, N.Y.